A Murder of of Crows

Edited by
Sandra Murphy

DARKHOUSE
BOOKS

A Murder of Crows
Copyright 2019 Darkhouse Books
All rights reserved
This story is a work of fiction. Any resemblance between
events, places, or characters, within them, and actual events,
organizations, or people, is but happenstance.

Anthology copyright © 2019 by Darkhouse Books
ISBN 978-1-945467-19-6
Published October, 2019
Published in the United States of America

Darkhouse Books
160 J Street, #2223
Niles, California 94539

Coming soon from
Darkhouse Books

Mid-Century Murder

Cozy to Cozy-Noir crime stories from
the age of tail fins and stiletto heels.

Fearrington Road

A collection of Lovecraft-inspired
tales of mystery and horror.

*What We Talk about
When We Talk About It*

Poetry and Prose

Table of Contents

A Murder of Crows

Continued on next page

Table of Contents

A Murder of Crows

Introduction

by Sandra Murphy

It's all Kaye George's fault. She's the author of multiple series of mystery books and the editor for Day of the Dark: Stories of the Eclipse, twenty-four tales about what could possibly go wrong, crimewise, during a total eclipse. She and I are e-friends because I've reviewed a number of her books. They were really good reviews.

In a Facebook post, she said she'd seen a large number of birds in her backyard. Upon closer inspection, they were crows. "How cool is this? I'm a mystery writer and a group of crows is called a murder of crows," she said. "And there's a murder of them in my yard."

I happened to see her post right after it appeared and replied, "That would make a good anthology topic. You should do that." I was not-so-subtly angling for a market for short stories, one that didn't involve a lot of hoops to jump though, wouldn't need research to find, and maybe, (this is the kind of subtle part), had a friendly editor who would like my story, whatever it turned out to be.

To my disappointment, she said due to deadlines, she didn't have time.

All was not lost. Andrew MacRae of Darkhouse Books, saw our comments. He and I talked. Before our conversation ended, one of my other personalities took over and agreed to the outlandish idea that I could edit an anthology. Other personalities volunteer me for a lot of things. This one left me a little note that said, "Oh, hey, you need to think up rules for this anthology thing so people can send you dozens of stories. Good luck with that." Then she went off to a Greek island to develop other plots against me and I was on my own.

The rules called for a cozy to cozy noir story. That means no excess violence, bad language, and for the cozy end of the spectrum, the bad guy gets what's coming to him in the end. For cozy noir, similar rules but nothing goes right for anybody.

Writers had to use the collective name for a group of animals as part of the story. It didn't count to just mention it in passing. Each animal would only be used once. If there was no official collective name, writers could invent one.

Killing or maiming an animal would be an automatic rejection. That included a coat with fur trim, a seafood dinner, feeding fish to another animal, squashing bugs, taxidermy, training dogs to hunt, or birds flying into a window. When I liked a story but one of these bloopers was used, I offered the writer a chance to make changes. Some worked, some didn't.

In all, I read 71 stories, wrote one of my own, totaling about 275,000 words. The resulting book is a mix of established and new authors, animals of all sorts, settings ranging from an island sanctuary to a farm, airport, forest, library, cave, a movie set, a church, or laboratory. Two stories are set in England, one in Australia. Two are written by authors from the UK. I read and reread them often enough that I can quote passages from every story.

Enormous thanks go to Kaye for the remark that started the process. Profound thanks to Andrew and Darkhouse Books for trusting I could select and edit the stories. They were all worthy but only twenty-one fit the final word count.

Thanks also go to Patricia Fry, author of the Klepto Cat mysteries. When we met, she asked, "Are you a writer too?" and then showed me how to be one. Writers Under the Arch, my critique group, made me a better writer. John Gilstrap, author of the Jonathan Grave thrillers, explained the "muddled middle" so the book keeps pace from beginning to end. Lorie Lewis Ham offered the opportunity to review truly good writing for Kings River Life online magazine. The late Bill Crider took the time to encourage and share what he learned over the years. Jay Hartman, Editor in Chief at Untreed Reads, published a collection of my short stories (From Hay to Eternity) because, he said, "You'll just let them gather dust in your hard drive if I don't."

Thanks everyone, for the push to do more, even when the push was really a kick in the pants. The anthology let me see into the creative minds of other writers. They've had patience with my questions and edits, were gracious if rejected, thrilled when accepted.

Thanks for finding time to read in spite of busy schedules. Enjoy the stories, share, and leave reviews. Via the written word, readers can have an out of body experience, time travel, and spend time in another world, if only for a few minutes.

Sandra Murphy
September, 2019
St. Louis, Missouri

Jack Bates is a three-time finalist for a Derringer Award. His shorts appear in The Killer Wore Cranberry and The Fakahatchee Goonch is in Florida Happens. He is a whiz with names.

His main character, Millie, was born when a group of crime writers used a common character. No one can verify their state of mind at the time. Millie had another adventure in her so he woke her up and put her to work.

A Tickle of Tarantulas
by Jack Bates

Millie Mornhinweg jumped at the bellow of the ooga horn behind her. She had just enough time to flatten herself against the exterior wall of Sound Stage E11 before a hook and ladder red fire truck, full of the Fumbling Firemen rocked around her on its way to the studio back lot. One of the comedic stuntmen, the handsome, squared-jaw one who always caught the beautiful ingénue, swooned as the truck passed Millie. Another Fumbler, the one who had a Fuller brush of a moustache and eyes as big and bright as saucers, sprayed the swooning man with seltzer water from a mock fire extinguisher.

"Teacher's pet! He's all wet!" the mustachioed man yelled.

A third member of Captain Klutzkee's Fire Brigade clanged the bell over the big, gold 13 on the hood as the truck disappeared into the façade of New York City.

Sometimes Millie marveled at her job. After earning her teaching credentials, Millie took what she thought was going to be a part time job at the Trentwood Pictures Amalgamated movie studio, tutoring the child actors of the TPA's 'Lil' Dickens' series. It wound up being more of a babysitting job. Trying at times, but the pay was good. So were the unspoken fringe benefits, namely her off camera relationship with Brad Jolly, the square-jawed Fumbling Fireman who also played the naïve soda-jerk in the 'Lil Dickens' shorts.

A green light glowed over the door to sound stage E11 indicating Millie could enter without the day's director chastising her. The opposite happened. Joe Clawson, the prop manager to the stars as he called himself, greeted Millie on his way to the set with a large, spinning globe of the world.

"Hi, ya, Millie."

"Hello, Joe. What do you know?"

"Hope you like spiders." He patted the globe.

Millie stopped. "Why? Is that globe filled with them?"

"Oh, you'll see." Joe continued on his way to the classroom façade used in the studio's 'Lil' Dickens' shorts.

Millie followed. It had been bad enough when they brought in the snakes for the one-reeler, 'For Goodness Snakes!' She kept her composure when two hundred chirping crickets escaped from the picnic basket and spilled all over poor, innocent Miss Weepington and the bumbling soda-jerk Halfpint Harrigan, during 'A Case of the Crickets'. After that one wrapped, Millie made Brad dispose of the clothes he wore before she'd let him in her bungalow. Even Edie Froehlich, who played the innocent teacher in the episodes, complained of something crawling over her skin for days after the scene was shot.

Spiders were a whole other worry.

Only three of the child actors were on set that afternoon. Freddy Hogan, who played Toady; Jenny Mitchell, who carried the role of cutie-pie Dolly Dimples with great aplomb; and, Georgie Reynolds, who was perhaps more known by his character's name, Lil' Stubby Dickens, than he was of his own. All stood around Miss Weepington's desk while a man Millie didn't know stood with his back to her and Joe Clawson. The man spoke softly to the children while patting what looked to be a large doctor's bag. He hooked his thumbs together and moved his eight fingers like legs across the desk. Jenny Mitchell wrinkled her nose. Georgie Reynolds looked a bit uncertain. Only Freddy Hogan looked excited.

The scene pleased Millie. Usually the boys chased one another along the catwalks twenty feet overhead. Millie, who wasn't wild about heights, would scale the rungs running up the wall to bring them down for lessons or filming.

Joe the prop man set the spinning globe on the desk. The man with the doctor's bag spoke to Joe. He was much older than Millie originally thought. She saw his light brown hair had white at the temples. A thin line of hair above his upper lip looked more like a tan caterpillar than it did a moustache. It wriggled when he talked and matched his eyebrows almost too perfectly.

"Doc, this is Miss Mornhinweg, our on-site tutor for these little dickens. Millie, this is Doc Vroman from L.A. City College. He's a teacher, too."

"I prefer professor," the man said. "And please, call me Stephen."

Millie shook his hand. "What brings you to the studios, Professor Vroman?"

"Doc is here to introduce the kiddos to some of his friends," Joe said.

"Friends?" Millie looked around the set. "Are they joining you later?"

"Ain't she a card, Doc? 'Are they joining you later?' No, Millie. They're already here." Joe opened the globe. A giant novelty spider on a spring sprung out and bobbed in front of a screaming Millie. The hardy-har-har gag put tears from laughter in the eyes of Freddy Hogan and Jenny Mitchell. Joe the prop man was pretty proud of himself. Professor Vroman rolled his eyes. Georgie Reynolds looked as if he might cry.

"Not… funny… Joe…" Millie said. It took her a second to find her composure.

Professor Vroman put his hand on her back. "Do you need some water, Miss Mornhinweg?"

'Water when gin is available?' Millie thought but didn't say. She nodded.

"Children," Professor Vroman said. "Would one of you kindly get Miss Mornhinweg a cone of water?"

"I'll do it," Jenny Mitchell said. She hurried over to the water cooler and pulled a paper cone from the sleeve. By the time she got it back to Millie, the cone was only half full. In her haste, the girl wound up spilling half the contents. Jenny turned around twice to refill the cone before realizing at her current rate she was putting most of the water from the bottle onto the floor. She handed the cone to Millie who knocked it back like a sailor on shore leave bellied up to the bar rail.

"I hope what I show you now won't trouble you," Professor Vroman said. "You see, I'm an entomologist who concentrates on arachnids."

"I only had two semesters of Latin, Professor Vroman," Millie said. "Spell it out for me."

Professor Vroman smiled. "I study spiders."

Millie's eyes went to the leather case he patted. She pointed a trembling finger at it. "Are there spiders in there?"

Professor Vroman opened the case. He pulled from it a metal cage containing three large, hairy spiders. "I give you the Chilean rose hair tarantula."

"Nope," Millie said. "You can keep them."

"Family Theraphosidae. Order Araneae. Class Arachnida."

Millie backed away. "Class dismissed."

"They're essentially harmless to humans. Their bite is more like a bee sting."

"Also not high on my list of preferred creepy-crawly-buzzy things."

"I've been bitten several times while studying them," Professor Vroman said. "I'm perfectly fine."

"You're carrying spiders in a doctor's bag, mister," Georgie Reynolds said. "That doesn't sound fine to me."

"I can see why you're the leader of the Lil' Dickens, son," Professor Vroman said.

Freddy Hogan waved his hand dismissively. "Aw, that's only in the shorts we shoot."

Freddy's comment triggered Georgie's defenses. "No it isn't."

"Yes it is."

"Here they go," Joe said.

"Boys," Millie said, her voice hoarse. She cleared her throat.

"Dare you to hold one of the spiders, then," Freddy said.

Georgie looked a bit nervous. His young eyes searched for a way out the snare. "I would but he won't let me." He pointed at the man who brought the tarantulas.

Professor Vroman opened the door on the top of the cage. "No, no. It's fine. Petunia loves to be held, don't you, my dear?" He wiggled a finger at the spider.

Millie felt as if she'd jump out of her skin. Petunia or not, if he took one out of the cage, she just might. Petunia reached with her front legs for his cupped hand.

The main door swung open. Edie Froehlich rushed in sobbing. Thankful for the distraction, Millie hurried to the young actress.

"Edie? What is it? What's wrong?"

"Oh, Millie, it's horrible. I've been sacked."

Joe the prop man and the three child actors gathered around Millie and Edie.

"Sacked?" Joe asked. "On the day of a shoot?"

Edie spoke through her tears. "Mr. Trentwood just told me I was through at this studio."

"But why?" Millie asked.

The door opened again. A cavalcade of studio types marched into the soundstage, led by Paul Trentwood, the head of Trentwood Productions Amalgamated, also her boss. Millie recognized a couple of the people with him. There was Oscar Baier, a stocky, bald, German man who oversaw distribution of American films in Germany and Chuck Wolfe, head of studio security. With them was a curly-haired blonde Millie didn't recognize. At the very back of the group stood a pair of uniformed guards.

"Why's none of your business," Trentwood said. "I made an executive decision. Children, this is Miss Aggie Bernhard. From now on Miss Bernhard will be playing your teacher, Miss Appleby."

The new actress flung open her arms. "I am so very excited to work with all of you!"

The three Lil' Dickens embraced Edie.

"All right, Edie," Trentwood said. "I gave you your chance to say goodbye. Wolfe. Get her out of here."

Chuck Wolfe barely moved. The guards pulled Edie away but not before she spat in Oscar Baier's face. He laughed and wiped his cheek with a kerchief pulled from his breast pocket. His jacket sleeve pushed back to reveal a cuff link that bore the emblem of the Nazi party.

Joe Clawson must have seen the pin as well. He leaned in close to Millie's ear and whispered, "There's your answer. Edna "Edie" Froehlich don't play vell in das Fahtterlund."

The amount of power Oscar Baier carried around the studio infuriated Millie. He had shut down more than one project that he deemed anti-Nazi or anti-Hitler. As if that wasn't enough, he turned his attention to individuals, taking away jobs and hampering careers.

Millie seethed. "Don't you fret, Edie. You'll be a star at any studio you choose."

"You think I deal only with the TPA?" Baier asked. He shook his head. "Cockeyed, American optimism."

Joe the prop man took a defensive step around Millie. "Hey, we beat you in the War to End All Wars, Kaiser Cue Ball. If we have to, we'll do it again."

Baier laughed. "The economic dependency America has on Germany is too great. If you're wise, you won't fight us a second time."

"I'll fight you right now—"

"That'll be enough, gentlemen," Trentwood said. "Little pitchers and all that. Come on, Edie. Don't make this any harder than it has to be. Mr. Wolfe. Please escort Miss Froehlich out of the studio."

"But I don't want her to leave," Jenny Mitchell said.

Trentwood glared at Millie. "You're in charge of the children. Get them ready to shoot."

"Do you mean with film or a gun, Herr Collaborator?" Millie covered her mouth with both of her hands as soon as she said it. Trentwood's fists clenched tight as his face turned red. Millie took Jenny's hand to lead her and the boys away from the scene.

Professor Vroman stood behind them. He seemed surprised by what was unfolding.

"Sarah?" he asked.

Millie knew the professor wasn't talking to her. She looked over her shoulder at Edie. Edie shook her head.

"Sarah, is that you?"

Aggie Bernhard looked up from the cigarette she was lighting with a gold-plated lighter from her gold-plated cigarette case. She scratched a bit of tobacco from her tongue with the back of her thumbnail.

"I'm sorry. You are?" Aggie Bernhard kept her eyes on her cigarette.

"Sarah, it's me. Your Uncle Stephen. I haven't seen you since you were this child's age." He indicated Jenny Mitchell with a sweep of his hand. "I know it's you. Do you remember I came to visit you and your family in Krakow?"

"Krakow?" She scoffed. She spoke through a cloud of smoke. "I've never lived in or been to Krakow." She twittered her reply while releasing tiny puffs of smoke from her nose.

"But it is you, isn't it? You have the same little mole on your chin."

Aggie Bernhard finally made eye contact with the professor. "I don't know who you are, buddy, but I am *not* your niece."

Trentwood intervened. "Who are you and why are you on my set?"

"My name is Stephen Vroman, sir. If I am mistaken, Miss, I apologize." He went back to the desk.

Joe Clawson answered in a calmer, restrained voice. "He's the bug wrangler your director brought in for today's shoot, Mr. Trentwood."

"Where is Bigelow?" Trentwood looked around the cavernous soundstage.

"I'll see if I can find him." Clawson glared at Oscar Baier as he stepped around Trentwood and his entourage. He hooked out his arm to Edna Froehlich. "May I see you out, Miss Edie?"

Edna slipped her arm through his. "Thank you, Joe."

As they left, Brad Jolly hurried into the soundstage. "Hey, sorry I'm late. Max wanted an extra take and—" He stopped. "Where's Edie going? Aren't we shooting 'A Tickle of Tarantulas' today?"

"We've made some changes, Brad," Trentwood said. "This is Aggie Bernhard. She'll be replacing Edna in the short features for now on."

Aggie held out her cigarette free hand. "A pleasure to meet you." The wink she gave Brad sent sparks of jealousy through Millie's bones.

"Aggie, let's get you to wardrobe since Bigelow isn't here. Miss Mornhinweg, please see to the children."

Millie nodded. "Of course, Mr. Trentwood." She still had her job. For the moment, at least. Millie turned to the three Lil' Dickens. "Go take your seats on set, children."

"Yes, Miss Mornhinweg." They moved and spoke in unison.

Brad waited until the children were gone to ask Millie what he had missed. She told him everything that had occurred. Like Millie, Oscar Baier angered him.

"I guess I just don't understand world distribution rights," Brad said. "If Trentwood is getting that much money for distributing in Germany, it seems like I should be getting a little more in my pay check."

"It's more than just the money, Brad. It's allowing a foreign nation to dictate what films we can make and who we can use in those films. Look what happened when Universal tried to release 'All Quiet on the Western Front' in Berlin. Nazi Party members showed up with stink bombs and rodents to chase people out of theaters rather than let them see the movie. They thought it was anti-Germany when it was actually anti-war."

"Edie's sacking has really got you steamed."

"I just can't believe this can happen in the twentieth century."

Brad took her in his arms. "It'll get better."

"It better. I don't want you going off to war anytime soon."

"That'll never happen. America isn't going to get dragged into another European problem."

Jenny Mitchell screamed. She and Georgie Reynolds stood on the chairs connected to desks. Freddy Hogan laughed and pointed at his peers. Professor Vroman slid prop books stacked sideways on the shelves and knocked piles of fake essays too the floor as he searched for the most important creature in his life.

"Oh, no," Millie said as she pulled away from Brad. She opened her arms to the frightened actors. "Children, come back over here."

Professor Vroman turned abruptly. "Please! They must remain where they are. Petunia is missing."

"I thought you said the tarantulas weren't dangerous."

"The tarantulas aren't. The children are. They might step on her in their panic."

"How big is this Petunia?" Brad asked.

"Like a grapefruit," Georgie Reynolds said. "Miss Mornhinweg, you have to help us."

"Professor Vroman, I have to get the children out of here. They are petrified."

"Aw, I'm not afraid of no spider." Freddy Hogan said. "I just can't stop laughing at those two scardey-cats."

"I'm not scared!" Georgie stomped his foot. Professor Vroman winced.

Brad whistled everyone quiet. "Line up single file behind Stubby. Walk straight at me."

"But my spider—Petunia—"

"I can see the path they'll take. I don't see any grapefruit sized spiders. You find Petunia. We'll take care of the kids."

"Brad," Millie said. "Take the children outside."

"What are you going to do?"

"Help the professor."

The children did as Brad told them. Millie went to the set.

"Please, step with care," Professor Vroman said.

"Of course. I can see this has you frazzled."

"It's not just Petunia. It's my niece."

"Aggie Bernhard is really your niece?"

"Her name is Sarah Dubinski. She is lying."

"A lot of actors and actresses change their names."

"She is lying about who she is. Twenty years ago, my sister married a nice man from Krakow. Benjamin Dubinski. A baker from a long line of bakers. Then the Hitler mess began and I haven't heard from my sister or her family until today."

"And if Oscar Baier finds out your niece is Jewish, she'll lose her job like Edie Froehlich."

"Or worse. There are stories out of Europe… Oh! What a troubled world in which we are living."

Millie didn't want to hear any more. Unlike Brad, she feared America's involvement in another European affair loomed.

A shaft of sunlight cut across the concrete floor from the opening of the soundstage door. Joe Clawson walked toward them carrying a butterfly net.

"Brad Jolly told me you lost one." Joe handed Vroman the net. He looked at Millie. "Mr. Trentwood wants to see you in his office."

Millie's heart dropped. She knew it was coming. Frankly, she was surprised he hadn't sacked her on the spot. Only fools spoke so candidly to Paul Albert Trentwood.

"Thank you, Joe." She turned to Professor Vroman. "Sorry I can't help you, Professor Vroman."

"It is all right, Miss Mornhinweg. I am sorry I cannot help *you*."

Outside Soundstage E11, Brad waited alone.

"Where are the children?" Millie asked.

"I sent them to the commissary to get some ice cream."

"Why didn't you go?"

"Joe told me Trentwood wants to see you. I'm going along."

"You don't need to."

"Yes, I do."

Millie looked back at the soundstage door.

"That's odd," Millie said. "The red light is on."

"I didn't see Max Bigelow go in."

"I didn't see anyone go in."

"Or come out. Of course, someone could have used the loading bay doors."

"Maybe I should check—"

Brad caught her arm. "Maybe you should go see Mr. Trentwood."

Millie relented. She squeezed his hand. "You're right. Will you check on the children? There's a lot of mischief they can get into on their own. If they think the soundstage is empty, they might go up in the catwalks to play Dead Man's Tag."

Brad tapped Millie's nose. "For you, I'll do anything."

The Fumbling Firemen's Fire Engine rolled to a stop with two of the actors from earlier on the driver's bench. Henry Kruk, now without his thick moustache, and Clive Yancy, who rang the bell, jumped down and walked over to Millie and Brad. Kruk slapped Yancy's arm.

"Pay up, Yance."

Clive Yancy dug a quarter out of his pants pocket. He plopped it into Kruk's palm.

"What's that for?" Brad asked.

"I bet him we'd find you swooning over Millie," Kruk said.

"Clive," Millie said with a smile. "That's a sucker's bet."

"There's one of me born every minute," Yancy joked.

"We're on our way to the canteen," Kruk said. "Care to join?"

"I have to corral some kiddies first."

"Those Lil' Dickens?" Yancy hooked a thumb over his shoulder. "Think they snuck into the soundstage. Back door is open."

"You guys go," Millie said. "I'll get them out of there."

She watched Brad and his pals head off to the commissary before she headed around to the back of Soundstage E11. Oscar Baier came from the opposite direction brushing a dusty white powder from his bald head and shoulders. Both he and Millie stopped when they saw one another.

"Mr. Baier, I was just on my way to see Mr. Trentwood."

Baier, uncertain as to what to say, nodded, causing some of the powder to spill onto Millie's shoes. Before she could ask what happened, the German hurried off toward the executive office building. Millie knew she shouldn't follow Baier as Trentwood awaited her. A trail of dry, white powder urged her to the back entrances where the loading bay door was closed but the standard door was ajar.

Joe Clawson approached from the opposite side carrying an apple box and whistling like it was no big deal a Chilean rose tarantula was on the loose. Millie ducked behind the back of Fire Engine 13 before he could see her.

"Jiminy," Joe said interrupting his whistling. "I thought Doc closed the door!" He rushed inside the Soundstage E11. Millie started to stand up when Joe ran out, still carrying the apple box.

He tossed the crate aside, looked back at the open door, and ran off yelling, "She's dead! Somebody help! She's dead!"

Running to the open door, Millie entered Soundstage E11 calling out to the children.

"Freddy? Georgie?"

The only response was the creak and squeak of the catwalk over her head. Something gray and gritty flitted down into the light cast by a lone lamp hanging from the overhead grid. Grit got into Millie's eye. She blinked as she came around the end of a set wall, her vision blurry

Aggie Bernhard slumped in the chair behind the teacher's desk. Her head lolled to the right. A large, red welt stuck out on the back of her neck. The spinning globe lay smashed at her feet. Behind her, the door to a fake closet was open. Millie could hear footsteps approaching. She stepped into the tiny four-by-four space and closed the door to hide. She crouched down on her hands and knees to watch what happened from the keyhole with her one clear eye.

Joe Clawson came into view. "See, Mr. Baier. I think she's dead."

"You did not check?" Oscar Baier came up behind Joe with his hand in the front pocket of his suit coat.

"I'm not a doctor but you've got to admit she looks dead."

"Yes. She does, doesn't she?"

"Yeah. I think that runaway terrible-rantula bit her."

Millie found that an odd thing for Joe to say given he was there when Dr. Vroman explained the tarantula bite wasn't deadly to humans. Of course, knowing this didn't stop Millie from being frightened of the missing spider.

"Tarantula, you meant to say?"

Baier held something inside his closed hand. His thumb drew back on a ring that lifted a silver shaft of a plunger. Baier raised a silver syringe behind Joe's back.

"Yeah. Come look at this welt. I think it's where it bit her."

Baier stepped closer to Joe.

Millie had every intention of warning the prop man of the danger he was in until she felt something tickle the back of her neck. Whatever it was moved from her neck into her hair one soft step at a time, steps that felt like fingers caressing her scalp with little, fuzzy, pads. The movement paralyzed Millie with fear. She knew exactly what crawled across her head.

Petunia.

A rush of voices filled the soundstage that culminated with Professor Vroman's anguished inquiry.

"Is it my Petunia?"

"No, Doc," Joe Clawson said. "It's your niece!"

With Petunia covering Millie's clear eye and gritty dust still irritating the other, Millie could no longer see what was happening outside the closet door. Millie, however, could hear what was being said, over her own thumping heart, as Petunia slowly moved down Millie's face.

"Ja," Oscar Baier said. "I believe she may have been bitten by your missing tarantula."

"Why do you say that?" Trentwood asked.

"Look at that red welt on her neck—"

"Mr. Baier! Do not touch the body!"

Though he said little, when Chuck Wolfe spoke, he wasn't ignored.

Baier persisted. "But look for yourself, Mr. Wolfe. She tried to smash the spider with that globe."

"Good heavens," Professor Vroman cried. "My Petunia!"

Unable to open her mouth because Petunia was using Millie's lips as a resting spot for her front four legs, Millie made tiny, little moans for help. One of Petunia's legs rubbed over Millie's nose generating a need for her to sneeze. Millie fought it back, afraid that the sudden burst from her nasal cavity would startle the spider causing it to bite Millie on the mouth.

On the other side off the door, voices grew louder.

"She tried to smash something, Mr. Baier."

"What are you implying, Joe?" Wolfe asked.

"For a bald guy, he's got a lot of dandruff, Chuck. I noticed him brushing off his shoulders."

Millie moaned. Petunia moved over her ear.

"What's that got to do with the globe?"

"That globe? Paper mache. I know. I made it."

Millie kicked her foot on the closet wall.

"Hold on," Trentwood said. "Do you hear that sound?"

The set went quiet.

"I hear nothing," Oscar Baier said.

Petunia made her way for the open neck of Millie's blouse. No longer to hold back, Millie sneezed and screamed simultaneously.

"It's coming from the closet!"

The door opened. Joe Clawson, Professor Vroman, Mr. Trentwood, and Chuck Wolfe stared at Millie.

"Gaahhnnnn…!" Millie said. She pointed at Oscar Baier.

"Don't move," Professor Vroman said. He swung the butterfly net under Petunia's front legs. He brushed at the spider with a manila file from the desk. After a couple of taps the tarantula dropped into the net.

"Baier!" Millie said. "It was him! He was going to inject Joe with a syringe!"

Everyone turned. Oscar Baier stared at the group like he didn't have a care in the world

"Your niece was an agent for the OSS, Professor Vroman. She was sent to investigate our party's influence and manipulation in the movie industry. She might have succeeded had you not exposed her cover."

"What have I done?" Professor Vroman covered his face in his hands. His shoulders shook up and down.

"You won't get away with it, Baier," Chuck Wolfe said.

"Get away with what, Mr. Wolfe? You must realize I did nothing." Baier took a step back. "Miss Bernhard lured me here to entrap me but when I arrived, she was already dead from the spider's bite."

"You intended to kill her."

"You cannot know my intentions."

"But it's impossible," Millie said. "The rose tarantula's bite isn't strong enough to kill a human, isn't that what you said, Professor Vroman?"

Professor Vroman lowered his hands. He hadn't been crying. He'd been holding back his laughter.

"He didn't know that, did he, Sarah?"

"No, he didn't." Everyone looked at a fully conscious Sarah Dubinski sitting at the desk. She winked at Joe as she pulled off the special makeup effect of a spider bite. "Thanks for the help, Mr. Clawson."

"My pleasure."

Agent Dubinski pulled out a gun she'd hidden in the teacher's desk. "Oscar Baier, I am placing you under arrest for crimes against the United States, attempted murder, and anything else I can think of to put a stop to your evil plans."

Oscar Baier walked backwards, his hand fumbling in the front pocket of his suit coat. "You forget, Miss Bernhard. I have diplomatic immunity."

Behind him the door opened and Jenny Mitchell entered.

"Hey! We shooting today or what?"

Oscar Baier spun to face Jenny Mitchell raising the silver syringe to jab her. He reached for the child actor with his free hand. Jenny screamed and backed away just as a spider bobbed in front of Oscar Baier's face. He looked up as a nettle of sandbags came down on his baldhead, dropping him to the floor. Everyone else looked up at the catwalk too. They didn't see anyone but they heard the patter of feet.

The door opened once more. Brad Jolly stood inside the frame. "Anyone seen the kids? I can't find them."

Jenny Mitchell crossed her arms. "You missed your cue, Mr. Jolly."

Aggie Bernhard knelt down to put handcuffs on Oscar Baier.

"I'll call the police," Chuck Wolfe said.

"Call the coroner while you're at it," Aggie said. "He's dead."

"Dead?" Jenny Mitchell said. She looked at Freddy Hogan and Georgie Reynolds moving cautiously out of the dark. "You idiots weren't supposed to kill him. You were supposed to scare him so the guards could get him when he ran outside."

"They didn't kill him," Aggie Bernhard said. "He fell on his syringe."

"Well," Joe Clawson said. "There goes our 'days without an accident' tally."

"Aw, we didn't drop the sandbags anyhow," Freddy Hogan said.

Georgie Reynolds dangled the fake spider on the string. "All we dropped was the prop spider."

"Was everyone but me in on this ruse?" Millie asked. She looked at Paul Trentwood. "Wait a minute. That's why you wanted to see me. To tell me Edie Froehlich wasn't really sacked and Professor Vroman's niece worked for the OSS."

Trentwood stretched his neck and his smile. "Ah, right. Of course."

"By the way, I'm not actually a professor," Vroman said. He pulled off the thin, caterpillar-like moustache, eyebrows, and wig he wore. "I'm Special Agent Dan Booker."

"So that stuff you told us about tarantulas…" Millie said. She held up a hand. "Never mind. I don't want to know."

"It was all true, Miss Mornhinweg," Agent Booker assured her. "I studied entomology and toxicology before being recruited by the Office of Strategic Services."

The door to Soundstage E11 opened one more time. Max Bigelow, the director, entered.

"Sorry I'm late but I'm ready to shoot—whoa! What did I miss?"

Millie cozied up to Brad and thought, 'End of scene. Circle swipe out on the happy couple.' She reached up to kiss her beau.

"I hate to be a killjoy at a time like this," Joe the prop guy said. "But has anyone seen Petunia?"

With over 1,300 short stories published in Alfred Hitchcock, Ellery Queen, and Mike Shayne mystery magazines, anthologies and periodicals, Michael Bracken still manages to think up ideas faster than his keyboard can keep pace. He's written a few novels too.

Now, thanks to his wife, Temple, the ideas are coming double-time. From NPR, she learned koalas have fingerprints. She insisted that bit of trivia would make a good story. She was right. Wives always are.

A Cling of Koalas
by Michael Bracken

The overwhelming scent of eucalyptus assaulted my nostrils when I stepped into the five-story faunal enclosure. I turned to my driver. "I thought it was illegal to own koalas."

"It is, Detective Inspector," Constable Sophie Robinson said. "This is a rehabilitation center. They care for the sick and injured."

I looked up, searching the eucalyptus trees for any sign of the marsupials. None were in sight in the branches above, but a single koala stared back at me from a wire cage near the door through which we had entered. After a moment I turned my attention to the dead man lying in a wide spot on the slate walkway.

"Marc Winston," Sophie said. I had stopped to examine the parking lot—the pickups, the SUVs, the police vehicles, the red Jaguar parked at the far end—so she had been briefed by the first responders before I entered the enclosure through the double-door airlock. "Single shot through the heart—unless the M.E. learns otherwise during the autopsy. One of the keepers found the body when he opened this morning, called triple-0, and here we are."

"Paramedics?"

"There was nothing they could do. Winston had been dead for hours."

I squatted next to the body and examined the dead man. Mid-thirties, short hair, too pale to have spent much time outdoors. He wore a blood-soaked white short-sleeve shirt, khaki slacks, and tan buckle boots—apparel more suitable for an office than for an animal enclosure. I stood and waved over the paramedics. "You can take him."

A derringer found at the scene before my arrival was already on its way to forensics, where its ownership would be traced. Once the bullet was recovered from the body, tests would likely prove the gun was the murder weapon.

I doubted I could learn any more by watching the removal of the dead man's body, so I exited the enclosure and crossed the parking lot to the sanctuary's main office with Sophie only a few steps behind.

"He's been with us almost a year," explained Alice Thompson, executive director of Koala Haven, speaking of the dead man as if he were still alive. "Always a pleasure to work with."

I sat opposite her, speaking across the top of a desk larger than my cubicle at the station, having forgotten that Sophie sat in the chair next to mine. "What did he do here?"

"Office manager," Thompson said. A shapely woman in her late forties, she wore her auburn hair stylishly short, her make-up light and accentuating rather than concealing, backdrops for a black cascade wrap dress with three-quarter sleeves and modest décolletage. She wore no jewelry beyond diamond stud earrings and a slim gold watch on her left wrist. "And he'll be missed. He's whipped things into shape during his brief time with us."

"He have problems with any of the other employees?"

She shook her head slowly. "Nothing I'm aware of."

"Mind if we ask around?"

"Not at all," Thompson said.

"And we'll want to look through his office."

"No office." She told us Winston's desk was one of the two in the wide-open reception area outside her office. "Feel free to look through his things, Detective Inspector."

She stood, indicating the end of our conversation, and I stood as well. So did Sophie. When Thompson offered her hand, I took it and we shook. She held my hand a moment longer than necessary and, as her blue eyes searched mine, I understood how she was able to raise money from the local businessmen whose charitable donations supported the sanctuary.

As we left the executive director's office, I found myself no further along in the investigation than when we'd entered. Sophie remained to talk with the sanctuary's receptionist and search the dead man's desk while I spent the day speaking with the sanctuary's other employees. The general consensus matched that of the executive director. The dead man was well liked.

I returned to the faunal enclosure for the last interview and found Hunter Lee—the keeper who had discovered Winston's body—holding the young northern koala that had been in the cage by the door when I'd first arrived. He held the koala against his chest much like he might a small child, his arm beneath its rump and the koala's arms around his neck. "This is Oliver," he said. "He's only been with us a few days."

Covered in thick gray fur, Oliver had a large round head with large ears, a big flat nose, and small dark eyes that watched me as I spoke to the keeper.

I asked, "What's wrong with him?"

"Hit and run," Lee explained. "Left by the side of the road until a Good Sam spotted him and called us. Oliver was banged up pretty bad but nothing serious. We kept him caged for observation, and I was about to let him out with the others."

I redirected the conversation to the events of that morning.

"The doors were locked when I arrived." The double-door airlock prevented koalas from escaping when a single door opened, though I doubted the marsupials could outrun any of the keepers if they did escape. Lee showed me how the locks worked. Because the doors did not automatically lock when closed, only someone with keys could have locked the doors.

I asked, "Who has keys?"

"All the keepers," he said. "The other employees."

"So then what happened," I asked, "after you let yourself in?"

"I saw Marc lying there," Lee said, "and I knew something was wrong. Nobody can lose that much blood."

"So you phoned triple-0?"

"Aye, mate. I checked his pulse, just in case, you know, and then I phoned for an ambo."

"What did you do while you waited?"

"Checked on Oliver here," he said. "Your lot ran me out, and I'm only now allowed back inside to care for the walas."

I looked into the trees again and still saw nothing. "How many are in here?"

"Oliver makes five."

———

After I finished the interviews, Sophie drove me to the medical examiner's office, where we examined the personal belongings found with Winston. Change. A key ring containing more than a dozen keys. A wad of tissue. A cellphone belt clip holster. His wallet, containing identification, driver's license, credit cards, cash, and a photograph of a slender young woman in a blue sundress.

I looked up. "No cellphone?"

"Found it on his desk," Sophie said.

"Why would he leave his cellphone on his desk? Why wasn't it in the holster?"

She shrugged.

"You learn anything from it?"

"Can't," she said. "It's password and fingerprint protected."

I thought about that for a moment. "Anyone notified his next-of-kin? Maybe one of them knows the password."

———

The potbellied young woman who opened the door of Marc Winston's flat collapsed when we shared the news of his passing. Except for the belly, the woman matched the photo we'd found in Winston's wallet. Sophie helped her to the couch and then sat with her arms wrapped around the young woman as she drained her tear ducts onto Sophie's shoulder.

Between sobs, we determined Matilda King had been cohabitating with the deceased for thirteen months and they had been engaged for two. She showed us the rather sensible diamond solitaire on her left ring finger.

"He was—we were—now he'll never—" She didn't finish whatever she'd been trying to say because another geyser of tears erupted from her.

"I think she needs a lie down," Sophie said. "She's preggers."

I'd missed that, so I let Sophie lead Matilda into the bedroom, where she settled onto the bed. Once Sophie ensured Matilda was comfortable, I overheard her asking, "Is there anyone we can call?"

I didn't hear the answer because I was nosing through the flat, learning what I could about the deceased without interrogating the distraught pregnant woman. There wasn't much to learn. The flat was sparsely furnished, and most of the furniture appeared to be the assemble-it-yourself kind from IKEA. Photos of an older couple, either Winston's parents or Sophie's, graced a bookcase that sported only a handful of books—all of them bookkeeping primers—held in place by a pair of ceramic koala bookends.

The only other decorative reference to the dead man's occupation was a poster featuring a near-life-size photograph of a koala wedged into the Y of a tree branch, chewing a mouthful of eucalyptus leaves.

Sophie joined me in the living room. "I've phoned Matilda's mum and she should be here in a few minutes."

I nodded toward the bedroom. "She tell you anything?"

"She said something wasn't right at the sanctuary. Marc told her he found invoices for things that were never delivered. A few hundred dollars here and a few hundred there, but—"

"But it adds up, doesn't it?"

Sophie nodded. "Marc told Matilda he was going to confront someone about what he discovered."

"And did he?"

"She didn't know, but he must have, mustn't he?" Sophie said. "Why else would he have been killed?"

I had yet to reach any conclusions, so I shrugged.

"She said he kept copies of everything on his phone." Before I could ask the obvious question, Sophie continued, "She gave me the password."

The front door opened, and we turned to see a grey-haired squab of a woman bustle in. After explaining the situation to Matilda's mother, we left her to tend to her grieving daughter.

Sophie drove me back to the station, and we watched over the shoulder of one of the young techs as he keyed in Marc's cellphone password.

Though the phone was not wiped completely clean, we found no incriminating evidence on it—no photos of receipts, no text messages arranging clandestine meetings, no threats sent or received. We also found no text messages from Winston's co-workers nor any from his fiancée.

"I'll keep at it," the tech said, "and see if I can recover anything that's been deleted."

We returned to my cubicle and discovered forensics had sent the report on the murder weapon while we were away. I called it to my computer screen. The killer had fired a single shot from a Remington Arms Model 95, a .41 rimfire over-under double-barreled derringer manufactured from 1866 until 1935, deadly primarily at close range because the .41 Short bullet moved slowly compared to the speed of modern ballistic weaponry. The gun had not been registered, and likely entered the country before the enactment of stringent gun control laws. Often carried by gamblers, derringers were also popular with women because they fit easily into a purse.

The day had disappeared rather quickly, and I wanted to talk with Alice Thompson again. I called Koala Haven and the sanctuary's receptionist told me I could find her that evening at a fundraiser for the local museum, a fête she felt obligated to attend because many of the museum's donors also supported the sanctuary. My badge granted me entrance despite my workaday apparel, and I found Thompson seated at the bar nursing a martini. She wore her evening attire a little tighter, her décolletage a little deeper, her hemline a little higher, and her lipstick a little redder. The same gold watch adorned her slim wrist, but she had exchanged her diamond studs for chandelier earrings, and a thin gold chain around her neck disappeared between the swell of her breasts. I settled on the stool next to her and ordered a shot of Sullivans Cove Double Cask, a single malt Tasmanian Whisky.

"To what do I owe this pleasure, Graham?" she asked.

"I wanted to see you in your natural habitat," I said.

She smiled and her eyes sparkled. She made a vague motion with her left hand that seemed to indicate our surroundings. "And you think this is it?"

"You appear much more comfortable here than you were at the sanctuary."

Thompson leaned toward me to provide a better display of her cleavage, and she rested a hand on my knee. "I am," she said, "but I'd be even more comfortable if we went somewhere private."

"Such as?"

"My place." She finished her martini, grabbed her clutch, and slid from the barstool. "Follow me?"

I didn't tell her I had lost my driver's license and Constable Robinson was waiting for me outside. "How about I ride with you?"

She smiled. "Even better."

I waved Sophie away and waited with Thompson while the valet brought her red Jaguar. The valet held her door and I let myself in on the passenger side. As we drove away, I said, "Rescuing koalas must be quite lucrative."

"Not as much as you'd think," she said with a laugh. "This was a parting gift from my ex-husband—this and a rather substantial monthly check."

When we reached Thompson's home, I realized how large the monthly check must be. Though she only parked the Jaguar inside, the three-car garage was larger than my flat, and the foyer we passed through on the way to the den could have served as a museum exhibit. I commented on the expensive decor.

"I can afford many things," she said. "What I cannot afford is a scandal."

"How's that?"

She did not answer my question immediately, instead offering me a shot of Sullivans from the wet bar. After I accepted, she continued. "Donations are down, expenses are up, and the discovery of a dead body at the sanctuary is unlikely to improve things."

"What if it came out that someone was diverting funds?"

"Highly unlikely," she said. "I double-check everything my—" She stopped when she realized the implication. "You think I would shoot my office manager to cover up embezzlement?"

I sipped at my Sullivans. "People have been killed for less."

"I'm certain they have, D.I. Kelly." She had resumed using my title, letting me know that any possibility of intimacy had passed. "But I didn't have anything to do with Marc Winston's demise, and I take offense at the implication that I might have."

I finished my drink as she spoke.

"I'll let you see yourself out."

I did, realized Sophie had not followed us, and had to phone for a cab to take me to my flat.

———

Sophie met me first thing in the morning.

"While you were visiting with the sanctuary director," she said, "I returned to Winston's flat to check on Matilda. I bumped into Hunter Lee in the parking lot, and he said he'd stopped by to console Winston's grieving fiancée."

"And?"

"When she opened the door to my knock, it was obvious they'd been engaged in some rather vigorous consoling."

"But isn't she pregnant?"

Sophie stared at me as if I were daft.

We were interrupted by the arrival of the fingerprint technician, a ruddy-faced bloke who walked his report to my office rather than emailing it.

After a quick glance through it, I threw the report back on my desk. "The fingerprints on the gun don't match any of the employees, we have other prints from the scene that don't match any of the sanctuary's employees, and no one was allowed inside except employees. That's what we were told."

"Aye, mate, have you printed the koalas?"

"Excuse me?"

"The little buggers have fingerprints."

"They what?"

"The fingers of chimps, gorillas, and koalas carry ridged patterns of loops, whorls, and arches, a biomechanical adaption to grasping."

"In English?"

"They have fingerprints, just like humans," he said. "The loops, whorls, and arches produce multidirectional mechanical influences on the skin, which help the koalas grasp eucalyptus leaves."

"You think Winston was killed by a marsupial?"

"What else was in there with him?"

"Jesus," I said. "Print the damn koalas, and don't let any of them get away until we've checked all their prints."

I'm uncertain how the fingerprint technician bumped our case to the top of his to-do list, but Sophie had the results that afternoon.

"Oliver," she said. "The fingerprints on the gun match a koala named Oliver."

She drove me to Koala Haven, and I learned Hunter Lee had taken the day off. One of the other keepers escorted me into the enclosure, where Oliver was once again in the wire cage near the air-lock door.

I stared at him and he stared back. I said, "You don't look like the criminal type."

He blinked.

"So you must be a witness," I continued. "So what did you see, and who would want to implicate you?"

Oliver blinked again. He could tell me nothing. Not directly. I turned to the keeper. "Who has keys to Oliver's cage?"

"Only the keepers," he said.

"Not Ms. Thompson?"

"No, sir," he said. "Just me, Tony, and Hunter."

We made two arrests early that evening, and I spoke with Matilda King first. She claimed she knew nothing about her fiancé's murder, but as recipient of his life insurance policy and the probability the baby she carried was not actually Winston's provided us sufficient reason to keep at her until she broke down.

Our other arrestee had already retained a solicitor, but I wasn't bothered by the shyster's presence.

I stared across the table at Hunter Lee.

"What bothered me is that the airlock doors on the faunal enclosure only lock with a key. Winston still had his keys, so whoever was in there with him locked the door on the way out. That means his killer was one of the employees."

Lee crossed his arms.

"Matilda tried to implicate Alice Thompson, claiming that Winston had uncovered embezzlement at the sanctuary, which, given Thompson's lavish lifestyle, was certainly worth looking into. But she didn't have a key to Oliver's cage."

When Lee glanced at his solicitor, I knew I was on to something.

"Here's what I think happened," I said. "You lured Winston into the enclosure, and you shot him. You wiped your fingerprints off the gun and pressed it into Oliver's hand or paw or whatever it is and tossed it near the body. Then you used the dead man's finger to unlock his cellphone and carried it with you when you left. You locked the doors behind you, deleted incriminating evidence from Winston's phone, and put it on his desk. The next morning you found the body—a body you fully expected to find—and you called the ambo, just as anyone would."

Lee broke his silence. "Why would I kill Winston?"

"Matilda's having your child—I'm certain DNA testing will confirm that—and his life insurance would have set the two of you up nicely. See, her breakdown was quite convincing when we told her of Winston's murder, and I likely never would have caught on if it weren't for Oliver. The fingerprints on the murder weapon matched none of the sanctuary's employees and weren't in our database, but they matched Oliver's. You would know that koalas had fingerprints, and you would know that we could not match his prints to anyone. But the real giveaway was that you locked the doors to the enclosure to prevent the koalas inside from escaping. Only someone who cared for the little buggers would take the time to do that."

———————

Lee ultimately confessed to the murder, claiming that it was all Matilda's idea, but determining the degree of complicity was a matter for the courts, not for me.

Two weeks later, Sophie and I accompanied Alice Thompson and one of the Koala Haven keepers when they released Oliver into the wild, the first time I was ever happy to see my prime murder suspect escape life-long incarceration.

Jeanne Dubois lives in Florida with a retired racing greyhound. Whenever it's too hot or raining buckets, she reads and writes mysteries. Visit her at www.jeanne-dubois.com

When a friend stocked her newly-built pond with koi, Jeanne was amazed at how expensive koi were compared to standard classroom goldfish. For this story, she asked herself: What if someone didn't want lowly goldfish swimming with their fancy koi? What if someone had a motive for creating chaos?

A Troubling of Goldfish
by Jeanne DuBois

I found the body, tripped over it as a matter of fact, minutes before dawn. If not the witching hour, then certainly the darkest one. I wasn't hysterical for more than ten minutes.

It started the previous Saturday. Tax season was over, along with its companion project, a backyard pond, and my husband Walter was happy: He was Googling *koi* and sipping iced tea on our screened-in porch instead of weekend-working on some procrastinator's returns. Ma was happy: Her handsome son-in-law was keeping her company while she lounged and watched the hummingbirds at the backyard feeder. I was happy, too. All my eighth-grade essays were graded, next week's lesson plans were complete, and fixing dinner was hours away. Happy, that is, until I caught sight of Walter's laptop screen. The koi he was ogling cost over four hundred dollars. Each. I bit my lip and looked away to contain my alarm. My mother, who lived with us while recuperating from a January hip replacement, read my expression and dove in.

"Cat got your tongue, Denise?" Ma wore her fluffy white hair like a badge allowing free entry into my business, any time, any place. "You look like you got something to say. You got a problem with the koi?"

Walter glanced at me. I smiled and shook my head, contemplating a cold drink. Limes for Cuba Libres were right up there with milk, bread, and toilet paper on my grocery list these days.

With innocence shining in her baby-blue eyes, Ma tried a different tack. "Find a fish you like for your new pond, Walter? After all that work, you'll only want the very best."

"I'm not going for the collector's cut," he said with a smile. "But there are some fine ones online. Where's Jimmy? He was going to help me decide." Walter turned and called his name.

I groaned inwardly. Our son shared Walter's expensive taste. If something cost more, it had to be better, right?

Jimmy appeared in the doorway holding a can of Mountain Dew. Taller and almost as muscular as his father, with long eyelashes and a mass of blond curls not yet reduced by age to a wispy tonsure, our high school senior attracted girlish attention like a flower does a bee. "What's up?"

"Take a look at this Gin Rin Showa," Walter said. "What do you think?"

Jimmy strolled across the porch and considered the image on the screen. "She's beautiful, Pops."

"What's a Gin Rin Showa when it's at home?" Ma asked.

"A Showa is a koi that's born all black and develops red and white markings as it grows," Walter said. "Gin Rin, also known as keen-geen-leen, refers to the gold and silver reflective scales which make this koi a Living Jewel."

Ma clapped her hands. "It sounds absolutely gorgeous! Don't you agree, Denise?"

"Naturally," I said, getting up to greet Sam and Terry Cassidy, our neighbors from across the street. They were approaching on the path that led around the garage and through the azaleas. Sam's car dealership—*You Better Hop Along to Cassidy's*—was famous for its wacky TV commercials with a Western theme. Hopalong Cassidy was, according to Ma, a beloved TV cowboy from the fifties.

"Don't worry, it's less than five hundred dollars," Walter said. "Free shipping," he added, as if that clinched the deal. *Click. Click. Click.*

Ma missed my wince. She only had eyes for Terry, a wrinkled redhead wearing pink lipstick and a Hawaiian-flowered romper, who took Ma with her everywhere. They ate gourmet lunches at cozy restaurants with gilded faucets in the bathroom, drove two hours to the beach to park and watch the lifeguards work-out, played bridge and bingo and went to matinee movies. Meanwhile, I was hammering English usage rules into hard-headed teenagers and hoping for a break to relieve my bladder.

Sam wanted to see Walter's pond so, leaving Ma and Terry to their gossip, we three went outside. Walter catalogued the aquatic plants for us and began to describe the pond's filtering system, in detail. I drifted away with Myesha and Caroline, two of the college students renting the house next door. When they saw me in the yard, they came through the gate to ask about substitute teaching at my school. Substitutes were always needed, but shapely Caroline with her turquoise eyes and long black hair, and elfin Myesha with her shy smile and Bambi eyes, would wreak havoc at the middle school. Middle school boys were like unstable gases. The slightest rise in temperature could cause an explosion. I gave the girls the name of somebody at the elementary school and we walked along the back fence admiring the tall gardenias, full of buds, before joining the men at the pond.

Sam wasn't afraid of flashing his new dental implants at the pair. "I bet comets cost twenty-five cents at PetSmart," he said, winking at Caroline. A jovial man, he liked his chances, no matter the game. His hair was brown, but his whiskers glinted silver in the sun.

Myesha said, "Are comets a kind of koi?"

"Comets are a kind of goldfish," Caroline said. "They come in different colors and have a long, forked tail."

"There'll be no goldfish in my pond," Walter said.

"How are koi and goldfish different?" Myesha was studying to be an art teacher. "I thought they were both carp."

"Both carp, but different species." Caroline, future scientist, was reading something on her phone. "Goldfish tend to be smaller and have more variety in their body shapes, while koi have more variety in their colors and patterns."

"And," Walter put in, "goldfish breed more frequently. As a result, they not only outproduce the koi, they adapt more easily to changes in the environment due to their smaller size. Goldfish will quickly destroy a koi pond."

"I doubt most people can tell the difference," Sam said, turning slightly away from his wife who sidled up to him with a proprietary smile.

Ma was walking toward us bent over, without her cane, which I encouraged, though not the like-a-hunchback part. "Between what and what?"

"Between goldfish and koi," Caroline said.

"Which do you like best, Walter?" Ma said.

"Koi, of course," he said.

After Caroline promised to have a look at Sam's dealership one day soon—"I'll make you an offer you can't refuse!"—the girls headed home. Sam and Terry came in for drinks and stayed for dinner.

"When's the koi fish due to arrive?" Sam said, helping himself to more salad.

"Have some more pasta and shrimp," I said.

Sam said, "No, thanks, I'm on a diet. Trying to get healthy."

"That explains why I see you jogging when I'm on my way to work," I said.

"He can't go very far," Terry said, laughing.

"Tuesday," Walter said, "between noon and four."

I said, "I can't be home before three-thirty."

"Farther than you," Sam said, no malice in his voice.

My mother was already shaking her head. "That's tournament day for our bridge club."

Terry agreed with a nod, her mouth full.

"Don't worry," Sam said, clapping Walter on the back with a grin. "The box'll probably say 'Live Koi' or something. Nobody's going to steal it."

"Somebody with a pond might," Walter said.

The Cassidys left soon after dessert, and Walter headed for BestBuy, open 'til nine.

He installed his new Door-Mate-*Ultra*, a battery-powered camera that provided motion-activated or live-view video, beside the front door, and spent the rest of the night sneaking peeks at our front yard on his phone.

———

Walter texted me at school as soon as the box was delivered at two o'clock on Tuesday, then again at two-ten, and at two-twenty, and... I succumbed to the pressure and went home.

The box marked *Live Fish* was waiting inside the front door when Walter arrived home at five-thirty, as per his instructions. Jimmy was at baseball practice. Ma was lying down after losing the bridge tournament on the last hand. I was in the kitchen assembling eggplant parmigiana, Lidia-style. Walter greeted the box with a cheer, changed his clothes, and called me to duty.

"The transfer will occur shortly," he said, handing me a clipboard with a checklist attached.

I grabbed a pencil and followed, wondering if we were going to have a countdown. Why he couldn't drop the fish into the water and be done with it was beyond me. But it was his project and he could, and would, complete it as he saw fit. Without a snide remark or a single eye roll, I placed a check in front of: *1 Carry unopened shipment to pond area.*

I read ahead to: *3 Wait 20-30 minutes for the water temperatures to equalize,* and armed myself with a folding chair. As I settled myself on it, Walter opened the box. He removed the sealed plastic bag containing the (one very large) koi and placed the bag in the pond. I checked off number two. Walter screamed.

Frightened, I jumped to my feet. "What's wrong?"

He turned a stricken face to me. "There's a goldfish in the pond!"

"What?" I went closer to investigate. Sure enough, a flash of reddish-orange gave the trespasser away. "Where'd it come from?"

Walter ran to the garage and returned with a brand-new fish-net as well as a plastic container from our recycle bin. He thrust the container at me. "Fill it with water."

"Pond water?" I said.

Walter said nothing, intent on catching the koi-pond destroyer. I shrugged, filled the container with water from the pond, and waited. Some time later, the goldfish was swimming around the container in my hand and looking rather pleased with itself. "What do you want me to do with it?"

Wordlessly, Walter snatched the pencil and clipboard from the ground, reviewed his checklist, and checked the time on his wristwatch. He opened the bag, released the dazzling koi into the pond, and watched it wriggle away. He made some marks on his checklist, then turned on me. "If you didn't want me to get the koi, you should have said so!"

"What? You don't think I—"

"Who else? It's not a bit funny." He stalked toward the house.

Ma was waiting for me on the back porch. "What's got into you, Denise?"

"But I didn't do anything," I said helplessly.

She gave me a pitying look.

Dinner was an awkward affair. I ate with Jimmy on the back porch; Ma and Walter ate in the kitchen. I washed the dishes, packed away the leftovers, and contemplated three-inch-long Goldie, waving graceful white fins and a forked tail in the crystal vase I'd filled for her. When and how and who were the obvious questions. The why was not a mystery: Annoy Walter Stevenson.

Walter was a light sleeper, thank goodness. The next morning when he discovered two more goldfish in the pond, I was off the hook, so to speak, as perpetrator. When I left for work, he was trying to net the interlopers while Jimmy aimed the flashlight.

———

Wednesday night's dinner was grim. Walter's Gin Rin Showa was in hiding, so he couldn't assess her health. Worse, he'd found more goldfish in the pond when he arrived home from work. The goldfish didn't appear to be nearly as disruptive to the peaceful pond as the hunters—a net swooping in and out of the water, feet stomping in the grass around it, loud cries of "Over here! Over here!"—but I kept that observation to myself. Walter and Jimmy removed four intruders before sitting down to meatloaf and garlic mashed potatoes, one of Walter's favorites.

Jimmy had talked Myesha into giving the two morning goldfish a home, but she turned down his early evening plea. I sent him to the playground with the goldfish, each in its own clear plastic bag of water, and suggested he find some kids.

Walter, meanwhile, removed the Door-Mate-*Ultra* video camera from beside the front door and took it out back. Ma lounged with a magazine, one eye on the hummingbird feeder, and listened to her son-in-law explain what he was doing as he drilled the outside wall and plugged in boxes on the back porch. He played around with the app on his phone, showed Ma a live-view of the backyard, and sat down with a cup of coffee. I fixed my mother an iced tea, mixed myself a drink, and joined them at the table. We put our heads together and instinctively lowered our voices.

"There are only three ways in," Walter said.

I sipped, coughed, and nodded.

He counted on his fingers. "The neighbors on either side, one-two, and our front yard, three. The front yard is out. The doorbell camera would have caught the movement."

Ma said, "What about through the woods?" Behind the houses on our side of the street was a forested conservation area.

"Tramping two miles through the woods like seems an awful lot of trouble for a joke," I said.

Ma shrugged. "It was just a suggestion. What about the sides?"

I looked at Walter. "Phil's fence does have a gate."

Walter stuck out his chin. "Let that renter try something. I've got motion zones activated all around the pond now. This goldfish nonsense has got to stop. I'll report him to his landlord if it doesn't." He drank more coffee.

I said nothing, but I knew exactly who he meant. Caroline-and-Myesha's roommate Todd, a freshman at the university, would think planting goldfish in Walter's pond good for a million laughs. Todd had placed rubber rats among the lady palms outside Myesha's bedroom window within days of moving in, and draped a plastic rattlesnake along Caroline's windowsill a week later.

Walter's upper body swayed slightly as he waggled his finger at me. "Phil'll put that kid's ass on the street in a New York minute!"

I wondered, *Am I the only one drinking rum here?*

In spite of the alcohol, which he wasn't used to, or perhaps because of it, Walter tossed and turned all night. I dozed in fits, my sleep full of weird dreams of boats and choppy seas and monster goldfish flying over the waves.

I yawned. "Why do you want coffee?"

"I have a math test first period." Jimmy pulled the cup from under the Keurig and dropped in some ice cubes.

"How about a healthy breakfast?"

Jimmy brightened. "Bacon, eggs, and pancakes?"

"That's not exactly what I'd call a healthy breakfast."

"I know," he said, "why don't I have some yogurt and a banana?"

I looked up in surprise, but he was making fun of me. I pressed the button on the coffee maker. "Hey, did you check to see if Todd put any more goldfish in Dad's pond?"

"Todd? Why are you picking on Todd?"

"I'm not picking on him."

"You're still mad about the rubber rattlesnake."

I made a face. "He threw it at me."

"It wasn't Todd who put the goldfish in the pond, if that's what you're thinking."

"Oh, no? And how can you be so sure about that?"

"Because Todd," said Jimmy, "is visiting his dad in Maryland and won't be back till next week. You really should get your facts straight before you start tossing out accusations, Mom." He finished his coffee and left me standing at the counter, openmouthed.

I followed him to the front door. "What about the others?"

"What others?"

"C'mon."

He acquiesced. "I don't see either of the girls sneaking around with goldfish in the middle of the night, do you? And Mark's been staying nights with his girlfriend on campus."

I pressed on. "What about our neighbors on the other side?"

Jimmy shrugged into his backpack. "Mr. Morris is about a hundred years old. You really think he's gonna climb a four-foot fence to play a joke on Dad?"

"What about his wife? She's a lot younger. I bet she could climb it."

He laughed. "Mrs. Morris? She never even goes outside! Face it, Mom. There's really only one person it could be." He smiled and opened the front door.

"Who? Not me. It wasn't me. I didn't do it."

"Bye, Mom." He kissed the top of my head and walked into the inky morning. The Cassidys' garage light shot across the street like a star.

"What about breakfast?" I called after him.

Jimmy's disembodied voice came back to me. "I'll get something at Roger's. His mom makes apple-cinnamon pancakes and baked ham every morning."

Ouch. I closed the front door and went to shower. Before I left for work, Walter shared his only night-vision activity-video with me: a large pale bird flying low across the yard. He hurried outside to check the pond.

I caught Sam in my headlights as I rounded the first curve. He was on the side of the road, bending over, hands on knees, trying to catch his breath. I slowed for a speed bump, lighted Myesha and Caroline in their skimpy jogging clothes, and then entered the second roundabout where another male jogger ran solo. My phone dinged. I viewed the text at the next stop sign.

Walter: *no gd gf grs ok :-)*

I had neither the wits nor the time to decode it, but figured lower-case letters and a happy face meant things in Walter's world were not-so-bad, maybe even good, and I could relax.

Ma was in a snit when I returned home from school Thursday afternoon. Her bedroom was too hot. The air conditioner was too loud. The back porch was too sunny. Then she started in on me. My dress was stained. My makeup had smeared. My hair needed combing.

"Hey," I said finally, "my work day is done," and went to change.

She trailed me, harping. "You wear that dress all the time. It doesn't even look good on you. Why don't you buy some new clothes? Seems like you spend a lot of money on food. Walter doesn't need meat every night. And speaking of Walter, he was shining his flashlight around at the crack of dawn again. How is a person supposed to sleep around here?"

I wheeled around. "What is it, Ma? Find a pea under your mattress again?"

She stomped across the house to her bedroom and slammed the door.

I washed my face, ran a comb through my hair, and changed clothes. After a few bracing sips of rum and Coke, I fixed Ma a cup of tea, arranged some lemon-butter cookies on a pretty plate, and carried them to her room. She was sitting in the dark. I set the plates on the magazine table beside her chair and opened the drapes. Sunlight streamed in, accentuating Ma's frown lines. I automatically smiled. I didn't want all those wrinkles around *my* mouth.

"Go away." She gave me a sharp dagger of a look.

"I'll have to try that one on the kids. It'll stop 'em in their tracks if it doesn't kill 'em."

Ma squeezed her eyes shut. I hung her bathrobe on the clothes tree, swept a pile of dirty laundry into my arms, and hazarded a guess. "Terry too busy for you today?"

"Who cares?"

I took that as a yes. "Want to help me make dinner? We could do homemade noodle soup, your favorite."

"Get lost."

Part of a pant leg hung outside Ma's closet door. I swung the door farther open with a toe, poked the pant leg inside the closet, and caught the flash of something reddish-orange on the floor. I dropped the dirty clothes, opened the closet door, and retrieved a large clear plastic bag of water. Three fancy goldfish floated listlessly near its bottom.

"What's this?" I held up the bag of goldfish.

Ma opened her eyes and a flush of fear passed over her face. "Sam's idea."

"Sam gave you the goldfish and told you to put them in Walter's pond?" I was floating on a cloud of disbelief.

Her voice was a whisper. "Sort of."

"'Sort of'? What does that mean?"

"Sam gave them to Terry and she gave them to me."

I was having a hard time with this. "But *you* put the goldfish in the pond? Is that right? Ma, look at me. Did you put the goldfish in the pond?"

Ma stared at me, nodding slightly.

My voice rose. "What about these three? Were they going in tonight?"

Ma shook her head.

"Tomorrow?"

A tear traveled down Ma's ravaged cheek and she looked away. Like a kid in trouble at school, Ma was shutting down. I had a sudden insight.

I lowered my voice, made it soft and soothing. "Why is Terry mad at you, Ma?"

After a minute, her mouth quivered. "I said I couldn't do no more."

I took a deep breath and continued in the same quiet tone. "All right, drink your tea and eat some cookies. I'll take care of the evidence."

Ma was staring into her lap when I left her.

I made a call, then drove the comets to the elementary school. The principal, a huge man with hands like baseball mitts, met me in the bus circle. He took possession of the bag of three, and Goldie in a bag by herself, and laughed.

"Looks like a good glint of goldfish." Dr. De'onte Hall took in my expression and sobered. "Or perhaps, a troubling?"

I tried and failed to form a convincing smile.

De'onte patted my arm. "I got this. You take care, Deeny-girl." We taught our first five years in adjoining classrooms. Friends for life.

I drove home, cooked dinner, cleaned the kitchen, and wondered why my mother would do that to Walter. *Because Terry asked her to, that's why. You jealous, Denise?* Maybe. Mostly, I was disappointed. Bossy, grumpy, and nosy were some of the names I pinned to Ma's changing moods. But underneath it all, I always believed she was *nice.*

I dusted our wood furniture, vacuumed the carpet, polished brass knobs, shined mirrors, and decided that putting the goldfish in Walter's pond was not so much a betrayal as a thoughtless prank. I resolved not to confront Sam or Terry about it. Eventually, I'd have to tell Walter, but I'd cross that bridge when I came to it.

The next morning, I opened the garage door preparatory to leaving, but instead of getting into my car and backing out as usual, I went outside and ambled along the driveway, sucking in a large amount of the spring-scented air. I flipped off the Cassidys' house and tried out my new dagger glare, then, turning, stumbled over something on the driveway near the street. My phone was in my pocket. I pressed its flashlight icon and found Sam Cassidy in his jogging clothes, covered with blood, lying across the pavers like a beached whale.

I must have screamed because Walter barged out of the garage in his bare feet, wrapped his arms around me, and pressed one hand over my mouth. "Hush. Hush. What's the matter? Did you see a snake or a spider?"

Which was exactly the right thing to say. He knew I hated it when people intimated that because I was female, I must be afraid of snakes and spiders. I straightened up, gave him a don't mess with me look, indignant at the idea. I pointed to Sam's body and handed Walter my lit up phone. Walter knelt beside Sam. I turned at the sound of footsteps in the garage. Ma, probably. Jimmy was… I searched the darkness, trying to remember when I'd last seen him.

After his conversation with 9-1-1, Walter returned my phone, said Sam had a pulse, and advised me to call work. "We're going nowhere fast."

But first I texted Jimmy: *You ok?*

When I received his standard green checkmark in reply, I phoned my school. The sky was lightening into pink and gray streaks on the eastern horizon. The Fire Rescue vehicle arrived with a squeal of brakes, disgorging two uniformed EMTs. Walter met them in the street. A sheriff's car followed a few minutes later. Before the strobe lights on its roof had time to dim, Terry was crossing the street, her red hair pinned around her head like a crown. Her green robe, covered with embroidered dragons, swept the pavement. She touched one slippered foot onto the driveway and turned into a tornado. Screaming and windmilling her arms, she came at me, ignoring the two men working on Sam. "What have you done to my husband!"

Walter stepped between us, physically blocking her.

I said, "I didn't do anything to him, I swear."

Ma let out a rush of words from the garage: "Denise backed over him, I'm sure of it, I shoulda saw it coming, she just gets in her car and goes out the garage without worrying about what's behind her, or who, never thinks of anybody but herself, such a shame."

I froze, stung.

Terry followed up with: "In such a hurry, Mrs. I-have-such-an-important-job-to-do. Now, just look at what you've done!" Terry burst into tears. Ma came out of the shadows and hugged her.

The deputy consulted with the medics carrying Sam on a stretcher, then walked back to us as the Fire Rescue vehicle peeled away from the curb in a blaze of blinking lights.

"Where are they taking him?" Terry said, holding Ma's hand.

"Northeast Hospital," the deputy said.

Ma said, "He's alive?"

The deputy nodded and turned to me. "You backed over him?"

I opened my mouth but no sound came out.

Walter shook his head. "No, sir. She never started her car this morning."

At Ma's and Terry's protests, the deputy cocked his head. "Sure about that?"

Walter pointed at the Chevy parked in the garage. "Feel the hood."

The deputy did as Walter suggested, then strolled out of the garage and surveyed us spread out on the apron. "Somebody's vehicle hit the victim. That seems likely at this time. But it wasn't this one. I don't see any damage to the front or the rear. And there would be."

Myesha and Caroline jogged up, mouths agape.

The deputy addressed me again. "How did he end up on your driveway?"

I said, "I don't know."

Myesha said, "Who?"

Walter said, "Sam."

"Hit by a car," I said.

"Here?" Myesha sounded surprised.

Caroline said, "That doesn't make any sense. Why is his SUV at the park then? We saw it there a few minutes ago."

"We thought he was jogging the woodland trail," Myesha put in.

Terry said, "His car isn't at the park, Bimbo. It's in our garage."

"My name is Caroline, and it *is* his car, I've seen him drive it plenty of times.

Terry snorted. "Lots of people drive Highlanders."

"There's a Hopalong Cassidy vinyl cut-out in the back window," Myesha said.

Caroline looked at the deputy. "Its back end is all smashed."

"I don't know anything about that," Terry said, tossing her head. "I know that Sam was salting Walter's pond with goldfish and Walter was getting really mad about it."

Walter wrinkled his forehead. "It was Sam? Why didn't he—"

"You know it was Sam!" Terry spat at him. "Your wife found the last three goldfish in her mother's room and told you all about it last night! That's why this happened! You just had to figure out a way to get even, didn't you!"

Ma pointed at me. "That's right!"

I frowned at her. "I didn't tell Walter about the goldfish."

Walter nodded slowly. "So that's why Sam didn't show up on the security camera. It *was* an inside job. I thought so, but I never dreamed—"

"Wait a minute," the deputy said, "you have a security camera? Let's see what it shows from this morning."

"It won't show anything," Walter said. "I moved the camera to the back when goldfish started appearing in my koi pond. After that, we didn't get any more goldfish. I was going to leave it there one more day."

I said, mostly to myself, "Terry wanted Ma to put goldfish in the pond because she wanted Walter to move his camera to the backyard." I turned to Terry. "You didn't want any record of what was going to happen out front on the street."

The deputy said, "What was going to happen on the street?"

I indicated the driveway with a sweep of my hand. "I guess she was going to back into him when he went jogging and blame it on me. Or somebody."

"Check the blue Highlander at the park," Caroline said. "I bet there's a ton of forensic evidence there, inside and outside the vehicle."

The deputy said something into the radio on his shoulder and stepped toward Terry. And she was off to the races. Walter, Myesha, and Caroline blocked her escape long enough for the deputy to get a grip on her arms. Screeching and cursing, Terry gave us what for about Sam and the two freaking college girls and the black-haired bimbo and that blankity-blank know-it-all, Denise. The deputy snapped the cuffs on Terry's wrists and hauled her, spewing obscenities, to the backseat of his patrol car.

Sam Cassidy survived, but he wouldn't be out of the hospital anytime soon. Terry, in jail for attempted murder, would probably be released before him. Ma went to live with my brother. He was glad to take her. With her new hip, Ma could babysit his two girls after school and over summer break. Walter added an orange and white koi to the pond, a ten-inch female. It reminded me of the goldfish, and I phoned De'onte. Goldie and her pals were doing fine.

Ma's words from that morning haunted me, more troubling than a group of goldfish could ever be. Like cold fingers, they poked me awake at three in the morning and kept me, trembling and hurt, at the edge of sleep. Walter said deeper cuts took longer to heal. But I never was much good at forgetting.

Kaye George (alias Janet Cantrell) is a short story writer, and the author of five mystery series. Her characters include Neanderthals and a Fat Cat. Her latest, The Vintage Sweets series, debuts in March 2020. She blogs at https:// writerswhokill.blogspot.com/ and www.killercharacters.com

The idea of bees as characters has been buzzing around in her head for a couple years. This was the perfect place for the swarm of characters to settle but it's not all sweetness.

Grist for the Mill

by Kaye George

Kevin Grady couldn't wait to get outside. The sunshine beckoned him from his office window, the first nice day since it started raining a week ago. It felt like he'd been cooped up in his home office forever. He hurried through paying the bills online and flung the back door open to suck in the warm spring air.

When he choked on it, he stopped and looked around, spitting out the foul taste he had inhaled. His property was two acres, not a large amount of land, but big enough for his vegetable garden and his bee hives. The new neighbor to the west, Vivian Sessions, was in her yard, head down, walking slowly. She had moved in over the winter. He had met her then, but they hadn't talked much. He often saw her at church and they greeted each other, but that was about it.

What was she doing? She was spraying her lawn, working methodically back and forth, covering the whole yard, it looked like.

Whatever she was spraying, the wind was blowing the smell of it to his yard. It was sulfurous, smelled the way Kevin imagined Hell might smell if he were to get there eventually.

It had been a long time since Kevin had contemplated Hell. In his younger days, his twenties and thirties, he had done some

55

things that would warrant eternal residence there. Except he had already served a period of confinement for those things in the state penitentiary. When he was feeling philosophical, he used to debate with himself whether his slate would have started fresh by now. Or not.

One of the reasons he liked keeping bees was that he hoped it would balance the scales. They were good for the planet, so he had the idea he was doing good for all his fellow humans by collecting and selling honey from his own hives. Some of his customers seemed to think he was wonderful. They gushed about being able to purchase "local" honey.

"Good morning, Ms. Sessions," he called. She looked up from her sprayer. No response. "What are you doing?"

"Spraying." She spat the word at him and went back to it. He couldn't read the printing on the plastic container, shielded by her rather substantial body.

"Ms. Sessions, what are you spraying?"

"My yard." She continued working her way closer to the property line, her permanent frown even deeper today.

His bees buzzed around their hives as usual. They seemed okay for now but there were a lot of sprays that could hurt them. They were delicate little creatures. He tried again. "What is in your sprayer?"

This time when she looked up, she glared. "That's my business. This is my yard."

That was the longest exchange of words they'd had since she moved in. She didn't seem to like him, but he had no idea why. He smiled to try to soothe her. "It's just that the bees, you know…"

"What about them?" The look in her hard eyes was mean. With a jolt of shock, he thought he saw real hatred there.

"I need to make sure it's not something harmful to them."

This time she turned her back on him. That's when he caught a glimpse of the label. It was the popular major brand of weed killer that contained Glyphosate, a substance banned in many countries, but not yet in the USA. He knew it would also kill not only the weeds, but her grass and his bees if she sprayed enough of it.

There wasn't even a fence between their yards to prevent it from blowing his way. Now he was getting mad. He crossed the invisible property line into her yard and came up behind her.

"Ms. Sessions!"

She raised her head, alarm in her eyes. "Get out of my yard. I can't keep your horrid bees from flying into the yard, but I can tell *you* to get out."

"You can't spray that around my bees. You'll kill them."

"Good," she said, walking to the other side of her property, still spraying.

Kevin stood watching her, fuming but helpless. What could he do? She was allowed to spray poison in her yard. There was no law against it, unfortunately. He walked to his hives, slowly, so he wouldn't alarm the bees. The wind had shifted, blowing the toxin away from his place. He didn't see any dead insects on the ground. Yet. The prevailing winds were usually from her place to his, west to east, so it was only a matter of time until the wind shifted back his way.

She kept spraying. Was she going to use the whole sprayer in one day? It was a huge container. He stuck his hands on his hips and stared at her until she quit and went inside, taking her sprayer with her. She hadn't used all of it, but she had slathered it thick on her yard. At that rate, her grass would probably die along with any weeds.

Kevin uncoiled his hose and washed off his vegetable plants, tomatoes, pole beans, small heads of lettuce just beginning to form, and some broccoli and other vegetables. He couldn't wash off the bees, though. Those poor little guys.

Sometimes he thought it was strange of him to feel that way, but he had an affection for them. They were cute, fuzzy, and made that soothing hum when they flew. He belonged to a local group of beekeepers who met a few times a year. They were all fond of their insects. Kevin had done terrible things to a few people, but wouldn't think of harming a single worker bee from his hives. They were great little fellows, toiling so hard to make honey for people to eat. Besides doing that, they also pollinated plants. Kevin thought that everyone should love bees.

Over the next three days, he didn't catch Ms. Sessions spraying again. Sometimes when he went out to tend the hives or his vegetables, though, he could smell it and knew she'd been at it. One evening, his indoor bookkeeping work done, the actual job that supported him and the bees, he strolled through his yard to do a routine check on the vegetables. He tied up some tomatoes and beans, then suited up and approached the three hives. The air was pure tonight. No spraying.

Tending his garden and his bees made a welcome change from his work, freelance from his home office. He had three regular major clients who gave him enough work to suit him. He didn't want to get rich. He just wanted to tend to his hobbies.

The three hives sat in a row with about a foot of space between them. He usually pulled the frames out twice a month to inspect them, but pulled out a few today, even though he'd done it last week. He wanted to see how the bees were doing after the attacks of his neighbor. It didn't seem like there were enough bees on the rack he held. He pulled out another. It, too, was low, by at least a third. He moved to the second hive, thinking he could maybe transfer some bees from there to the ailing hive, as he sometimes did, but eventually discovered that all three hives were missing a lot of worker bees.

Tears sprang to his eyes. His poor bees. It was because he lived next door to a monster.

He wondered if he could appeal to her again. Maybe she didn't mean it when she intimated that it would be good to get rid of his bees. How could that be good? He still had a few jars of honey from last year. It lasted forever. Everyone loves honey, he thought. Maybe even her. After getting a jar of it from his basement shelf, he rang her doorbell.

"Ms. Sessions," he started when she came to the door. He showed her the jar and smiled. "I don't think I've ever given you any of my honey. I'd like you to have a jar."

"Don't want any honey. I have allergies."

"Ah. This is very good for allergies. Local honey is recommended by everyone when you're allergic to—"

"Bees," she said. "I'm allergic to bees. I'll die if they sting me. If you come on my property again, I'm warning you, I have a shotgun." And she slammed the door.

Kevin stood, stunned, for a moment. Is that why she sprayed? Was she actually *trying* to kill his hives? Did she want to kill him, too? He stomped home and fumed for a couple of hours. What a stupid woman. Being allergic to bees didn't mean she couldn't eat honey but she wasn't going to stop. She was going to continue until his bees were gone and she was going to be happy when that happened.

He paced his living room, wearing a path. He had to save his bees from a sure death. There was time to save them, but not much. What could he do? He slumped on the couch, envisioning abandoned hives, no honey, no fuzzy creatures humming through the yard. Then a different vision appeared.

A calm came over him. He imagined one of the bees, writhing on the ground, changing shape and as it grew, it developed into a human form. It looked remarkably like his neighbor as it struggled against the poison.

How could he make that vision come true? This thought occupied him every evening for a few days, then inspiration struck. He got online and did about ten minutes of research to find what he needed.

The church was having their social next weekend. Would that give him enough time? He thought so, if he got to work right away. He ran to a couple of local stores and procured the equipment he would need. The collection kit was more expensive than he thought it would be, but it would be worth it, he was sure. He took care setting everything up as the instructions directed, aided by some online videos to show him exactly what everything should look like.

The bees were drawn to the plates he set out, just as the online instructions said they would be. After landing on the strategically placed plates outside the hives, they reacted to the electric shock and stung the surfaces of the plates, depositing their loads of venom there, but, as it said online, with no resulting harm to the bees. When he had enough, he scraped the venom off the plates and brought it into the house.

Saturday, he prepared a salad and mixed up a vinegar and oil dressing. He used lettuce from his own garden, and sliced a few radishes, carrots, and tomatoes. After he made the vinegar and oil dressing, he poured a bit of it into a smaller container and added bee venom. He hoped the vinegar would mask the bitter taste. When he sampled a tiny drop on his tongue, he decided it needed a lot of herbs. His crops of oregano and thyme were lush, so he ground up even more, adding the pungent flakes as he muttered, "Grist for the mill," amused at his own pun. Besides being the stuff ground up at a mill, a gathering of bees was also called a grist, a fellow beekeeper had once told him. He wondered if Ms. Sessions knew the term. He couldn't wait to see her at the church dinner after the service on Sunday. He sealed his small vial of "special" dressing and shook it. The tiny pieces of herbs looked a bit like a swarming hive. No, he corrected his thought. A swarming Grist of Bees.

Sunday was so fine that the early afternoon dinner was outdoors on long tables carried from the fellowship hall and placed in the shade of the tall sycamore trees behind the church. Kevin put his salad and his larger container of dressing on the table near the other salads and looked around for Vivian Sessions. He hadn't seen her at the service, but there she was, driving up for the social.

"Yoo hoo, Vivian," called one of the many widows of the church. "Come sit by me."

Kevin was glad to see where she would be sitting. He made his way to that table and put his hat on the seat next to the one being saved for Ms. Sessions, Vivian, at the shady end.

After everyone filled their plates and the pastor blessed the food, Kevin took his seat next to his neighbor, slightly late on purpose, so she wouldn't move away from him.

"Hi Ms. Sessions," he said with a smile. "It's good to see you here."

She frowned at him, that hatred he'd seen before, shining through her eyes and she leaned away.

"Come on, we're next door neighbors," he persisted. "We need to get along." He pointed with his fork. "I see you took some of my salad."

She looked at her plate. "Your vegetables do look very good. I see you out in that garden all the time taking care of them." Her words were friendly, but she sounded wooden, like it was hard for her to say something nice to him.

"Yes, gardening is my joy, Ms. Sessions. I could bring you some of my crop if you'd like."

She frowned again and turned to the woman on her other side.

"Who is this, Vivian?" the woman asked.

"This is my neighbor, Kevin Grady," she added. Grudgingly, it seemed to Kevin. "This is Alice," she said to Kevin, half facing him.

They all said hello and started eating. Kevin fingered the small vial in his pocket, waiting for his chance. "What did you bring?" he asked her, staying alert for his opportunity, while trying to appear relaxed.

"The brownies. I see you took one."

"Looks delicious."

Kevin's chance came when he "accidentally" knocked over her ice tea. She jumped up and swatted at her dress with her napkin. Several people handed her extras since her clothing was sopping. Kevin, concealing the small vial in the palm of his hand, passed it over her salad as he reached to set the glass upright. He refilled it from the pitcher on the table. She gave him a small, but grateful nod of thanks.

When she was reseated, she ate some corn casserole, then worked on the salad.

"My, the dressing is heavy on the vinegar, isn't it?" she said, turning her scowl on him.

"I don't think so," Alice replied. "It's good, I think. And your brownies… yum."

Kevin made an apologetic face. "Maybe I got the proportions wrong. I like the brownies, too, Alice. You're a good cook, Vivian." He finished both the brownies that were on his plate.

She leaned close to him. "I have a special surprise for you in one of the brownies. I raise some plants too, on the other side of my house. Do you know what belladonna is?"

Kevin frowned. Belladonna. You weren't supposed to eat that. Had she given him poison brownies? Wait, he had eaten two. He had only taken one. Where had the other one come from?

He stared at her as his vision started to blur. His mouth felt dry, but, in a macabre replay of events, he overturned his own glass when he reached for a drink. He could hear his heart getting ready to burst.

Vivian, almost to the bottom of her salad, dropped her fork. "I... don't feel too good. Faint. Dizzy." Her eyes stared ahead, not focusing. "Kevin, what did you..." Then her throat started making gurgling sounds.

As he fell to the ground, he thought, at least she'll die, too. I hope someone will... take care of my... bees. He also had a brief thought that he would now discover just what Hell was like. The last thing to run through his slowing, numbing mind was that... Vivian Sessions... would probably... be there, too. His thoughts turned gray.

And stopped.

An early influence for EJ McFall, Scooby Doo inspired her to read and write mysteries. Her short stories have a decidedly odd bent, as shown in her book, Interview with an Ax-Murderer.

On her family tree is an uncle, a Chicago lawyer, who is rumored to have helped a client dispose of an inconvenient body. Family members claim it's a tall tale. EJ knew, true or not, it was the basis for a short story.

Banks, Bats, and Bodies
by EJ McFall

The post-Prohibition celebration was still going on at the Black Cat tavern, despite the fact alcohol had been legal again for the last six months, and despite the fact, that for many of the tavern's occupants, the party had never stopped—it had just gone underground. Lou LaPage had been one of the thousands of Americans who had considered Prohibition more of an annoyance than a law.

Lou was in a fine mood as he entered the familiar bar—scene of many of his most cherished teenage indiscretions. The Black Cat had been christened with great fanfare in 1915, only to be hit by the Volstead Act in 1919. Like many other such establishments, it survived the dry years by selling lemonade at the bar and bathtub gin in the alley. As far as Lou was concerned, Prohibition had been a boon to his profession. If not for the restrictive laws that turned honest drinkers into smugglers and bootleggers, his legal career might never have taken off. He had feared a downturn in business once alcohol became respectable again, but the Depression happened along just in time to change honest workers into bank robbers and kidnappers. Fortunately, the key word being fortune, his office was in the center of it all—Chicago.

At the moment, however, he was on a well-earned vacation from the Big City. He'd come home to peaceful little Rockville to attend his parents' 50th anniversary. Of course, that required him to spend time with his large and eccentric family—which is why he'd ducked out to grab a quick shot of whiskey at the Black Cat. Most of his old friends were still spending their nights at the tavern so had no shortage of hands to shake and pleasantries to exchange as he walked through the establishment. Frank, who'd been tending bar since opening night, automatically poured him a drink of their best whiskey. Lou was about to retreat to his favorite table, the one that would allow him to remain in the shadows while monitoring all the comings and goings—when he spotted a familiar face.

"Hello, Counselor." A wiry man in his late twenties waved from that remote table. It figured that John Dylan would gravitate to the one spot where he could keep the front door under surveillance while protecting his back. He was a bank robber—one of those dubious Robin Hoods who had crisscrossed the Midwest for most of the summer. The public seemed to tolerate them as long as they weren't violent. Afterall, only the rich still had any money left in banks. John was very charming, causing more than one pretty witness to become deaf and dumb when the police tried to interview her. He had his dark side too, but he reserved that for authority figures.

Lou was happy to see his less-than-reputable clients when he was back at his Chicago office. It was a different story in his hometown, where he did his best to keep his reputation unsullied. He considered side-stepping the man, but it was too late. He could feel the eyes of the locals on his back already.

"Hello, Mr…Johnson…What brings you to my town?"

John took a deep draw on his cigarette while gesturing for Lou to join him at his table. "Heard so much about it, I figured I'd better come see it for myself. It seems like a friendly place, with nice friendly banks."

"Those are off limit to you, if you want me to keep as your lawyer. My family has their life savings in those banks" Lou looked around before he took a seat. "This is not a good time for you to visit. You know damn well that Hoover's boys are scouring the Midwest for you."

"G-Men don't bother me. They couldn't find their way out of a wet paper sack." John employed his most charismatic smile, the one that made bank clerks fall in love with him even as they were handing him all their cash. Lou was immune to it, being something of a charming ne'er-do-well himself. It gave him a distinct advantage in court when he tried to convince the jury his clients—who were usually caught red-handed—were victims of circumstance.

"I heard your family's having a big to-do for their anniversary. I'd sure love to drop by and say 'hey' to your folks."

"I'm afraid that's out of the question." Lou spoke in a low but firm voice. "My parents are law-abiding, god-fearing people. I've never introduced them to any of my clients and I don't intend to start now."

John sent a smoke ring Lou's way. "They sound nice to me."

"They are. I aim to see that they have a wonderful anniversary party." Lou's voice hardened. "With no unpleasant surprises. Or unexpected visitors."

"Suit yourself. I was just trying to be hospitable." John looked hurt, gestured at the eavesdropping old man at the nearest table. "Seems like there's no pleasing some people."

"Cut the crap, John. What are you doing here?"

"Just looking for a safe port in a mighty big storm." John glanced about the noisy bar, but no one appeared to be interested in their table at the moment. "Hamilton's dead, Lou. The Feds got him."

"I heard he'd been shot. Sorry to hear he bought it." Hamilton had been John's partner in crime. The news hounds reported that he'd been shot during their last job, but Lou had long since learned not to believe everything he read. "What'd you do with the body?"

"Got it out in the trunk." John spoke in a whisper. "Need someplace to dump it."

"The hell you do!" Lou struggled to keep his voice as low. "What's that got to do with me?"

"Thought you might know a good place to get rid of it." John dropped the butt of his cigarette into Lou's glass. "It's a shame not to give him a decent burial, but times are hard all over."

"Damn you, you—" Lou bit his lip in frustration. "Finish your drink. We need to get away from all these people."

"My thoughts exactly." John chugged his drink, set it down with a thunk. "Shall we?"

Lou tossed some money onto the table and followed his client outside. "You've done a lot of ballsy things in your life, Dylan, but showing up in my town with a corpse in your trunk has got to be the worst one yet."

John shrugged. "I've done worse. Why, once back in Indiana…"

"Never mind." Lou glanced up and down the street. "Where's your car?"

"That shiny maroon sedan over there." John fished in his pocket for the keys. "Come on. I'll take you for a ride. It's no race car, but it can get up to a respectable speed if it has to."

"No, thanks. I'll take my car." Lou considered for a moment. Rockville lacked Chicago's convenient dumping ground—Lake Michigan—but it had once been home to several thriving lead mines. They were mostly closed now, but one of them might be able to provide Hamilton with an adequate resting place. "Okay, here's what we'll do. We leave separately and meet up outside town, on the road to Greenville. I've got an idea of where we can park your cold friend."

"Where's that?"

"Not here." Lou indicated a group of men milling about outside of the Black Cat. "Once we're out on the road."

"Okay." John patted his coat pocket, indicating the shape of a pistol. "You'd better not be planning a double-cross, LaPage."

"Nothing of the kind. I'm just trying to get you and your partner out of town before my family gets word of this mess."

"Better be the case." John nodded curtly, headed for his sedan.

Lou exhaled, took one last look around, then walked toward his black LaSalle. His mind was reeling as he started it up. He knew helping his outlaw client dispose of a body was beyond the scope of his professional obligations, but he also knew John well enough to know that he wasn't just going to disappear. The only way out of the predicament would be to do what needed to be done, done fast and without drawing any attention.

Lou entertained a brief hope that John would realize the folly of hanging around in a small town where he stuck out like a sore thumb and return to bustling, anonymous Chicago, but his client's stolen car was waiting for him just outside of town. Lou pulled his own vehicle onto the shoulder and gestured for the bank robber to come to the window.

"What now?" John considered the rolling pasture that spread before them as he walked to Lou's car. The landscape offered little more than a ravine as a hiding place. "Roll him into a crick?"

Lou shook his head. "There's an abandoned lead mine a mile or so down the road. We can take care of your problem there."

"Sounds good." John started for his sedan. "We'll follow you."

Lou glanced at John's car, assured himself that 'we' meant only the bank-robber and his dead partner, then pulled onto the road. He kept the sedan in his rearview mirror as he drove down a series of winding back roads until he came to the headframe of an abandoned mine shaft. He pulled his own car behind a group of pine trees, making sure that the license plate was unreadable by any passing motorists. The old Bull Moose mine was miles outside of town—far from the vision of any of Rockville's citizens—but still he worried about ending up on the front page of the local newspaper.

Shoving his misgivings firmly to the back of his mind, Lou retrieved a small flashlight from his glove compartment and used it to direct John's car onto the darkened field. "Pull up beside the old supply shack. Let's get this over with as fast as we can."

John complied and lost no time in tugging a bundle wrapped in a blanket from his trunk. "Still seems wrong, just getting rid of the poor guy like this. He did a lot of stuff in his life, but nothing deserved this."

"He knew what he was getting into when he decided to rob banks. You reap what you sow."

"I suppose." John dragged the blanket to the mine shaft. "Seems like some folks have more say over how their lives turn out then other folks do, though."

Lou mumbled something noncommittal, his attention focused on getting the unpleasant task over with. He shone the light around the headframe until he noticed a stack of old discarded metal parts from the days when the mine was active. "Have you got a rope in your trunk?"

"Don't rightly know." John grinned. "The car hasn't been mine very long."

"Well, go check." Lou grumbled. He didn't want to risk another trip into town, but he didn't want to risk someone finding John's late friend while the LaPage family was in the midst of their celebration.

"Found something." John returned with a length of old, fraying rope. "It's not in great shape, but it should serve our purpose, don't you think?"

"Let's hope so." Lou indicated the pile of old metal. "Shake a leg. We don't need any witnesses happening by."

"Keep your pants on." John hastened to wrap the rope around the body, using the metal discards to give it weight. "You got a river around here you're not telling me about?"

"Down in the mine." Lou led the way inside the headframe, shone the light down the shaft. An underground river had seeped into the tunnels and swept away any chance the owners had of making their fortune in the lead market. "That's why it was abandoned."

"Made to serve, then. Where does that end up?"

"Don't know for sure, but with luck it doesn't go anyplace where anyone's going to be for the next few days." Lou shone the light over his pocket watch. "Let's get out of here before someone drives by and wonders what we're up to."

"I don't know. I kind of like this place. It's nice and peaceful. I think I'll hang out here for a while and take in the local sights."

"You're going to stay here?" Lou shook his head. "Why? It's nothing but a rickety old mine. You can't get at the lead, if that's what's on your mind. Not enough to make it worth your trouble, at any rate."

"I'm not so broke I'm gonna go digging in the ground, but I need a quiet spot to hide out till the cops get tired of looking for me. This place will be just fine."

"That won't happen until you're dead."

"You're probably right. But I'm still going to stay here for a bit while things cool down. Then I'll head back to Chicago."

"No. No way." Lou chose his words. "You can't stay here. It's not safe."

"For who? Me or your reputation?"

"Both." Lou exhaled in an attempt to regain his composure. "This is my hometown, John. We can't have bank robbers lurking around. People won't stand for it. They'll call the Feds."

"I ain't planning on doing anything to attract attention. And since you're the only one who knows I'm here…" John paused. "Well, I guess we don't have to go into all the bloody particulars. Do we, Counselor?"

"Doesn't seem to be any point in doing that." Lou held up his hands in surrender. He knew what John did to those who crossed him. The only thing he hated more than a G-Man was a traitor. "Ok, do what you want. It has nothing to do with me."

"I don't know about that. It's been some time since I had anything decent to eat. You wouldn't want your favorite client starving to death in the middle of nowhere."

"No way. I'm not going to be your errand boy."

"Suit yourself." John's tone hardened. "Maybe I'll just drop into your big shindig and ask your Ma for a piece of anniversary cake. That should hold me for a while."

Lou sighed in defeat. "That won't be necessary. I'll bring you something to eat."

"That's what I like about you, Counselor. You always know which side of your bread is buttered."

"I'm warning you, though—you can't stay here long. Hoover's got a bee in his bonnet about all the bank robbery going on around the nice, quiet Midwest. The Feds aren't going to stop until they've locked you all up. Or mowed you down in a corn-field."

John shrugged. "I'm not worried. They're not exactly the sharpest tacks, if you know what I mean."

"Maybe not, but even morons get lucky once in a while."

"Which is why I need to find a safe place for good old Hamilton." John wrestled the body over to the shaft and groaned as he struggled to get him into the metal cage that was used to lower workers into the mine. "A little help might be nice. The S.O.B.'s plenty heavy."

"I'm keeping lookout."

"Uh-huh." John grunted as he managed to dump Hamilton's remains down the shaft. "You city boys are all the same. Lazy as hell."

Lou listened for the splash, then shone his flashlight onto the body as it slowly sank into the water. As Hamilton disappeared, the light caught a cloud of black wings flying above the water and heading their way. Lou backed out of the headframe.

"What the hell?" John shouted as dozens of wings filled the air around him. He struck out blindly as an unseen creature brushed against him. "Get him off me!"

"Calm down. It's just bats, heading out for the night. Stand against the wall and let them pass." Lou raised his voice above John's screams. "They're not going to hurt you. Stop banging around in there. You're going to start a cave-in."

John continued to shout and lash out against the bevy of bats that swirled around him. In his terror, he jumped into the metal cage and slammed the door shut.

"Don't rock that thing!" Lou admonished as the cage swayed, banging from one side of the shaft to the other. "No one's used it for years. It's not safe."

John continued to rock in the cage as each new bat that bumped against it sent him into a panic. Lou trained the flashlight on him, hoping to calm his client, but the man only screamed more as he was able to identify his companions, one of whom had flown into the cage with him. John swatted at the lone bat as it tried to catch up with its bevy. That sent the metal cage slamming against a weathered support beam. The wood cracked as the cage swung to strike the opposing beam with a loud thwack. The cage door popped open, freeing the bat and sending John into another round of panic as it flew past his ear.

"Stop it, you idiot! You're going to bring the whole damn thing—" Lou swore as the sound of disintegrating lumber sent him running. A cloud of dust and debris—along with a few last bats—blew out of the mine entrance. Inside he heard a last agonized scream and a splash as the cage fell into the river.

"John?" Lou drew closer to the pile of rubble that blocked the mine entrance. He managed to peer inside through a small opening in the debris, only to see the last of the cage sinking into the river. "Dylan! Can you hear me? John?"

Lou heard the flutter of a bat over his head, but no sound from beneath the rubble that separated him from his client. He yanked a few rocks from the pile, only to have more cascade down to replace them. He called John's name a few more times, then backed away from the mine.

He stood at a safe distance considering his options. He could speed into town and get together a crew to dig through the rubble, but the chances of John being rescued were slim and none. And the chances of the authorities asking hours' worth of questions he had no intention of answering were overwhelming. John had no family and only a bleached blonde moll that would have no trouble finding herself another bank robber to support her. So… the choice seemed fairly obvious.

Lou whistled as he went to John's stolen car and scanned it for any incriminating evidence. He found an article from the Rockville Journal that announced his parents' upcoming anniversary. He would shred it and dispose of it, piece by piece, on his way home.

Prodded by a last vestige of conscience, Lou backtracked to the mine, called out for John once last time. Satisfied that there was no one to rescue, he returned to his own car and set out for his parents' party. It would be some time before anyone noticed John's car parked in the trees and stopped to investigate. With any luck he'd be back in his Chicago office by then, padding his pockets with fees from whatever bank robber rose to take over Dylan's territory. It seemed there was no shortage of desperate men willing to turn over their loot to a fast-talking lawyer in hopes of avoiding prison.

Lou paused before pulling his car back onto the road, watched as a small bevy of bats circled above him in search of bugs. He supposed he should feel guilty for abandoning his client, no matter that he was no angel and was most likely dead, but if the Depression had taught him anything, it was it was every man for himself. John had lived by the same philosophy and would have abandoned his lawyer to a watery grave if their situations had been reversed.

No, he had nothing to feel guilty about. It had been John's turn to die today. It might well be Lou's time tomorrow. In the meantime, he tipped his hat to the remaining bats in the sky and whistled *Happy Days Are Here Again* as he drove towards a pleasant evening of cake and champagne.

Kari Wainwright lives with her husband Tom, son Travis, and Shih Tzu, Oscar Wild. The Desert Sleuths and Mesa Writers critique groups are on the lookout for plot holes, grammar gaffs, and blatant bloopers in her short stories.

Once she found a sleuth of bears was the group name, she looked no further. Dumpster diving, a bear's favorite pastime, is a perfect way to discover a body and killer. Hint: the bears didn't do it.

A Sleuth of Bears
by Kari Wainwright

September 7, Thursday morning, 8:37 a.m. I remembered the precise time I pulled into the library parking lot for a reason. Actually, three reasons—a trio of dumpster-diving bears. Little ones, big one, cubs and mama. A sleuth of bears investigating the Juniper Library trash.

I assumed not a lot of people know that a group of bears is called a sleuth, but as a librarian I possess quite a bit of arcane knowledge.

The cubs were cute, roly-poly and cuddly-looking. Even the adult was endearing, until one considered what she might do to a person who got too close to a young one. The large brown bear, Big Mama, clambered on top of the shuttered half of the metal container, then disappeared through the open lid on the other side.

The janitor should have shut and locked both lids after he finished cleaning the building last night. He must have forgotten, which was unlike him. Johnny Dobbs was usually reliable.

I considered the distance between my car and the library's front door. It wasn't really far, but then again, I wasn't nearly as fast as a bear if one decided I looked like breakfast.

Big Mama reared her head up over the dumpster's edge, her mouth full of something green. As she pulled herself up and over, she tugged and tugged and tugged on something, bringing it out with her. Finally, she managed to toss it over the edge. It hung up for a moment, and then toppled to the ground, swatting one of the cubs as it fell. The cub roared his indignation.

It was no longer an "it." "It" was a sweater-clad body. The second cub became interested in playing with the new toy. It looked like a man and he was probably dead, but on the off chance he was alive, I couldn't let the bears maul him. I honked my horn, over and over. The sound got the bears' attention, but not for long.

I restarted my car and drove on the dirt pathway toward the dumpster, still honking. The cubs galumphed off into the woods like furry "persons of interest." Big Mama was last, but she didn't leave with empty paws, so to speak. She grabbed a dirty gray backpack from a pile of trash before she, too, lumbered away.

My heart thundered in my chest as I parked as close as I could and got out. Leaving the door open, I ran toward the body, keeping a wary eye out for returning bears. A man was crumpled on the ground, slashes of red staining his green sweater—Christmas colors. He wore pieces of paper and remnants of sack lunches—pathetic holiday ornaments. There was no sign of life from his bloody chest. At first, I thought the bears must have killed him, but I realized the gashes were too tidy for bear claws.

The stink of death did not mingle well with the stench of garbage. I gagged, retching like a drunken party-goer.

When I was done, I held my nose with one hand and reached out the other to feel for a pulse. His wrist was cold and slimy to the touch. I moved away from him a few feet at a time, headed for the car, wiping my dirty hand on my black slacks.

I recognized the poor guy. Blackjack Robbie—a homeless man who sometimes frequented the library, using its facilities to tidy up a bit or to keep warm during a frosty Colorado Rocky Mountain morning. No one was supposed to use the restrooms for hygiene purposes, but Blackjack was always polite, always soft-spoken, with brown puppy-dog eyes.

His favorite part of the Juniper Library was the history section, especially local Colorado authors. To me, Blackjack Robbie belonged with the mysteries. I often wondered why such a seemingly gentle soul was living the hard life of the homeless. Now I wondered who had harmed this poor wretch of a man.

I suddenly returned to my senses. I needed to call the sheriff's department. I retrieved my cell phone from the car and dialed 9-1-1 with trembling fingers.

Soon, sirens echoed through the canyon, the sound bouncing off boulders and mountainsides as sheriff deputies, the coroner, and Colorado Bureau of Investigation personnel raced to the scene.

The first car that skidded to a halt in the parking lot belonged to the sheriff's department. A tall, lanky deputy approached me—Deputy Sheriff Benjamin Wells. We'd met before. His laser-beam blue eyes always disconcerted me. I felt like I was unable to escape.

He took out a notebook. "Morning, Ms. Parsons. I see you've had a startling beginning to your day."

"Deputy, you can call me Abigail. And, yes, I never expected to witness a sleuth of bears discovering a body."

"A sleuth? As usual, you are a fountain of information. Was the dead man in that position when you got here?"

"No. Big Mama, er I mean…"

Small lines around his eyes crinkled. "You name the bears?"

I stammered out the rest of my story of the bears and the body.

"Have you had problems with bears before this?"

"No, usually the janitor locks the dumpster before he leaves. He must have forgotten."

"How many bears were there?"

"I saw three."

"Did you see any human activity? Other cars?"

"No. I'm the only one here before the library opens at nine. A group of third graders is scheduled to come in about an hour."

"You need to cancel that."

He studied the dirt passageway that led from the parking lot to the dumpster. I turned and surveyed it, too. Two sets of tracks merged and blended into each other. "Did you have to drive your car this close to the dumpster? You've disturbed my crime scene."

I cringed. "It was the only way I could scare the bears away. I didn't want Blackjack to be eaten."

He looked surprised. "You know this man?"

"Only a little. Everyone calls him Blackjack Robbie."

"But his clothes, his… well, his everything. He looks homeless."

"He is, but he would come to the library sometimes. We get a few of the guys who hang out around here."

His voice took on a lecturing tone. "Don't you realize how dangerous that could be, letting these men into your library?"

I shrugged. "So far no one has been out of line. And Blackjack was one of the nicest ones."

He tucked his chin down and stared right at me, as if my words were the most incredible he'd ever heard.

"Really, he was," I insisted.

His eyes nearly rolled right out of his head. "Okay, here's what we're going to do. You're going to cancel the school children's visit. The crime scene tech is going to take pictures of the tire tracks in the dirt, as well as pictures of your tires. After that, they'll make impressions of the tire tread marks. Once that is done, one of my guys will back your car into the parking lot, and you can go home. The library will remain closed for the day."

"But—"

"No buts. If you think of anything else, you can call me later." Pen in hand, he waved a dismissal.

I took the hint and sat on a bench in front of the library to phone the Crystal Peak Elementary School principal. She was shocked at such violence in our neighborhood, but appreciated the call. I sat there for the rest of the morning, watching the two-legged sleuths swarm the crime scene. I doubted Blackjack Robbie had gotten that much attention for a long, long time.

I wondered if he had a family. If anyone would want to know about his passing. If anyone would cry if they knew. I didn't realize tears were trickling down my face until a drop splashed on my hand. I could swipe the tears away, but it wouldn't relieve the ache I felt for Blackjack, or remove the despair in the pit of my stomach.

I watched patrons get turned away at the other end of the parking lot. The small town of Juniper would soon be a swirl of talk and hushed speculation.

Once my car was returned to me, I drove to the Camping World store, where I purchased a can of bear spray. I wanted to be armed and ready should I meet Big Mama again. I drove home, where I sat in my recliner, my Shih Tzu dog Oscar Wild on my lap, a glass of merlot by my side and my attention on mindless old movies resuscitated by TCM.

That night I tossed and turned. I managed to get some sleep, but not enough. At six a.m. I pushed back the bed covers and dragged myself to the bathroom. My reddish-brown, wavy hair was even more tousled than normal. A bird would have been quite content to lay her eggs in the wiry nest on my head. I stuck my tongue out at my reflection, pulled off my nightgown, and ducked into the shower.

Later, after half a pot of coffee, I grabbed my car keys and with dragging feet, headed to my car. For the first time in ages, I didn't want to go to work.

At the library, I parked on the opposite side of the lot from the dumpster. I didn't want to see it. That is, until stupid curiosity tickled my mind and told me I needed to see it with Blackjack gone. I grabbed my bear spray, had it ready to use as I slid along the library wall to the other side. Once there, I took as quick a peek as I could. No bears in sight. The container was locked tight, bear proof once again. No body rested on the ground in front of it. I looked around the woods for signs of bears. All was quiet.

I turned to go back to the library door when suddenly I remembered—Big Mama had run off with a backpack from the dumpster. Might it have belonged to Blackjack?

I scribbled a note on a Post-It and pasted it to the front door. Back in half an hour. I took off in the same direction as the bears, armed with my bear spray.

For a while, I tiptoed through the woods, but that was hard to keep up. I kept a sharp eye out for critters and for the backpack. I spotted papers strewn about the area. Shredded. Crumpled. Tattered. I knew the papers would be evidence but the breeze was getting stronger. To keep them from blowing away, I decided to take them with me. I saw a wool hat hung from a low bush. I grabbed it too. I'd seen Robbie wear it last winter. A little further along, there was the backpack itself, large gashes in its sides and an empty Twinkie wrapper beside it.

The mangled backpack was heavier than I expected. I looked inside and pulled out a book. A library book, its cover torn. A book Blackjack had not checked out. I'd started to examine it when I heard a rustling sound off to my right. Not very far away. I dropped the bag and started to run. Branches tore at my hands and I dropped some of the papers in my wild dash through the trees, but I held onto the spray can and the book even as prickly bushes jabbed me. I couldn't have gone any faster if the headless horseman himself had leapt off the pages of a story book and chased after me instead of Ichabod Crane.

I didn't slow down until I burst out of the woods and saw the benign walls of the library. Rounding the building to reach the door, I slid to a stop when I saw a sheriff's car and Deputy Wells pacing near the steps. He hadn't spotted me yet.

I put the book on the bench and went to meet him, still trying to catch my breath.

He turned toward me, then halted as if surprised. Those startling blue eyes of his grew even more intense. He took two large strides closer and grabbed my shoulders. "What's happened? Are you all right?"

"I'm…" Pant, pant, "okay."

"You don't look it. You're out of breath, pale as a ghost, scratched and bleeding, and your hair…" He left that part of the comment unfinished.

I could imagine how crazed my hair must have looked. Even after being washed and brushed, my curls often behaved like truant children. Running through the forest had totally unleashed them.

"A bear." I pointed toward the pine trees. "At least I thought there was one. I found the backpack, then I heard a noise so I ran. I was afraid it was Big Mama or one of her cubs."

This time he didn't smile at my name for the bruin. "What backpack?"

"Didn't I tell you yesterday?"

He shook his head.

My hand flew to my mouth. "I'm sorry. I must have forgotten. When Big Mama left, she had a backpack in her mouth." I heaved one more big breath. "I went to see if I could find it, and I did. She'd ripped it apart to get at a Twinkie. Papers and stuff are strewn all over. When I heard a noise, I got scared. I'm afraid I dropped the backpack and most of the papers."

An exasperated sigh escaped him. "Why didn't you call me when you remembered?"

"I was going to, but first I thought I'd see what I could find."

"You are not a sleuth. You are not a detective. You are a librarian. You should now go into the library and deal with books." He looked as if he wanted to shake me.

"Yes, Sir." He didn't look amused.

I thought about the book, but didn't want to lose it to the evidence locker just yet. I'd find out what it was first. *Then* I'd call him.

He stalked off to his car without looking back. I realized he hadn't told me why he had come. He must have been really irritated with me. I retrieved the book and opened the library doors. It didn't take long for patrons to start strolling in. Usually, I enjoyed chatting with them, learning about their lives and their taste in books, but this morning my attention was drawn to that black book with the torn cover.

Finally, I was able to read the title and scan the table of contents. The tattered cover revealed a partial picture of a log cabin close to a stream and a grove of aspen trees. I had to remove the torn paper to reveal the name of the book: *Homesteader Hannah Jones*. Inside, I learned that the widow Jones had brought her five children from Massachusetts to Colorado in 1863 to establish a homestead in the Crystal Peak Valley, only a few miles from where

Juniper thrived as a mining town. In between patrons, I skimmed a couple chapters, reading the details of the hardscrabble life she led. She'd been one tough woman.

I glanced at the end of the book where there was a family tree denoting her descendants up to the 1980's. I gasped when I saw a name I recognized—our janitor, John Dobbs. I looked up his phone number and left a message for him to meet me at the library as soon as possible. I wondered what the connection was. Since Blackjack Robbie was intrigued with this book, I wondered if he was connected to the family as well. There were a couple of Roberts—one Carlton and one Jones.

The name Carlton sounded familiar, but I couldn't remember why. I'd ponder that over lunch as I read more about Hannah. Seated in my office I noticed sheriff's cars pulling into the lot. No one came into the building. Instead the deputies headed toward the neighboring forest, I guess to retrieve as much of the backpack's contents as possible.

That reminded me. After lunch I'd have to face the music and call Deputy Wells to confess I had the book. I'm sure he'd consider it long overdue. I braced myself for his displeasure. I'd rather face Mama Bear.

And displeasure was exactly what I got.

His voice was a low, controlled growl. "You mean, you found this book this morning and withheld information from me? Deliberately?"

I gulped and nodded.

"Why?"

"It obviously was one of our library books and I just really wanted to know what book it was, and maybe why Blackjack Robbie took it."

The deputy took a deep breath. "I could charge you with obstruction."

"But I'm giving it to you now."

He flung his head backward, his vision directed toward the heavens. Maybe he was seeking spiritual help to deal with me, then his eyes pierced mine again. "Have you learned anything else pertinent to the investigation that you've 'forgotten' to mention?"

"Maybe, but it's hard to tell. The book is about a woman homesteader in the eighteen hundreds who settled near here. At the back of the book, there is a family tree. One of the names listed is Johnny Dobbs, our janitor."

Wells cocked his head. "That's interesting. Anything else?"

"Do you know what Blackjack Robbie's full name is?"

"Yes, he was Robert Carlton. We've learned he had a bad gambling problem. Lost everything and became homeless."

"His name is in here, too. For some reason, the name Carlton sounds familiar but I can't quite place it."

"If it comes to you later, call me this time, immediately." He held out his hand for the book. "And next time you find evidence, don't touch it. Call. Got it?"

He slid the book into an evidence bag. Although it had been through so much already, I wasn't sure what else he could find. At least he hadn't singed me with his anger. I knew I'd disappointed him. "I hope there is no next time."

A few minutes before closing at 5 p.m., I heard a slight movement and a tap on my shoulder. I yelped and jumped, almost knocking over my high stool. I was relieved to see fingertips instead of bear claws. At least it wasn't Big Mama, Ursine Sleuth.

I whirled around to see Johnny Dobbs standing behind me. He looked a bit sheepish. "Sorry, Miss Abigail. I didn't mean to scare you. Why did you call? If you're going to chew me out about not locking up the dumpster the other night, I'm sorry. I cut my hand on a can lid and came back inside to get something to stop the bleeding." He held up his hand to show the bandage wrapped around it.

"Did you need stitches?"

"No, I just cleaned it myself and held pressure on it."

I shuddered. "You should go to the ER. The wound could get infected."

"I'll be okay. Germs don't scare me none." Johnny shrugged.

Rather a cavalier attitude, even stupid, I thought, given all the nasty viruses and things that can attack us.

"Did you know about the book, *Homesteader Hannah Jones*?" I asked. "It has your name in it. As well as Robert Carlton's. Did you know him?"

"Was that the guy the bears found?"

I nodded.

"Can't say I ever met the man."

"I'm wondering, was it possible his body was already in the dumpster before you emptied the trash?"

"Can't say, Miss Abigail."

"Was Blackjack Robbie actually Robert Carlton?"

"Can't say."

"Is there anything you can say, Johnny?"

"Yeah, I was related somehow to Homesteader Hannah. Leastwise, according to my grandmother."

"That's cool. So, your family has been in the area for decades."

"Yeah, guess so."

"Maybe you can help me out. The Carlton name seems to ring a bell for some reason, but I can't figure out why."

"Maybe Uncle Jason Carlton's death is why you recall the name. He was a recluse, but had a lot of money, so his death made the news recently."

"So, if Blackjack Robbie was a Carlton, he probably stood to inherit."

I was answered with another Johnny Dobbs shrug.

"Did you inherit anything from your uncle?"

"I don't think that's any of your business, Miss Abigail." His voice dripped ice water tones. "Why are you asking all these questions?"

Maybe I had asked one too many. A chill threaded down my back and I leaned away from Johhny.

I injected as much innocence into my voice as possible. "I ask questions because I find local history fascinating. Since I've only worked at the library for two years, there's a lot I don't know. I especially find Hannah interesting." My tone must have worked, because Johnny's shoulders relaxed a bit. Dare I ask more pointed questions now? I decided to risk just one more. "Robert was your uncle's son, so your cousin? Maybe you knew each other when you were kids."

"Maybe. I don't recall. My family didn't get out much."

"Would Blackjack Robbie have inherited?"

"Maybe, if he was really related."

"Well, it is rather a coincidence that his body turned up in our dumpster."

Johnny shook his head. His hands turned into fists. I backed up again.

"You just can't let it be, can you?" He reached for my throat.

I grabbed the bear spray I'd left on the counter, and blasted it right in his face. I got a little choked up from residual spray, but Johnny took the brunt of it. His face reddened and he clutched his throat as tears streamed down his face. He staggered away from the desk

I pushed him to the floor and knelt on his back to hold him down. Then I picked up my cell phone and pushed the emergency button. "Send help to the Juniper Library. I have the man who killed Blackjack Robbie."

The dispatcher responded. "Deputy Wells is already on the way. Said he has to talk to you about the library janitor. I'll stay on the line with you until help arrives."

Johnny bucked his body below me. I held the spray can where he could see it. "Want more?"

He quieted.

The library's doors burst open and I heard a loud bellow. "Johnny Dobbs, you are under arrest."

Wells and two other officers, guns drawn, were a welcome sight.

"Why were you already coming here?"

"One of our men saw Dobbs' truck in the parking lot. He knew Dobbs had become a person of interest, *he* knew to call me and wait for backup."

"Lucky for me."

Johnny lunged at me, still crying from the spray as the officers dragged him to his feet and handcuffed him.

After our soon-to-be-ex janitor was led away, Wells coughed and asked what I'd sprayed on Johnny. I picked up my trusty spray can. "I figured if it works on bears, surely it would work on humans, too."

"I can't leave you alone for a second, can I?"

I laughed, then realized my legs were about to give way. The adrenaline that had surged through my body was exiting, fast.

Deputy Wells took my arm and led me to a chair at a nearby table. He sat down across from me and we traded stories. I told him about my afternoon, then he told me about his visit to the Carlton family lawyer. "Old man Jason amassed more than five hundred thousand dollars, to be split between Johnny and Robbie. Apparently, Robbie hung around here for the past few months. His mistake was to look up his cousin Johnny."

"Wow," I said, "if the bears hadn't found Blackjack's body, Johnny could have gotten away with murder. The body would have wound up in the dump with tons of garbage. Since nobody misses a homeless person, there would have been no search for him."

Deputy Wells reached across the table and took my hand. "You're right, Abigail. Your Big Mama bear was one hell of a sleuth."

John M. Floyd's award-winning stories have appeared in AHMM, EQMM, Strand, Saturday Evening Post, and Best American Mystery Stories. His seventh book, The Barrens, is the latest.

When an insurance investigator goes undercover to search for a stolen animal and lands on a private island, it's no ordinary assignment. That could lead to all kinds of complications—and it does.

The Blue Wolf originally appeared in the Feb 2000 issue of Alfred Hitchcock Mystery Magazine and in Rainbow's End and Other Stories (Dogwood Press, 2006)

The Blue Wolf
by John M. Floyd

Jason Plumm lay on the beach for three hours before he was found.

His rescuer was a four-foot-tall native islander named No Sin Kahano, who was working in a field of sugar cane with a machete as long as he was when he saw the body lying on the sand just above the waterline. No Sin, a man unusual in both name and appearance, was typical in his dislike for manual labor: he promptly dropped his knife and trotted down the hill to investigate. He was also, as Jason Plumm would later discover, typical in his choice of employer. He worked for Colonel Hanson McDade, who owned everything and everyone on the island.

It took the small man five minutes to drag Plumm's limp body to the shade of a clump of mango trees, ten to retrieve a battered truck and load him inside, and another ten to drive the bumpy jungle road to the Colonel's estate. Once there, the truck's horn attracted enough servants to help carry the groggy and sunburned American into the Main House and put him to bed.

Plumm recovered quickly. He was awake and coherent by midafternoon, and around six o'clock he was brought supper in bed by his host, a smiling and gracious Colonel McDade. The two men hit it off right away; the Colonel was grateful to have a visitor from his homeland and Plumm was grateful to be alive. Their conversation stretched far into the night.

Plumm's sailboat, he said, had been blown off course in a storm several days ago. Lost and desperate, he had headed north, hoping he would eventually hit one of the Marquesas Islands. He didn't. On his third day at sea he encountered another storm, and this time he capsized. He had no idea how long he had been in the water—he just swam aimlessly until he could go no further. The next thing he remembered was waking up in one of the Colonel's upstairs bedrooms, under the watchful eye of No Sin and the household staff.

Colonel McDade listened closely to the account, and when it was done, he told his own story. This was a private island, he said, small and fertile and almost entirely self-sufficient. Its human population was less than fifty souls, its crops were sugar cane and pineapple, and its coordinates were largely unknown. Simply stated, the island was unnamed and uncharted. To all but a very few, it did not exist. "It's better that way, really," the Colonel said. "For the animals."

Plumm looked at him and frowned. "The animals?"

"Sugar cane and pineapple aren't all we raise here," McDade said with a smile. Over the course of the past three years, it turned out, Hanson McDade had established quite a facility—a kind of specialty zoo, stocked with unusual examples of wildlife from all over the world. Through the Colonel's determined efforts—and at tremendous expense of time and money—animals from the farthest reaches of the globe had been captured and transported (under the supervision of McDade's men and in the secret holds of his supply vessels) to this tiny and remote location. As a result, at least one representative of almost every rare or endangered species on earth could be found right here on the island.

"I have them all," Colonel McDade said, unable to conceal his satisfaction. "Platypus, white rhino, sable antelope—this is their home now. I can see and study them anytime I want. I've even given them a name, as a group."

"A name?"

"A collective name, like a troop of baboons or an army of ants or a colony of badgers."

"So what are they?"

"I call them an exotica," McDade said. "An exotica of rare species."

The only drawback he had found to life on the "zoo" island, he explained, was the isolation. There were no telephones here, no radios, no telegraph, no airstrip. By choice and by design, the island was cut off from the rest of the world. Only then, the Colonel reasoned, could he have the freedom to run his facility the way he wanted it. So far, it had worked out well. Most of his employees were Polynesian natives, well trained and well paid, and all of them understood and accepted the circumstances that went along with the job and location. The island's one and only lifeline to civilization was the Colonel's supply boat from Papeete, which came once a month. And it was due again, McDade informed his visitor, less than a week from now. "You're here for at least five days, I'm afraid, like it or not," the Colonel said.

Somewhere in the house a clock chimed the hour. With a sigh the Colonel rose to his feet, then wished his new houseguest a pleasant night's sleep. He also offered an invitation—and a word of caution. The invitation was that Plumm was welcome to remain here on the island as long as he liked; the restriction was that he must stay away from the walled compound directly behind the Main House. That was off limits.

"The tree of forbidden fruit?" Plumm asked, with a grin.

"Don't worry, Mr. Plumm—I am not God, and this is not Eden." McDade considered this for a moment, amusement gleaming in his eyes. "Though I suppose I could be mistaken."

Both of them smiled and shook hands. After the Colonel had left, Jason Plumm sat in bed and stared at the door for a long time, reviewing in his mind the long story he had told his host.

Not a word of it was true.

Radar had been Plumm's biggest worry. A needless concern, as things had turned out, but he hadn't known that two days ago, on the chartered pleasure-boat out of Bora Bora. All he had known then, for certain, was that Colonel Hanson McDade ran a very expensive and secure operation, and he knew that if anyone was watching a monitor in an operations center somewhere on the island, the forty-foot Bayliner would make a sizable blip on his screen.

But no intercepting vessels had come out to challenge them, and in the darkness of last night he had slipped into the water two miles from shore, dressed only in his carefully tattered sweatshirt and jeans and clutching a watertight plastic bag attached to a cord around his neck. As he started the long, easy breaststroke that would take him to the island, he heard the boat turn and begin the long trip back to port. He had no worries about the crew—they were chosen by his own hand, and had been paid generously for their silence. His worries lay ahead.

The moonlit swim to the beach, however, proved to be easy going. Plumm was in good shape, except for a recent bout with the flu, and had been a champion swimmer in his college days. His newly-acquired sunburn was painful but necessary to his plan; if anything, the caress of the water felt good to it. When he reached the island, he hid the plastic container in the grass beneath a palm tree and, when dawn came, stretched out on his stomach on the white sand a few yards above the waterline.

Plumm saw No Sin long before the islander saw him, and had watched the little man from the corner of his eye for almost an hour before he was finally spotted and rescued.

And now here he was, safe inside the stronghold he had come all this way to conquer, with a fine meal in his stomach and a soft bed underneath him. A suitable end, he thought, to a trying journey... and a good beginning to the most challenging assignment of his career.

For Jason Plumm was no frustrated businessman on sabbatical from his ex-wife and his job, as he had told Colonel McDade.

He was an insurance investigator. In fact, he was probably the best insurance investigator in the business, and certainly the most sought-after. Again and again, using a formula that mixed equal portions of planning and ingenuity and daring, Plumm had broken cases that everyone else—including the police—had declared impossible to solve. Though his fees were high, his reputation was solid and his results were real. He was known as a man who could get the job done.

It was for that reason that Plumm's name was the first one recommended in the aftermath of the sensational theft that had occurred almost three months before. That same night, the St. Louis people had flown him in and made him an offer, and the very next day he had begun the investigation that had eventually led him to this island, and this house.

He was smiling when he drifted off to sleep.

———————

Plumm spent the following day "regaining his strength"—he was a passable actor when he had to be—and getting the general feel of the place. Colonel McDade stayed near his bedside most of the morning, chatting about this and that and making sure his guest was comfortable. At one point, the Colonel introduced him to Dr. Toshiro Sumoru, the resident veterinarian (and McDade's second-in-command). When Plumm jokingly asked Sumoru if he worked on people as well as animals, the sour-faced little man gave him a cold stare. Looking amused, the Colonel repeated the question in Japanese. Sumoru's only response was a steely gaze.

"To effectively treat human patients," McDade explained, "Dr. Sumoru would need to acquire more advanced equipment."

"What he needs to acquire," Plumm said, "is a sense of humor."

The Colonel just chuckled. "Don't hold your breath," he said.

Around noon, when it was evident that Plumm was much improved, McDade led him on a tour of the Main House and the surrounding area. Once, when the two of them were crossing the vast green lawn that lay west of the house, Plumm got a distant look at the fenced compound the Colonel had mentioned the night before. Nothing was said about it this time, but Plumm caught McDade watching him closely until the tall wooden walls were out of view.

That afternoon both the Colonel and Dr. Sumoru were called away for several hours, after an employee reported that one of the Grevy zebras had been injured by damaged fencing. Since Plumm was left to his own devices, he decided to take the Colonel up on his suggestion to continue exploring the grounds.

Over the next few hours Plumm wandered every part of the estate that was accessible and within walking distance. What he found was that Hanson McDade—retired Army hero, nature enthusiast, and only son of a Kansas millionaire—had created a world that far surpassed the information revealed by Plumm's prior research. For one thing, the island seemed larger and more primitive than he'd thought. And the zoo itself—actually more of a wild animal park, like the one east of San Diego—was an absolute wonder. By the time Plumm returned to the Main House, he had seen koalas and anteaters and eagles and at least half a dozen varieties of deer and antelope. Exotica was an appropriate name for this group of creatures. Many of the species he didn't even recognize.

But there was one animal he hadn't seen… and he thought he knew why.

———————

That night Plumm began to make preparations. Silently he scouted the house, squirreling away the items he would need: a flashlight, spare batteries, gloves, a paper clip, a pocketknife, even an old pipe tool he found in a desk drawer. By the time he and the Colonel met in the dining room for dinner, Plumm had everything he required, including a black poncho-style raincoat that had been hanging in the guestroom closet. With these resources in his possession and the details of the plan in his mind, he was ready to go.

At the stroke of midnight, long after the Colonel had left him—and after the last light had winked out in the block of workers' quarters visible from Plumm's bedroom window—he gathered his wares and his nerve and crept out onto the roof and the ladder-like rose trellis and down into the shrubbery beside the house. Within minutes he had made his way to the gate of the forbidden compound, and seconds later, using the paper clip and the pipe tool the way he had used similar implements a hundred times before, he sprung the simple padlock that held it shut.

Inside the fenced area, the layout was exactly as he had hoped. In the shielded glare of his flashlight he saw a network of pathways flanked by barred cages. Only the first few were visible, but from what he knew of the size of the place, he estimated there were probably dozens of cages in all. Already, as he began inching his way along the dusty path, he was breathing easier: he had worried he might find that the interior of the compound was a huge open area where its occupants could roam free. If that had been the case, he might have gotten himself eaten before he had a chance to do any investigating.

Most of the cages, Plumm found as he moved among them, were empty. The ones that were not, he left strictly alone. At each enclosure he took a moment to check its contents with a sweep of the flashlight's beam—a giant rabbit here, an emu there, a black leopard across the way—then moved quietly on. Very quietly, as a matter of fact. The last thing he wanted was to start a chorus of roaring and bleating and screaming from the inmates of this bizarre prison. The truth was, none of them seemed very interested in him, and that suited him just fine.

When he finally found what he was seeking, it didn't happen the way he'd planned. He was crouched outside the last cage on the first row, playing his light along the darkness inside, when he heard a low, rumbling growl. Then, too suddenly for him to react, a shape came flying out of the shadows, rammed its snout through one of the gaps between the bars, and grabbed his hand in its teeth.

Actually, it grabbed more glove than hand, and Plumm's cry of surprise made his attacker open its jaws and retreat. Plumm fell backward into the dirt, clutching his right hand. His assailant melted into the darkness, still growling with a sound like that of a poorly tuned outboard motor.

Inspecting his hand in the beam of the flashlight, Plumm saw with relief that the damage was slight: he had a red scratch on the bottom of his palm, where a flap of torn glove hung down from it like a sixth finger. Nothing serious. He was lucky, and he knew it: another inch and he'd need a set of left-handed golf clubs.

Once more Plumm turned his attention to the cage, and when he trained the circle of light on the thing that had attacked him, his breath caught in his throat.

It was even more beautiful than he'd suspected.

Crouching ten feet away in the beam of the flashlight, baring its fangs and glaring at him with pure yellow-eyed hatred, was a full-grown timber wolf. Its head was held low to the ground, ears laid back, powerful shoulders hunched as if ready to spring again. Its bushy tail twitched like a tiger's as it tried to figure out exactly what it was that stood looking at it through the bars.

And what Plumm noticed at once was its coloring. Even in the harsh glare of the flashlight he could tell this was no ordinary wolf. Its coat was a beautiful bluish-white, the shade of a snowy mountain stream or a summer sky streaked with clouds.

The Siberian blue wolf.

There were only a handful of them left in the world, and only two in captivity. One was rumored to be at the palace of King Qasani of Bandar-Kalam; the other was at the famous St. Louis Zoo.

Except that the one from St. Louis was missing.

Plumm spent another moment gazing into the animal's eyes, then turned and crept back down the path to the gate. Carefully he relocked it, made his way to the trellis, climbed it to the roof, and crawled through his bedroom window. Moments later, in the bright lights of his locked bathroom, he saw that he had been right about the bite: it had hardly bled at all. He'd had paper cuts that were worse. He dabbed his hand with everything he could find in the medicine chest, then applied a Band-Aid. Walking back into the bedroom, he considered for the first time just how close a call he'd had. If the wound had been serious—or if the wolf had happened to snatch the glove off and pull it into the cage with him—Plumm's master plan would have been finished before it started. As things stood now, he was right on target. He had located what he had come here to find. All he had to do now was secure the proof.

He'd take care of that tomorrow.

As things turned out, he had to wait a bit longer. Getting proof meant getting photographs, and to do that he had to retrieve the camera and film hidden beside the beach in the little plastic bag he'd brought ashore with him two days ago. His plan was to arrange a trip to his landing spot this morning, where he would elude his host long enough to find the hiding place and stuff the bag inside his shirt—but a sudden change in the weather kept that from happening. Heavy rains began just after daybreak, and it was a storm such as Jason Plumm had never before seen. It lasted two days, and during that time no one ventured far from home.

When the skies finally cleared, Plumm moved quickly, approaching the Colonel with a casual but well-rehearsed request to visit the area where he had washed ashore. With McDade's permission, Plumm borrowed one of the trucks and made the trip alone; it took him half an hour to drive to the beach, locate the palm tree where he had hidden the watertight container, and return to base. That night, after dinner and a game of chess with Colonel McDade, who had spent the day checking on flood damage, Jason went to his room to prepare for another midnight foray into the mysterious fenced compound behind the house.

Armed now with a miniature camera and film—in addition to his set of makeshift tools and the flashlight—Plumm retraced the route he had taken three nights ago. This time the trip was quicker, since he knew the way. It took less than fifteen minutes to get down off the roof and through the gate and down the long pathway to the cage. Keeping well clear of the bars this time, he sat down in the dirt outside the cage, took out his camera, and aimed his flashlight.

The cage was empty.

Plumm blinked. He looked all around; nothing was there. The wolf was gone. On impulse he reached up and tried the door to the cage. It was unlocked. In a panic now, Plumm rose to his feet, dashed inside, and searched every corner of the cage, as if the animal weren't gone at all, but had somehow become invisible.

"Where *is* he?" he wailed softly. He couldn't believe something like this had happened. He had been so close…

Frustrated, he made his way out of the compound and back to his room. What was going on, he kept asking himself. Only three nights had passed; what had happened? Why had they moved him? Did they suspect something?

Did they suspect *him*?

Plumm swallowed. That was a sobering thought. Maybe he hadn't been so lucky that night in the compound after all. Maybe the Colonel or his helpers had found a drop of his blood on the ground, or on the bars, or his footprints outside the cage, and decided that Plumm had come to kill the wolf, or steal him…

But that would be stupid. What reason would anyone have to kill it, and if an animal were stolen in a place like this, what could the thief have to gain? It wasn't as if you could escape and run away. There was nowhere to run.

He just couldn't figure it out.

Long after he'd returned to his room, and as he lay awake and confused in his bed, Plumm finally accepted the only possible answer: they had moved the wolf for reasons that had nothing to do with Jason Plumm. It was as simple as that. And it wasn't the end of the world, either—just a setback. It made his job harder, yes, but not impossible. The wolf was here, he knew that now. And if he found him once he could find him again. He just had to be patient.

But he wouldn't make tomorrow's boat.

The arrival of the supply boat was quite an event for the island. Almost every employee was present, either to help with the unloading or to chat with the crew or just to observe from the grassy ridge above the dock. As the Colonel had said earlier, this was the only lifeline to the outside world. That made it special. Even if all it brought was news, it would still have been welcome.

Plumm stood beside Colonel McDade at the foot of the dock, watching the proceedings like the others. McDade's foreman and a grim-faced Dr. Sumoru were supervising the transfer of goods. The morning was cool but humid.

"I'm glad you decided to stay a bit," the Colonel said, squinting at the boat.

"I don't have a lot to go back to," Plumm said. "No wife anymore, no kids, a crummy job… everybody thinks I'm dead by now anyway, I might as well stay a while longer and get my head on straight." He turned and looked the older man in the eye. "I appreciate the favor."

The Colonel regarded him a moment, smiling. "Just don't start beating me at Scrabble."

The next two weeks passed quickly. Jason Plumm went out on horseback every day to look for the wolf, using his long-neglected engineering degree to help advise McDade and his men on the placement of culverts and the repair of storm-damaged roads. It was the perfect cover, since it allowed him to earn his keep but also afforded him open access to all corners of the island without having to constantly think up reasons for his absences. His interest-in-wildlife excuse had been wearing a little thin.

It was on one of these excursions that he finally saw the wolf. The animal was standing on a ridge fifty yards away when Plumm spotted him, and for a moment both man and beast remained completely still, each studying the other. Staring at him now, Plumm was reminded again of the quiet beauty of this unique and magnificent animal. The pale-blue coat rippled and shimmered in the afternoon sun, and even from this distance Plumm thought he could sense the intelligence—even recognition, perhaps?—in the small yellow eyes.

But he waited too long to act. Even as he reached for the camera in his pocket, the wolf turned and bolted into the brush. Cursing himself, Plumm urged his horse into a gallop, skirting the entire area in hopes of catching another glimpse. It didn't work. Half an hour later he headed back toward the Main House, but for the first time in many days he felt encouraged. Certain types of animals were often restricted to specific parts of the island, and by now he knew most of the boundaries. Now that he had found the wolf's assigned area, all he had to do was concentrate on it alone, and keep his camera ready. Very shortly now, he would have what he needed.

It happened five days later, when he had stopped on the trail and was drinking from the canteen he took along on his outings. The wolf was above him on a shelf of rock, no more than twenty yards away, and outlined perfectly against the overcast sky. Moving with great care, Plumm raised the camera and shot a full roll of film. When he returned to base that afternoon, he knew he had what he required. The pictures he had just taken, when compared to the existing photos of the wolf before the theft had occurred, would be conclusive evidence—certainly enough to convict the Colonel and restore the prized animal to its owners. More importantly, the staggering insurance settlement would be prevented, and Plumm could collect his fee.

He smiled to himself as he loped his mount through the grassy meadows to the dirt road that led to the house. His job here was done.

All he had to do now was catch a boat.

A week later Plumm said his goodbyes to the staff, with a special thank-you to No Sin and those who had nursed him after his arrival. Under Dr. Sumoru's parting glare, he climbed into the passenger seat of the Colonel's Jeep for the ride to the dock.

It was a gorgeous day, the sky clear and the wind brisk through the open windows. Several of the field workers and animal handlers waved as the Jeep passed them on the rutted road. Neither of its occupants waved in reply: Plumm was feeling a little under the weather—his flu symptoms had returned during the night, leaving him weak and feverish—and Colonel McDade was moody.

"I truly hate to see you go, Jason," he said. "It's been damn fine having a companion to talk to around here."

"We've had a few debates, haven't we?" Plumm agreed.

In the silence that followed, Plumm came to a decision. Partly because of his sluggish feeling and partly because they were about to part forever, he felt a very uncharacteristic pang of guilt at what he was about to do to this kind man who had befriended him for almost six weeks.

"Why is it, Colonel," Plumm asked, "that in all those talks we've had, you've never told me about the wolf?"

McDade fixed his passenger with a stare. Then his face softened and he turned again to face the road. "So you saw him," the Colonel said quietly.

"Yes. A week ago, up in the hills."

They rode on in silence for a moment. At last McDade explained, with a sigh, "I'm a little funny about my animals, Jason. When bad things happen to them it affects me deeply. I find it hard to even talk about."

Plumm frowned. "What kind of things? The wolf I saw seemed to be in the best of health."

"Oh, he is. None better." The Colonel paused. "We had a hard time with him at first, of course—the temperature and humidity here are far different from his previous home—but with time he has adjusted well. A magnificent animal."

Plumm felt, above the flush of his fever, a little twinge of satisfaction. *That* was why the wolf had been in the compound behind the house, he realized: it had had trouble becoming conditioned to the climate, and was being treated.

Plumm decided to press a little.

"Actually," he said, watching the older man from the corner of his eye, "I wouldn't have thought the weather in St. Louis would be that much different from here."

McDade frowned. "St. Louis?"

Then, slowly, the Colonel's face cleared. "Ah," he said. "I take it they are missing their Siberian wolf."

"That's right."

A silence passed. "My friend," the Colonel said, "I do not indulge my… hobby, shall we say… at the expense of others. I would not be so unfeeling, or so presumptuous, as to attempt to purchase a rare animal from a public zoo."

Despite his headache, Plumm kept his eyes on McDade's profile. "I wasn't referring to a purchase, Colonel."

For a moment it was quiet in the car. Ahead, the dock moved into view, and McDade, expressionless, steered the vehicle onto a patch of gravel near the water's edge. The supply boat had already begun unloading; the wooden platform was busy with golden-skinned workers moving carts and boxes.

Hanson McDade sat there awhile, studying the blue ocean beyond the boat, then cut the engine. Without looking at his passenger, he said, "You think I… abducted him. That's it, isn't it? You believe I had him stolen, and brought him here."

"What I think, Colonel," Plumm said, "is that you were a victim of your own obsession. I think you meant no harm."

"So you're a policeman, then?"

Plumm sighed. His headache was worse now, and it hurt to swallow. "Nothing so noble, I'm afraid. I was hired by the company that insured the animal. They hope to restore him to his owners, and reclaim their loss."

"And how is it," the Colonel asked, "that you suspected *me*?"

"I have contacts in Papeete. The men on your supply ship are not all quite so loyal as you believe."

McDade thought that over, then smiled. "Ah. Joe Pintana. I might have known. He remembered the delivery?"

"No, but he'd heard others talking. It's hard to transport an animal like that one without attracting attention. The odd color, you know."

The Colonel nodded tiredly. After a short silence, he blew out a sigh and looked the younger man in the eye. "The truth is, son, you've made a mistake. A rather large one, I fear, but still only a mistake. You were trying to do your job, and I bear you no grudge because of it."

Plumm just stared at him. "What do you mean, a mistake?"

"The wolf you saw didn't come from St. Louis, Jason. He came from Bandar-Kalam. I bought him myself, a short time ago, from King Qasani."

Plumm blinked. "Qasani?"

"You don't have to take my word for it. I have the cancelled check, and both our banks can verify the transfer of funds. Besides, I am familiar with the wolf at the St. Louis facility. I have photos of him, which you are welcome to compare to the photos I assume you took last week, when you saw my specimen." He paused. "Theirs is a smaller animal, and lighter in color."

Jason was stunned. "But… where could he be, if not here?"

"I have no idea."

"But I—"

Colonel McDade held up a hand, stopping Plumm in mid-sentence. Their eyes remained locked.

"I'm telling you the truth, my boy. I believe you know that now."

Plumm swallowed hard. He did indeed know it. As he had said a moment ago, he was no policeman—but he had dealt with criminals and cheats and liars for many years now, and he knew with a terrible certainty that the Colonel had spoken the truth. He could see it in the man's eyes, for one thing. Also, Plumm had neglected to follow up on the small inconsistencies he had noticed recently—things that hadn't seemed to matter at the time, like the wolf's larger size that night in the compound, and the slight difference in coloring last week. With a sinking feeling he realized that he had screwed up, and on a grand scale. For the first time in his long career, Jason Plumm had shot himself squarely in the foot.

Neither of them said anything for a while. Outside on the dock, the unloading had finished. Plumm sat there, slack-faced and staring, until the silence was broken by the droning of the boat's horn.

Plumm blinked and looked around, feeling dazed.

'They're ready to sail," the Colonel said.

It occurred to Plumm then, with the force of a punch in the stomach, that he couldn't leave. His bosses were waiting for an answer—no, not an answer, a *solution*—and even now they must be wondering what the hell was taking so long. Plumm had left them no word on where he was going or who he was after, and now that almost two months had passed they would be furious to learn that their star investigator had been off chasing shadows while the real trail grew as cold as a Canadian winter.

"What do I do now?" Plumm murmured.

The Colonel sighed. "That's your choice. But I meant what I said—I hold you no ill feelings. I like you, Jason Plumm, and I believe we could work well together."

Plumm turned to look at him.

"You've already done wonders assisting my men with their construction work," he continued. "And I desperately need an irrigation system for my outer fields, and bridges over the ravines north of the lake." He studied his passenger a moment. "You think you could handle that?"

Plumm swallowed and winced at the pain in his throat. "Are you... offering me a job?"

"That's the idea. There is one condition, at the request of Dr. Sumoru—but it's just a formality."

"What kind of condition?"

"You'll see."

Plumm thought a moment. "When would I start?"

"How does tomorrow sound?"

Plumm hesitated.

Could he just abandon his life and profession—at least for a while—and stay here, on the island?

The answer, of course, was another question: Why not? He loved the island, he enjoyed the work, the outdoors, the animals. The exotica of wildlife.

Why not, indeed?

Trying to keep from smiling, he raised his head and looked the Colonel in the eye. "I accept," he said.

"In that case, welcome to the family." McDade reached out and clasped Plumm's hand in his, then frowned with concern. "You're hot as fire, boy," he announced, studying Plumm's face. "I can't have a sick employee on my hands. Let's get you back to the house and fix you up."

With a reassuring wink, the Colonel started the Jeep and pulled out of the lot. As they made the turn away from the coastline, they could see the supply boat heading slowly out of the bay that sheltered the landing. McDade waved through the window, and the boat's whistle blew.

"You'll come to love it here, Jason," he said. "It grows on you."

Plumm nodded, still a little overwhelmed by this turn of events. The movement made his neck ache; he was trying to rest his head against the seatback when he had a sudden thought.

"You never did tell me what happened," Plumm said.

"Excuse me?" McDade's eyes were fixed on the curving road.

"You said something about 'when bad things happen to your animals.' But then you agreed that the wolf I saw was in top shape."

McDade nodded. "Right. He is. I was talking about the other one."

Plumm raised his head. "What?"

"His brother. You see, I didn't just buy one wolf from Qasani. I bought two."

"You mean… there was a second wolf?"

The Colonel's eyes turned sad. "Even bigger and prettier than the one you saw. He was in isolation when you arrived, in the holding compound." He paused and sighed. "He died two days later."

"Died?" Plumm felt a cold tremor go through him. "Died… of what?"

"Rabies," the Colonel said. "One of the few things Sumoru can't treat."

———••———

Jason Plumm woke up an hour later, flat on his back on a couch in the living room of the Main House. At first, he didn't know where he was. Gradually he recognized the faces of Colonel McDade and Dr. Sumoru, and the memories came flooding in.

He was going to die, and he knew it.

"You fainted," the Colonel told him.

"The least of my troubles," Plumm murmured. And then, just as he was about to close his eyes again, he saw something in their faces. Miserably, he asked, "What?"

The Colonel and his vet exchanged glances. "I have a confession to make," McDade said. "As I told you earlier, we have no advanced medical resources here…"

"But?" Plumm said.

"But we do have a communications facility." McDade paused, studying Plumm's face. "If you're going to play at being a spy, you really shouldn't use your real name, you know. I checked out your story. Within an hour after our conversation that first night, I knew about the St. Louis theft, and your investigation into it. I also found out, later, about your little scouting expeditions, into the holding compound. No Sin followed you, both times."

Plumm swallowed, his mind racing. "So… you knew I was bitten?"

"I knew everything."

"Then why didn't you *tell* me? For God's sake, if the wolf was rabid… you could have *saved* me. I could have boarded the next boat, or you could have called for help—"

Another look passed between McDade and Sumoru. And this time Plumm thought he saw a flicker of amusement there.

They were *trying* to kill me, he thought feverishly. This was their plan all along…

Even in his despair, he felt a warm rush of anger.

But then the Colonel said, his eyes narrowed: "Tell me, Jason: Did the wolf *look* sick, when he bit you? Staggering, maybe? Foaming at the mouth?"

Plumm blinked. "What?"

McDade smiled. "The holding pens were off-limits," he said, "because we were mating Chinese pandas there. Nothing else."

"What do you mean?"

The Colonel leaned forward, watching him. "There is no second wolf, Jason. There never was. And the one I got from Qasani isn't rabid."

Plumm's jaw dropped. "You mean... I don't have—"

"What you have is the flu. And hopefully not for long; we have work to do, you and I, on that irrigation system." Still grinning, McDade stood up, as if he were ready to go get started right now.

Plumm could only stare. "You... lied to me?"

The Colonel somehow managed to look both guilty and pleased at the same time. "There's been a lot of that going around."

"But... *why*? You scared me half to death—"

"I had to. If I wanted to hire you, that is."

Plumm just gaped at him.

"That," McDade explained, "was Dr. Sumoru's condition."

During the silence that followed, both of them turned and looked at the little veterinarian.

Sumoru shrugged. In perfect English, he said to Plumm, "I have been working on my sense of humor."

And, very slowly, all three of them smiled.

After a decade investigating financial crimes, Heidi Hunter now puts crime on paper in mysteries and short stories. Follow her author blog at https://hollyhyattauthor.wordpress.com/ and her travel blog, https://wanderwoman376.wordpress. com

Watching a television veterinarian visit an alpaca ranch, she saw cute, curious alpaca milling around their corral. In her mind, she saw a herd of alpaca gathered around a dead body instead. Alpaca provide more than fiber and cuteness. They provide motivation to solve a murder.

Killer Alpaca

by Heidi Hunter

The alpaca's warm, placid eyes gazed at me over the fence, almost distracting me from the man lying motionless at my feet.

"Recognize him, Janet?" the detective asked.

The hefty man's scruff-covered face did not ring a bell. I shook my head, baffled. "No, I've never seen him before in my life."

"He's been dead a while." Dwight Weezil, the coroner, kneeling on the other side of the body, squinted up at the detective.

"Can you tell what killed him?"

"Not yet." Weezil was a short, lean man, who knew his job. "He has a broken leg. Multiple contusions. Cracked skull. Struck hard, I'd hazard. You'll know more after the autopsy."

I glanced at Freddy, the alpaca watching me, as if he could explain what happened. Freddy's wide eyes radiated bewilderment.

My partner and I had left home the day before, rushing to see my sister who'd called with an emergency. We arrived back at the house this morning to find alpaca and police milling around a dead man in our corral.

Three more alpaca approached the fence and joined Freddy in scrutinizing our every move. The herd was closing ranks. It comforted me to have them nearby.

"Could the alpaca…" the detective started, but a shrill voice interrupted his question.

"Absolutely not!" Sibyl Atkins, my partner and the co-owner of the Happy Alpaca Ranch, stomped over to us. Dressed in a vest she knitted from our alpaca fiber, she waggled her finger in the detective's face. "You get that right out of your head, Rod, er, Detective Rodnitski. Our alpaca did not trample that thief to death!"

Detective Rodnitski ignored her misstep on his name. Sibyl and I were friends with his mother and had known him since he was a rug rat. He was the newest detective with Holdingford's police force. It was difficult getting used to calling him 'Detective.'

"Thief?" He examined tan-colored Freddy with a section of fleece sheared off his right side. The fleece and the shearing implement, what appeared to be a barber's clippers rather than livestock shears, lay near the body.

"Poor Cinnamon and Penelope are missing!" Sibyl's hands clenched into fists, wanting to strike out in frustration.

"Are they alpaca?"

"Cinnamon is our stud," I tried to remain calm, although my stomach churned with anxiety about their fate. "A handsome red male who earns us a lot in stud fees. Penelope is expecting a cria—that's a baby alpaca—any day now."

More animals joined those observing us from the fence, all eyes focused on me as if imploring me to find their herd-mates. A low hum ran through the group, an indication of their nervousness. Jenny, a lovely cream alpaca, nudged me, seeking a comforting scritch.

"They are worth a lot of money." I scratched Jenny on the neck, reassured by the calming feel of her warm, furry body under my fingertips. "Ten thousand or more for a stud or pregnant female. They're our two most valuable alpaca."

"So, either they are familiar with alpaca in general or with your animals specifically," Rod surmised. "Who would know about your alpaca?"

I said, "Anyone who takes our classes meets them." We offered classes in fiber preparation, yarn spinning and knitting at our ranch. "Alpaca have an eleven-month gestation, so anyone who's taken a class in the last year would have known Penelope was expecting."

"I'll need names." Rod jotted in his notebook. "Who knew you were out of town?"

"Our neighbor across the road, Dale Withers, was looking after them. He has sheep," I added as if that qualified him for alpaca care.

"Dale called us," Rod informed me. "Said he arrived to turn your animals out to pasture and found the body. Who else?"

"Glinda knew," Sibyl said, and I winced. Glinda Godwin was the biggest gossip in Holdingford, so it was possible everyone knew we were gone. "I talked to her yesterday evening. She called to find out when our next yarn spinning class is. I mentioned we were out of town and I would check the schedule this morning when we got back."

"Would Glinda want to steal your alpaca?"

Sibyl's wrinkled forehead likely mirrored my own as we considered it.

"I can't imagine," I replied. "Glinda's been wanting to get in the business of spinning yarn and has taken several of our classes. But resort to kidnapping?"

Sibyl snorted. "And where would she keep them? In her back yard? It's the size of a postage stamp."

Glinda lived in a small house on a quarter acre lot in town, not quite enough land to house two alpaca. She had neighbors close enough they would notice livestock grazing in the front yard. Besides—

"Could Glinda have wrangled them by herself?" Rod asked.

Many of the herd stood up to my chin and weighed an average of 150 pounds. Glinda was at least sixty, bony and several inches shorter than me.

I shook my head. "No, we usually handle them together, sometimes along with a third person if we're shearing. They're strong, and they will kick if they get agitated. But they don't trample."

One of our bolder alpaca, a gelded male, sidled over to Rod.

The detective eyed the animal with suspicion. "Don't they spit?"

"Yep," I said.

He backed away from the curious animal. "Anyone else interested in your herd?"

Sibyl's expression darkened. "Roger Pickens."

I cringed. Roger was the town bad guy. Always angry, always drunk and always broke. He could be involved in something like this.

I elaborated for the detective. "We bought our original trio from him. He couldn't make a go of it. And now he's unhappy at our success. Wanted to buy them back to restart his herd. He's trying goats right now."

I eyed poor Freddy, as the rest of our shaggy-headed fur babies gathered around him in commiseration. Freddy was one of the three we purchased from Roger. Was that a coincidence?

"Is there any reason to steal the fur?" The detective pointed at the pitiful pile of fleece next to Freddy.

I shrugged, mystified. "No. The fiber itself isn't valuable. Maybe a few dollars per pound. It's only after it's been washed and carded that the value increases."

"This is the wrong time of year to shear too," Sibyl added. "We shear in spring, not fall. The fleece isn't long enough now."

"I'll remove him to the morgue if it's ok with you," Weezil said, referring to our John Doe. The detective nodded. Officers had been taking pictures and bagging evidence since we arrived home.

"Let me know if you think of anything else." Rod bade us goodbye and headed to his car.

The next day, Sibyl and I were in the outbuilding where we processed fleece, spun yarn and conducted classes. We were spinning roving—washed and carded alpaca fleece—into yarn for the knitting shop in Old Town Holdingford when Rod dropped by.

"Just wanted to let you know your animals are off the hook for murder," he reported.

"I should think so!" Sibyl bristled like an angry porcupine, even though I knew Rod was joking. At least we had proof our alpaca weren't hardened killers.

"What did him in?" I asked.

"The coroner thinks he was hit by a car. Maybe not even here, but dumped later."

"Why back here?" This whole crime wasn't making any sense.

"My theory? The killer was trying to make it appear the vic was trampled by the herd while shearing them."

I groaned at the criminal's stupidity.

Rod continued. "We identified the vic too. Fingerprints in the system. Jamison Gunderson. Sound familiar?"

Sibyl and I shook our heads. I would remember meeting someone with that unusual name.

"Mind if I take another walk around your corral?"

I nodded. "What about our missing alpaca?" I didn't mean to appear heartless about the dead stranger, but members of our family were missing.

"We're working on it."

"I don't think they care about our babies at all." As Rod walked away, tears sprang to Sibyl's eyes. "He's more concerned with the dead guy."

"Of course he is, that's his job," I pointed out. "But he'll search for our alpaca. That's how he'll find the killer."

"How can you be so calm about our missing children, Janet?" she moaned, gearing up for a meltdown.

"I'm not," I admitted. The missing animals weren't just our babies, they were our livelihood. I'm not sure we'd receive enough from insurance to replace them if they were gone for good. A weight settled in my chest at the thought of never seeing Cinnamon or Penelope again. Trying to ignore the sensation, I took one of Sybil's hands in both of mine. "I have faith they'll come back to us."

However, Sibyl was inconsolable. "It won't be soon enough." She gripped my hands tighter. "Penny is due any day. If she doesn't feel comfortable, she could have complications during the birth."

I wrapped an arm around Sibyl's shoulders and gave her a squeeze. "Don't worry. We'll find them and bring them home." Her apprehension was rubbing off on me. What if Penny had problems? Who would help her? "We'll check with Dale and see if he saw anything unusual during the night."

Sibyl marched toward the car. "Let's go now."

Dale Withers lived on several acres across the road from us. As I drove up the rutted gravel drive, I spotted a large flock of brown and white sheep in a pasture to the left. While his home needed a fresh coat of paint, his barns were well-maintained and his fencing recently repaired. Typical prioritization for a farmer.

I pulled in behind his truck, which sported a new dent in the rear fender. Dale ambled out of the barn when I honked to announce our arrival. He was in his fifties, clad in worn but tidy work clothes of jeans and a t-shirt.

"Heard you found the dead man in our corral," I said.

"Yeah, ain't seen nothing like it." Dale removed his hat and scratched his balding head.

"Did you know a couple of our alpaca are missing?"

"No! All Rod talked about was a dead man. Who's missing?"

"Cinnamon and Penelope."

"Ah, too bad." Dale nodded in sympathy. He understood the financial and emotional devastation of losing members of your herd.

Out of the corner of my eye, I glimpsed Sibyl sidle toward the barn.

"When were you last at our place before you found the body?" I asked Dale, to keep his attention off Sibyl sneaking around.

"Evening before, around dark. I herded them into the barn and set out fresh hay and water like you asked. Shut up the barn. Made sure the gate was closed." Dale did know how to care for livestock.

"Did you see anything unusual at our place, or anywhere in the area that night? Or hear anything?" Alpaca can issue a piercing scream when forced to do something they didn't want to do.

"Didn't see nothin'. Didn't hear nothin'. I go to bed early, you know. Up with the light to tend to the flock."

I understood; that was our routine as well.

Sibyl walked back toward us, disappointment etched in her face.

"When did that happen?" I pointed at the dent on his truck's back fender.

"Oh, last month. Backed into a fence post by accident. Won't have money to fix it until the next shearing."

Sibyl and I thanked him for his time and left.

"Not in the barn," Sibyl reported on her surveillance. "I think he's lying. I saw him in town last week, and there weren't no dent in his truck then. Maybe he backed into our fence while gearing up to run over that guy."

"Dale at least would know how and when to shear an animal," I pointed out.

"Maybe he did it wrong to throw us off his scent." Sibyl crossed her arms.

"I can't fathom one reason Dale would take our alpaca. He's doing well in sheep."

"Alpaca fiber is more in demand. He had the best opportunity."

I conceded it was possible, but why?

"We'll have to search his place tonight while he's asleep," Sibyl said.

The alpaca, if he had them, could be anywhere on Dale's several acres. I pictured Sibyl stumbling through his fields in the dark and shuddered.

"No, we won't," I stated. "It's dangerous and he's been a good neighbor."

Sibyl huffed in frustration and ran her fingers through her short, greying hair, causing it to stand on end in inadvertently stylish spikes. "We're wasting our time. Let's go see Roger. He has to have them."

Visiting Roger Pickens called for caution. He was a card-carrying member of the NRA and no fan of "unnatural" lifestyles as he termed them. He lived closer to town on much smaller acreage than Dale. When we pulled into the weedy yard, his small herd of goats greeted us. A couple of kids cavorted around the yard in joy, butting heads. I had to grin when one bounced over toward me. They appeared well tended, but the farmhouse and barn were dilapidated.

Roger stormed out of the house, waved his arms and yelled. He appeared as rundown as his farm.

The goats fled. We didn't.

"Git! You're not wanted here." Spittle flew from his mouth. "Why did you lezzies sic that detective on me? I ain't done nothing."

I tried not to show my offense at his epithet, but it smarted. Fortunately, most people in town appeared accepting of our relationship. "Our lifestyle didn't bother you too much when you wanted to unload your alpaca."

"And you repay my generosity by trying to get me arrested?" His hands clenched at his side.

Sibyl held his fierce glare with her own. "A couple of our alpaca are missing. Know anything about that?"

"You sure they didn't just run away?" Roger sneered, baring his yellowing teeth.

"We take good care of our alpaca, unlike you."

Roger spit on the ground, barely missing Sibyl's boots. She didn't flinch.

Sibyl stood firm. "Where were you the night before last?" she asked.

"What business is it of yours?" he shot back, looming over her by several inches.

I jumped in to de-escalate a situation I felt was about to spiral out of control. "You tried to buy them back not long ago." I stepped toward him. "Maybe you didn't want to take 'no' for an answer?"

"Don't need 'em. Goat milk is big business these days." His farm belied that statement. "Lots easier than alpaca."

"Please, if you have our alpaca, we'd be willing to give you money to return them. No questions asked." I hoped I didn't sound as desperate as I felt, but Roger was our best suspect, and I was afraid to alienate him.

He swung toward me. "How much?" His weaselly eyes gleamed.

Before I could answer, Sibyl butted in. "Can we look in your barn?"

"Go to hell!" Roger stormed back into his house and slammed the door.

My shoulders slumped. That did not go well.

"Now's our chance." Sibyl hustled toward the barn but didn't get far before Roger reappeared from the house, shotgun in hand.

"Leave before I shoot you as trespassers!"

I fully believed he would too. We hurried back to the car.

Sibyl grumbled as we left the driveway. "It has to be Roger. You heard him. He hates lesbians. Let's search his property until we find them."

"Not right now." *Not ever,* I said to myself, trying to still my shaky hands on the steering wheel. I wouldn't put it past Roger to shoot us on sight the next time he found us on his property.

"It has to be now," Sibyl moaned. "He'll probably sell 'em. He obviously needs the money."

I was concerned he would get rid of them now that he knew we were onto him. And not just sell them but *dispose* of them.

"Since we're out, let's try Glinda," I suggested to remove that awful image from my head. "She knew we were gone and maybe she's heard some gossip."

As we entered town, I detoured through Glinda's neighborhood. A neat and tidy ranch-style house near the school, no one was home, not even alpaca. Sibyl rattled the doorknob, then peeked in the windows as if expecting to find two alpaca lounging on the living room sofa.

"Stop that!" I warned her, in case one of Glinda's neighbors was watching.

"She has *Alpacas Magazine* on her coffee table," Sibyl reported.

"Unless she has an actual alpaca on her coffee table, I'm not interested." We suggest in our classes subscribing to the official magazine of the Alpaca Owners Association for those interested in learning more about raising alpaca. It didn't surprise me that Glinda checked it out.

"Let's go into town and have lunch," I suggested. "See if anyone's heard anything."

Old Town in Holdingford, our destination, sprawled along the Mississippi River. Lined with small city parks and an extensive bike trail system, it used to be where its residents came to shop. Now, its stores sold baubles useless to everyone but tourists while the residents shopped at the big box stores that sprouted north of the city. However, locals still patronized one or two Old Town cafes for breakfast and lunch.

I parked in front of Tillie's Café. When Sibyl and I alighted from the car, we spotted Glinda arguing with a ferret-faced young man a few stores down from our parking spot. As we approached, I caught fragments of their quarrel.

"You promised…" Glinda hissed. "…what kind of son…"

"…got it all wrong… Jumbo assured me…" the young man was saying.

"…lied…"

"…doesn't matter now." The man spotted us approaching and limped off toward a beat-up Toyota.

"Is that your son?" I asked Glinda. I'd heard her son had returned to town, but I hadn't seen him in ages.

"Oh, hi Janet. Yes, that's Teddy." Glinda frowned after him, knuckles white as she gripped her purse to her stomach.

"Have you heard about the dead guy in our corral?" I asked, trying to draw her attention back to us. "And our missing alpaca?"

Glinda's eyes focused somewhere beyond my right ear. "Yeah, I heard. Bad luck for you. Hope you find them." She wandered away, apparently not up for gossiping.

"What's up with her?" Sibyl wondered. Glinda was always ready to jaw.

"Trouble with Teddy?" I suggested, but something about this whole encounter bothered me. "Let's go to the café."

Tillie's was a narrow space sandwiched between an antique shop and a small art gallery. The inside had room for five tables with the rest of the room filled with display cases packed with fresh bread and baked goods. Tillie's was known for its caramel rolls at breakfast and custom-built sandwiches at lunch. The yeasty scent of fresh dough filled my nostrils as we entered.

We commandeered the last free table. As soon as we sat, a heavily tattooed woman, the owner-waitress, Tillie, appeared. "Usual?" she asked.

I did order my usual, a turkey and Monterey jack sandwich. Sibyl seemed distracted and didn't answer, so I requested a veggie panini for her.

"Hear anything about our missing alpaca?" I asked Tillie.

"Not really. All anyone's talking about is the dead guy. Is it true your alpaca trampled him to death?"

"No!" Sibyl's face reddened in anger.

"He was hit by a car." I wanted to nip that rumor in the bud. No one would attend our classes if they thought the herd would attack them. "Did anyone say they knew who he was?"

"Not that they would admit." Tillie strode away to put in our order.

We waited in silence, me musing about the confrontation we witnessed outside, Sibyl still mourning our missing children.

I stopped Tillie when she arrived with our colas. "Did Glinda come in today?"

"Yeah, left not too long ago. Didn't say much, which now that you mention it is weird. Glinda can talk the spots off a leopard. But she hurried off when that boy of hers came in." Tillie hustled off to grab our lunch.

I turned to Sibyl. "Do you know anything about Teddy?"

"I know almost nothing about him, except what Tillie told me when he arrived back in town a few months ago."

Tillie reappeared and dropped our lunch on the table.

"Didn't you tell me Glinda's son was drummed out of the service?" Sibyl asked her.

"Yeah, dishonorable discharge, that's the rumor."

"Not an injury?" I asked.

"Nope." Tillie was certain. "Glinda's been tight-lipped about what he did, though. He was always her golden child."

"Does he live in town with Glinda?"

"No way would she take him back in. I don't know where he's staying."

When Tillie left, I picked up my sandwich. "I'd like to go visit Teddy," I told Sibyl before taking a bite. I savored the tang of basil pesto with the mild cheese.

"Why?" Sibyl hadn't—unusually—touched her sandwich.

"Because we have no other leads right now," I admitted.

I put aside my sandwich and took out my phone to search for an address for Ted Godwin. There was one in Hampton, a few miles south.

Sibyl regained her appetite with the possibility of a fresh lead. We gobbled down our lunch and returned to the car.

A piece of paper peeked out from under the windshield wiper. Had I parked in a no-parking zone? No signs, no yellow paint on the curb.

Sibyl snatched up the paper, ready to lay into any cop who'd write us a ticket. Her hand trembled as she passed it to me, her eyes agog.

"*$5000 FOR YOUR ALPACA. AWAIT MY CALL.*"

The ransom note—what else could it be—was hand-printed in all capital letters.

"I knew it!" Sibyl said. "Roger has them. He's the only one we've offered to pay for them."

"But he wouldn't have to leave us an anonymous note since we've already made him the offer." But it was a big coincidence. I scanned up and down the main street, trying to identify Roger's Ford pickup. If he'd been here, he was gone now.

Sibyl thrust out her jaw. I knew that look. She wanted to rush to Roger's farm and snatch back our alpaca.

"Let's give him time to call us before dashing off to another meeting with his shotgun," I said.

Sibyl's eyes pleaded with me, and my resolve melted into a puddle.

"Fine." I gave in.

I was apprehensive about seeing Roger again so soon after our previous encounter, but if he wanted to sell us back our alpaca, I would take my chances. Unfortunately, we didn't get that chance. When I pulled into Roger's driveway, I saw the beat-up Toyota Teddy drove parked in front of the house.

"What's he doing here?" Sibyl asked. "Do they even know each other?"

I wondered what business Teddy and Roger had with each other. "I dunno, but this gives us a chance to check out Teddy's house without him there."

Teddy lived in a mobile home parked on a couple acres of open land at the end of a dirt lane. Neighbors were sparse, which was fortunate for him as a dog howled as we pulled in.

Parked in front of the trailer was a white van. I peered in the back windows and spotted wisps of hay on the floor. I opened the back door and found more hay covered with bits of alpaca fleece.

"I think they were in here," I said. Alpaca can be transported in a van. It was big enough, and they typically lay down to travel. We used a horse trailer ourselves.

Circling around to the front of the van, we discovered the damage. A deep dent on the fender with a smaller one on the hood containing a smear of blood. A cracked windshield on the right side. For the first time, I felt some sympathy for the victim. The van struck him hard. He didn't have a chance.

A familiar shriek sounded from the back yard.

"Cinnamon!" Sibyl cried and ran toward the call. Our beautiful babies were in a small, fenced-in section of the yard meant to contain the resident dog.

"There's no shelter here." Sibyl was appalled. "And that fence is too low. Coyotes could have gotten them."

"And he has Cinnamon and Penelope together," I added, also upset. You can't keep stud males with pregnant females.

Cinnamon and Penelope crowded around us as we entered the enclosure, dare I hope, happy to see us.

Sibyl herded the alpaca out of the pen. They trotted easily ahead of her, eager to go.

"Where are you taking them?" I asked. "We can't fit them both in the backseat of our car. Let's call Rod."

Crunching gravel heralded the arrival of another car. My heart dropped. Teddy was home, and with two alpaca, we had no place to hide. I quickly punched in 911 on my phone and stuffed it in my jeans pocket.

The tall, rangy man we saw arguing with Glinda leaped from the car, squinting at us with suspicion. "Who the hell are you and what are you doing on my property?"

Sibyl reacted like a mother wolverine protecting her young. "You framed our alpaca!" she screamed, storming toward him as if to smack the fillings from his teeth.

Teddy pulled a gun from the back of his waistband and Sibyl froze mid-step.

The alpaca stirred next to me, sensing the tension. I crept away from them, hoping if Teddy fired, he wouldn't hit them.

"Stop!" He had noticed my movement and swung the gun toward me, then back at Sibyl. "Stay back!"

He pointed his gun in the direction of the fenced-in area. "Get in there."

Feeling safer with members of our herd than with him, we joined our animals in the pen. The agitated alpaca shuffled around the area. I stroked Penelope's neck to calm her.

"It will be so sad. You two killed by these mangy creatures." He waved his gun toward Cinnamon. "That one's particularly ornery."

Sibyl and I closed ranks, trying to protect our alpaca. We clasped sweaty hands, ready to meet our fate.

"That didn't work the first time you tried it," I reminded him. "With Jamison."

"Are you trying to make him shoot us?" Sibyl whispered out of the side of her mouth.

"Jumbo!" he spat. "This is all his fault. Thought we'd rake in a bundle sellin' 'em instead of keeping 'em for Ma.

"Why'd you run down Jumbo?" I asked to keep him talking.

"Yeah, sorry I had to do that. He was my bud." Teddy shrugged, exhibiting no remorse. "But he wanted more money because he was doin' all the work. It was my idea though. Mine and Ma's," he corrected.

"Your mother was involved in this?" I never seriously considered that Glinda would be involved in not only theft but murder.

"Ma said we'd make lotsa money raising these things. We just needed something to start with. You had a lot. Who'd miss a couple? Ma pointed out the ones she wanted."

My jaw dropped, and Sibyl and I exchanged horrified glances. We'd never miss them?

"Now let's get on with this." Teddy brandished his gun at us again. "Have a buyer coming to pick them up tonight."

"Roger?" I asked, thinking perhaps that's what the meeting we encountered was about. Did Roger plan to keep our alpaca or ransom them back to us?

But Teddy didn't answer, instead striding over to Cinnamon, waving his arms and shouting, "Go on! Attack!" He raised a hand as if to swat the alpaca on the rump.

Cinnamon stutter-stepped backward, then spat green bile in Teddy's face.

Teddy swore and wiped away the foul-smelling goo. Cinnamon twisted away from him in disgust, then squealed, reared up and bucked his hind legs back, nailing Teddy in the knee.

Teddy crumpled. "Dang it. I hate that thing!" he snarled as he fell to the dirt, losing his grip on the gun as he grabbed for his injured knee. It was clearly not Cinnamon's first attack on the man.

Sibyl pounced on Teddy, pummeling him in retaliation for stealing our alpaca. I snatched up the gun.

Cinnamon and Penelope lingered nearby, watching the whole scene with mild interest.

"How did you know it was Teddy?" Sibyl asked in awe as we tied him up as best we could with belts and vests to await the police.

"It was a guess," I admitted. "Of all our suspects, he's the one who doesn't know anything about alpaca, and he was limping."

The cria's warm, placid eyes gazed at me, almost distracting me from Detective Rodnitski's words.

"Glinda wouldn't say anything at first, but we couldn't stop Teddy from relating the entire scheme and his mother's role in it," Rod reported. "After that, Glinda put all the blame for the death on her son. But Teddy claimed she was involved, angry that Jamison wanted to sell her alpaca."

Her alpaca. Glinda's presumption angered me more than anything else that happened in this affair. I gazed with affection at the newest addition to our herd.

We had rescued and reunited our herd of alpaca just in time. Penelope gave birth, without complications, to an adorable, fawn-colored female the next morning, safe in the familiarity of our barn.

"Glinda admitted putting the note under your windshield when you went into the cafe," Rod continued. "She wanted to get rid of the alpaca since they would tie her to the murder, but she was greedy enough to try and get something for her efforts. And Teddy left a fingerprint on the shears he left behind so we can tie that to him as well. I think your alpaca are safe. The Godwins won't be around to try again."

The cria moved closer to the fence and butted her small head into my hip, her mother standing proudly next to her. I stroked the baby with affection. Belle, as we named her, was such a joy I almost felt sorry for Teddy and Glinda. They would never know the love of an alpaca.

Jacqueline Seewald has written nineteen books plus stories, poems, essays, reviews and articles for The Writer, L.A. Times, Reader's Digest, Sherlock Holmes, Over My Dead Body!, Gumshoe Review, Publishers Weekly and The Christian Science Monitor. Her blog is: http://jacquelineseewald.blogspot.com

Elderly neighbors who lived with a houseful of cats, walked them on leashes, and were willing to help others, a daughter-in-law's cat, and a real case added up to a unique crime story. Cats rule!

Touch Not the Cat

by Jacqueline Seewald

As Julia Matthews walked into her neighbor's rambling Victorian house, it was all she could do to keep from tripping over a tiger-striped tabby. Two other curious felines scrutinized her before they scattered and hid.

"Sister and I have talked it over and decided that you are the logical person to ask for advice." Miss Vanessa Valentine, resplendent in a royal purple caftan, glided toward her, hands outstretched.

"Yes, it's quite fortunate you decided to become a lawyer and move back to the neighborhood." Miss Vivian, Vanessa's younger sister by several years, was dressed in a vivid Pepto-Bismol pink pantsuit. She spoke in a more reticent but equally amiable manner.

Julia was fond of both sisters, although she knew Vanessa better. Vanessa's students referred to her as the Lavender Lady. She'd been Julia's favorite teacher and neighbor when Julia lived with her grandmother in a quaint, Victorian house just up the street.

Julia's parents divorced when she was six-years-old, each of them going their own way and leaving Julia to be raised by her grandmother. She'd been devastated and lonely, but Grandmother and teachers like Miss Valentine had made up for her lost family. Vanessa, as school librarian, had encouraged her to read. She'd loved books ever since. No one could read a book aloud with more vitality and expression than Miss Valentine; she made the characters come alive. For Julia, books had become more real and better friends than most people she knew.

The Misses Valentine were now well into their sixties and considered eccentric by some, but Julia regarded them with affection.

"We really miss your grandmother," Miss Vanessa said. "And we know how very proud she was of you."

Grandmother had referred to the sisters as "unclaimed treasures". Somehow that fit.

"We're so glad you decided not to sell the house," Miss Vivian said.

"I can work here in town just as well as New York or Philadelphia. I'll just be practicing a different kind of law."

The two sisters exchanged significant glances. Julia observed that although they were not twins, they looked very much alike. Both were short in stature, plump with ruddy complexions. They also shared a love of cats. In fact, their house was full of cats of every size, color and kind. The soft-hearted sisters saved as many cats as they possibly could.

"Perhaps you'll sit down and have some tea with us? Then we can tell you about the help we're seeking."

Vanessa led Julia through a cluttered living room that had dark mahogany furniture of another era. They settled in a cozy kitchen that caught the afternoon sunlight through cheerful aquamarine curtains blowing at the windows. Vivian served tea and scones from a well-polished silver service. A cat jumped onto Julia's lap.

"That's Desi. She's our Russian cat," Miss Vivian said.

Julia petted the white cat that purred at her appreciatively. "Desi? Isn't that a Spanish name like Desi Arnez?"

"Well, a Russian immigrant, who worked as our handyman for a time, found her and named her. When he moved away, he asked if we could take care of her. She seems to like you very much," Vivian confided. "Cats always know when people are kind. Desi hisses at anyone who's nasty. She has attitude. Then again, most cats do."

"So nice of you to take time out on your Saturday afternoon to talk to us. We have an odd story to tell you. Something of a perplexing mystery. Not the sort of thing most people would care to solve but we believe you could help. You see, we know this man who's gotten into trouble. We met him one day when we were buying cat food. He's very nice, though just a bit odd. The police think he murdered a woman, but we know that couldn't possibly be so. However, he's been arrested. He needs a lawyer, and of course we thought of you." Trust Miss Vanessa to get to the point.

Julia set down her delicate teacup. "Miss Valentine, I don't do criminal cases."

"But you could. You just finished law school. They've taught you all about it, haven't they?"

"I suppose, but a murder case is quite a serious matter. Your friend should have an experienced attorney representing him."

"Julia, dear, you were always so bright and curious, just like our cats. Sister and I talked it over and we don't think anyone else would do as good a job of it as you. Besides, poor Charles, well, he really doesn't have funds for an expensive criminal lawyer."

"What about a public defender?"

The sisters exchanged looks again. "The fact is, he has one and the fellow doesn't believe Charles."

"Charles has a very good heart. Desi likes him and he was very pleased when she rubbed up against his leg. He's a cat lover just as we are. But people, the police in particular, believe that makes him peculiar in a bad way. Will you talk with them and with him?"

"I won't promise anything," Julia said, "but I'll try to find out what the situation is as a favor to you."

Detective William Ferguson eyed Julia with dark, narrowed eyes. There was a cynical quality to his chiseled features that made Julia distinctly uneasy. "So, you've been asked to represent Charles Latham."

"I'm looking into the matter."

"Well, Ms. Matthews, Latham's misguided cat-loving friends haven't seen the evidence we've collected."

"Nor have I."

"Latham lives across from the park where Linda Raymond and her husband jogged regularly. The morning she was killed, they ran in different directions. When Joseph Raymond returned to the parking lot, he found his wife dead, stabbed multiple times. There were footprints in her blood and the trail led directly to Latham's house. We discovered that Latham has been in and out of mental institutions, lives the life of a recluse with a whole herd of cats, your basic weirdo. I understand he has half a dozen cats he takes for daily leashed walks in the park. We think the victim said or did something to enrage him. We questioned the husband and according to him, his wife disliked cats. In fact, she had no liking for pets in general. Neighbors say she had a sharp tongue. Apparently, she and Latham had words on a prior occasion at the park when one of his cats scratched her leg. She retaliated by picking up a stick and hitting the cat with it. It wasn't hurt but Latham was furious, warned her never to touch any of his 'clowder' again or she'd be sorry. What the hell is a 'clowder'? The husband clearly remembers the incident and the threat. It all fits."

"A clowder is what you call a group of cats, it's the collective name," Julia said as she looked at her notes. She recognized how damaging Ferguson's testimony would be when heard in court, but she wasn't about to give up and walk out. "Were there any witnesses?"

"None."

"What about the murder weapon? Did you find it at Latham's house?"

"No, but that's not a surprise. We didn't find it at the park either and we combed the area. He was obviously smart enough to ditch it."

"Who found the body?"

"Other joggers."

Julia persisted. "How do you know the husband didn't kill her?"

"There were witnesses. Couple of people driving into the parking lot spotted Mrs. Raymond just about the time as the joggers. Sorry, this one's cut and dried."

Julia was pensive. "It seems everything you have is circumstantial and inconclusive."

The detective's eyes narrowed into bullets. "If I were a fresh-faced kid like yourself, I'd stay clear of slime like Latham. I wasn't going to mention this, but just so you realize what a wacko Latham is, he has cats living all over his house and has converted his whole garage into living quarters for more. He calls it a 'catio.'"

Julia felt sick to her stomach, but hell would freeze over before she'd give the policeman the satisfaction of observing her reaction. She thanked the detective for his time and asked to see Latham.

As Detective Ferguson told her, Charles Latham did seem odd. He appeared distracted and his eyes never met hers as she explained who she was.

"How are my cats?" he asked. "Do you know what was done with them?"

"I'm afraid they've been taken to a no-kill shelter."

Latham broke down and cried. "They were all I had," he said. "They're my family."

Julia's gut reaction was that he seemed too pathetic to have killed anyone. But would a jury see it that way?

"Mr. Latham, why were you hospitalized?"

"I got very depressed. So depressed, I couldn't work anymore."

"Have you ever hurt anyone?"

"No, never. I fix hurt things."

"Did you try to take care of Mrs. Latham?"

He nodded. "I saw her on the ground and there was lots of blood. I went out to see if I could help her, but she wasn't breathing."

"Why didn't you call the police?"

He hung his head. "I was going to, but two men came and started shouting. I got scared and ran back to my house."

"Did you see anyone stab the woman?"

125

Latham shook his head. "It was real early in the morning. I pulled up the blind. I was getting ready for my morning walk. That's when I saw her. I didn't hurt her. But the police, they think I'm lying."

"Mr. Raymond said that you and the lady had an argument before. Do you remember that?"

Latham's expression was vague. "I guess she was the lady who tried to hit Aristotle. I told her not to touch him. She was very mean. But I didn't hurt her. Honor bright." Speaking in a child-like manner, Latham sounded entirely innocent and guileless.

"Mr. Latham, why did you keep so many cats in your garage as well as your house?"

"I put them there because I love them. They're feral and afraid of people, kind of like me. They don't hurt anybody. I never hurt anybody either."

Julia spent a sleepless night and around dawn decided to take the case. She would do some investigating on her own. She was convinced that the Misses Valentine were right about Latham, with their assessment of peculiar but not vicious.

The Raymond's neighborhood was not far from her own, but the houses were smaller and newer, the streets not as stately, lacking the huge, old trees planted in straight lines in front of each house. There was more of a development feel to the area. The homes loomed before her in modern non-distinction with bland, manicured lawns.

She wanted to talk with Mr. Raymond but he was getting into his car in the driveway when she pulled up. He was a trim man of average height in his middle thirties, very well dressed.

"Mr. Raymond, might I have a word with you?"

"I have to get to work. Who are you?" The way he was looking at her made Julia think Raymond might be something of a womanizer.

"I represent Charles Latham."

Raymond frowned. "That man killed my wife in cold blood. I don't have anything to say to you."

"Wait a moment. Did you actually see him do it?"

"No, I was jogging when she was attacked."

"Then you don't know it as a fact. Why weren't you running together with your wife?"

"I put on a faster pace and cover more miles. We each liked to do our own thing. Look, I have to get going." With that, he pulled out of the driveway in a BMW and took off down the street.

Just as well, she very much doubted he would have told her anything of significance. She looked around. Someone was at home next door. Julia rang the doorbell, a little nervous since she'd never done anything like this before but it was necessary. A young woman wearing jeans and a dirty shirt, holding a baby in her arms, came to the door after the second ring. She looked frazzled and eyed Julia, and her neat business suit, with suspicion. Julia introduced herself and explained the reason for her visit, wangling an invitation from Ellen Randall to come inside.

"There's toys scattered all over," the young woman said with some embarrassment.

"No problem," Julia said as she removed a large doll from a recliner and seated herself. "I just want to find out whatever you can tell me about the Raymonds."

"We didn't know them that well. They both worked. Didn't have any kids."

Julia smiled, hoping Ellen Randall would manage to relax. "How long have they lived here?"

"Oh, about two years." The baby started to complain about being held and Ellen let her down. The child grabbed for the doll.

"Did Mrs. Raymond like children?"

Ellen bit her lip and thought. "I don't think so."

"What about animals?"

"They didn't have any pets."

"Do you have any?"

"We have a dog."

"Did she ever express an opinion of dogs?"

"Well, she didn't like ours. She claimed he barked too loud and too often." Ellen smiled.

"What about cats? Did she ever say anything about them?"

"Oh, she didn't like them either, claimed they smelled. One came into the yard once and she threw rocks at it."

Julia knew that wouldn't go over very well in court. The prosecutor was bound to ask the very same question. It would go toward establishing motive. "What about people? How did she get along with the neighbors?"

"The Raymonds kept to themselves. They weren't particularly friendly."

Julia was discouraged but she wasn't going to give up. She was no quitter. "Ellen, did Mrs. Raymond and her husband seem happy?"

The young woman tensed. "I don't think that's for me to say."

Was Ellen Randall hiding something? "It really could be important," she pressed.

"Well, I could hear them argue sometimes. Not that I was eavesdropping, but in the spring and fall when windows are open, you hear things."

"What kind of things?"

"I don't know exactly."

"Well, did they argue about Mr. Raymond seeing other women for instance?"

"Oh no, nothing like that, just about money."

"What about money?"

Ellen shrugged, obviously thinking she'd said too much. Julia wasn't about to let the matter drop.

"Was he stingy with money?"

"No, she was. He wasn't. I don't know what they were arguing about except that she said some stuff and he got angry."

"How angry?"

Ellen worried her lower lip. "I believe he hit her. And someone called the police. Not me. Maybe she called them herself."

When Julia left Ellen Randall, her mind was clicking. There was definitely something here that needed further investigation.

She visited Detective Ferguson for a second time one week later. He was not particularly pleased to see her. He folded his arms over his broad chest and stared as if she were a criminal herself, but she wasn't about to let herself be intimidated.

"Mr. Latham did not kill Mrs. Raymond."

"You can't be serious! The guy's a lunatic, certifiable."

"His doctors say he was never a danger to anyone. The way he cares for stray cats proves he's got a good heart. I'm sorry, Detective, I believe you've got the wrong man. Have you ever looked for another suspect or did you simply settle on him for the sake of expediency?"

Detective Ferguson's posture stiffened. He wore a short-sleeved white shirt with a gun holstered over it and carried himself with the erect bearing and demeanor of a soldier. "We arrested Latham because of the evidence. It wasn't anything personal."

"You weren't prejudiced against him?"

"He fits the profile of a sociopath, but that wasn't why we arrested him."

"I won't debate the issue with you. But I would like to know if Mr. Raymond was in financial trouble. Could he have taken out a life insurance policy on his wife recently? I need your help. I talked to the neighbors and found out that the Raymonds were having serious arguments about money on a regular basis. I discovered Mrs. Raymond called 9-1-1 several times. Can you find out the details? There must be reports on file."

"I'll check it out," the detective said, more polite than he'd been before.

It was two weeks later that the Misses Valentine invited Julia for tea again.

"We can't thank you enough for what you've done for poor Charles," Vanessa said. "I understand the husband confessed to stabbing his wife before they were to start jogging."

"Detective Ferguson got the confession, not me."

"We're glad you were able to put him on the right track," Vivian said.

"Detective Ferguson did follow up on police reports and discovered Mr. Raymond had assaulted his wife and was arrested for domestic violence. Although Mrs. Raymond dropped the charges, she was in the hospital with a broken arm and assorted bruises and contusions. Her sister said she was talking about divorce. That was when Detective Ferguson got into Mr. Raymond's financial situation. He was heavily in debt. He was also the beneficiary of his wife's insurance policy. Honestly, I don't think Mr. Raymond would have confessed if his lawyer hadn't worked out a deal. Raymond was able to cop a plea."

"But how did Mr. Raymond manage to kill his wife without anyone knowing it in the first place?" Vanessa asked, raising her silver brows.

"Apparently, he picked a very early hour when no one was around," Julia said, "then simply caught her by surprise, stabbing her before she knew what was happening. He'd been looking for just the right opportunity for several mornings. The medical examiner verified the first blows were struck from behind. Then he ran for a time, threw the knife in the lake, and came back giving someone else time to find her. I think he planned to blame Charles all along. He knew Charles lived opposite the parking lot, had seen him go into the house. Anyway, he waited until there were witnesses before he decided to make an appearance."

"Charles managed to reunite with most of his clowder and we let him take several of our newest strays. He asked to take Desi; she was quite cordial toward him, but we saved her for you," Miss Vivian added. "We hope you'll accept her as your fee."

Julia heard a cheerful meow as a furry white creature leaped into her lap and thumped an elegant tail against her arm. She supposed there were far worse things than being a cat lover. She just hoped Desi wasn't the starter kit for a clowder of her own.

Kathryn Gerwig writes fiction and non-fiction about pets, nature, and vintage style. Her tale, Buried in Bressingham, appears in Landfall: The Best New England Crime Stories 2018. She publishes and posts through www.thepennymasonpost.wordpress.com. website: www.pennymasonpublications.com

Martens became the stars of her tale after she learned of them through field guides and met one at a wildlife farm in Maine. She aspires to move to New England although without the difficulties and danger her character faces.

The Martens and the Murder Attempt
by Kathryn Gerwig

Moving here was his dream, not mine, Ellie mused, as she stomped the mud of Northern Maine off her boots before stepping over the threshold of the small log cabin, home since the previous weekend. A hint of spring was in the air. The snow was melting, making the ground mushy in spots, especially so outside the back door.

Ellie had been willing to relocate, but had hoped they'd be living within an hour's drive of a city featuring modern events and amenities, not in a remote forest location more than one hundred miles from what she considered civilization.

Bob Kysor, Ellie's husband, loved the outdoors more than anything. As a kid in northeastern Ohio, he'd shared a love for nature with his father. As he grew older, his focus became conservation. The stocky but fit young man had asked Ellie to marry him when he was in third grade, she in second. In junior high he suggested they take a rain-check until he had earned a degree from Ohio State University and begun a career with The Ohio Department of Natural Resources.

A year before, after a fourteen-year engagement, the young couple had married, when Ellie turned twenty, Bob twenty-one. They made a sufficient living, in Shaker Falls, an eastern suburb of Cleveland, where they had occupied an upper floor apartment in a house next to a Wendy's.

Ellie had just finished her bachelor's degree in English at Cleveland State. Now that she was ready to start earning more money, she looked forward to moving to a nicer place. Perhaps in a few years they would have children, live the American Dream in the suburb of Cleveland where they'd both been raised.

Ellie felt the honeymoon was over the morning Bob received the call from the Maine Department of Wildlife, Fisheries, and Conservation and was offered a job with the Maine Cooperative Fish and Wildlife Research Unit.

The position was precisely what he'd been planning for. His first assignment would be to assess the status of some of the Northeast's threatened species. Ellie knew if she refused to move it would likely mean the end of their marriage.

She didn't want that. It was a harsh reality, in today's world, she reflected, that often a person was forced to choose between a career and a relationship, when one partner or the other made a professional move necessitating a relocation. She couldn't live without Bob, so she would do her best to live with him, in the middle of the woods.

It wouldn't be easy. Bob was stationed in a location so remote, there would likely be no opportunity for her to find a job at all, much less where she might apply her education. Not to mention the fact that they would face an extended car trip across primitive roads, and an overnight stay if they wished to see a play or shop at a place more civilized than a store that sold fishing bait and the basics, bread and brew.

This morning she found herself alone in their rented, and don't forget, with an option to purchase, log home. She was still searching for the perfect spots to hang pictures, position objects they wished to display, and stow clothing she wouldn't need for life in the woods.

Suddenly, she heard the sound of tiny paws pattering across the roof. Multiple species of wild creatures that didn't live in the Midwest could be found here in Maine. She'd already seen a moose and a porcupine. She pulled a hat over her shoulder length light brown hair, jumped into her L.L. Bean boots, pulled on her parka and rushed outside to see what it could be.

A small, long-bodied creature with catlike ears and a cute pointed muzzle peered at Ellie from the roof's corner. It was a beautiful brown with shadings of light honey on its underside, and little black lines that highlighted its facial features. It made a cheerful chattering sound as it leaped from the roofline to a branch of the maple tree that would shade the cabin during the upcoming summer.

"Sounds like a marten," said Bob, when Ellie described the encounter soon after he arrived home that evening. "They make little chatters and chuckles like you described, and they can live in the trees, though they prefer to remain on the ground most of the time.

"They're normally nocturnal unless it's a cloudy day like today. If you see it again, maybe you could follow it for me. It's one of the species I'm supposed to study. Find out as much as you can about its activities, where it's staying. I'd track it now, but after that squall that moved through an hour ago, I'm sure its prints are obscured.

"Martens are making a comeback, but they've lost a lot of habitat to logging. Poaching is always a danger when there's a richness of them concentrated in an area."

"A richness. That's a cool term for a group of them. I can try to see where this one goes, but it moves pretty fast. And I might get lost," Ellie said.

"Don't follow it too far. Just see what direction it heads, if you can. Maybe you should put the GPS in your pocket, just in case a squall moves in. You could get disoriented even close to the cabin, if there's a whiteout."

"You know I hate that thing. I'm not even sure how it works. I'd rather just tie a rope to the door before I head out, like farmers used to do in the olden days when they went to the barn to do chores."

"Oh, Ellie. Forget following the animal. I don't want you to take any chances."

The creature returned the next morning, just before noon. Ellie donned her gear, and, traditionalist that she was, put an old-fashioned compass she'd inherited from her grandfather in her pocket. She wasn't totally sure how to use it either, but preferred it, in principle, to the GPS. She wasn't a wilderness girl; she was old school.

The little elflike entity led her deeper into the forest than she liked, but she felt destined to follow. Suddenly, another of its kind appeared, and they romped off together into the snowsquall coming from the west. Ellie could just make out the shape of a small shack, wood neatly stacked outside. Someone must live there, or frequently visit. Unsure whether it was wise to proceed, she hesitated.

A figure appeared at the door as one of the martens disappeared into a burrow nearby, within the roots of a tall fir tree. Clad in a heavy wool shirt in a black and red lumberjack plaid, the grizzled old man waved her in. "Come take shelter, miss. Have a cup of tea with me."

Ellie was reminded of one of the old children's tales, the one about Hansel and Gretel. No one in their right mind would enter a shack in a remote forest, when beckoned in by a grizzled character like this one. Then again, no sane woman who'd just graduated from college with a degree in English would move to this godforsaken wilderness in the first place.

She sensed social norms were much different here, where the population was sparse. One needed to make friends when the opportunity arose. She offered a return wave and jogged toward the open doorway.

"You must be the wife of that new young forest ranger," said the man, as he offered Ellie a cup of Earl Grey. Surprised at his knowledge and choice of tea, Ellie was momentarily speechless.

"Yes, how did you hear of us?" She stuttered as she took the warm fragrant mug from the man, Sam. Samuel T. Rumford, he said.

"Word gets around. Another of the rangers stops in now and then. He told me. I saw smoke rising from your chimney the other morning. I'm glad you're here. I could use a new neighbor. That cabin's been empty the last year."

"I'm pleased to meet you too," Ellie told him, staring at the solid white wall outside the window. The snow squall had moved in, obscuring the trail she'd followed to get there. The room held the warm, faint glow from a woodstove with a see-through panel in the door. Pictures of ships lined the walls of the small living/ kitchen area. A tiny, crude bedroom and bath could be seen through a curtained doorway at the opposite end from the cook stove. A computer occupied a table between the front door and a picture window. Curious.

"You have electricity?" Ellie marveled, not seeing any wires outside.

"Sure do. Road's just down over the hill that way. Cable's buried. Cost a pretty penny but I don't often lose power."

"I'd love to have you stay awhile, but when you've finished your tea and the sky clears, you better head for home before the next squall comes. Nothing more dangerous than a whiteout when you're in strange territory. Bad enough ten feet from your own doorway. What brings you out on such a day?"

"I was following a little animal, a marten, I think. My husband wanted me to see where it lives. It went into a burrow just outside. There was another one too. I'm not sure where it is now."

"Yes, they're martens. I've always been able to tame them. Well, not tame them, really, but I've always got a richness of them living quite close to me. If this one came to your home, that's a good luck sign. They don't like just everyone. I sure hope the poachers don't hear about them."

"Poachers?"

"There's a group of guys that've been stopping on the road down below my cabin at night trying to bag bucks out of season, when no one's looking.

"If these guys thought there were martens around here, they'd set traps. I wish the warden would do something about the poaching but he doesn't have the manpower. You two just be careful. They only seem to hunt at night, so don't go far from your cabin if you head out to see the stars. I'll take care of those boys one of these times so we can all feel safe again," he said, jerking his head toward a rifle that hung on the wall.

Ellie must have looked a bit unnerved, as Sam said, "Oh, I won't take them out or anything like that. Just put a scare into them," he smiled.

Before she closed the door behind her, Ellie had to inquire about the computer.

"Oh, I write articles for newspapers, conservation agency newsletters, wildlife magazines. I wasn't a writing professional, I worked in logging when I was younger. But I've lived among the wild creatures all my life. I'm a good observer, and I know how to use a camera."

"How interesting. May I bring Bob over to meet you? I'm sure he'd love to hear about some of your stories. I'm definitely interested. I always intended to pursue a career in journalism or English education. Guess that idea's shot now that we're living up here."

"I wouldn't say that. Everybody does things on the Internet now. I don't have the best connection here, but I get by. Send me some writing samples. If I think you're a good fit for some of the publications I deal with, I'll recommend you. Come see me anytime. Bring your husband. I'm most always here, except on Monday mornings when I go for groceries."

"Thanks, Sam. See you soon."

Ellie took Bob to meet Sam the next evening. Bob was amazed how close the wild creatures came to Sam's shack in the woods, especially the marten that lived next to the building. Sam mentioned the poachers and Bob promised to tell his superiors, see if he could trigger the proper authorities to arrange an investigation.

"I appreciate that, Bob, but up here, we're pretty much on our own in dealing with things. We've got 911, but it takes a while for law enforcement to get here."

"I still can't believe you have a marten living right outside your door," Bob said, as they prepared to leave. "Oh, look, there's another one."

Sure enough, another of the little creatures, this one darker in color, was shyly approaching from the edge of the small clearing.

"I'm surprised there seem to be others hanging around just now, too," said Sam. "I had a richness of the little guys when they were courting Mimsy here," he gestured toward the little female who lived beside his home. "But it's not common to see a group, other than when the males are competing or after the female gives birth. Other times, they mostly like to live alone."

"An old guy I worked with in Ohio said there used to be a richness of them in the northeastern corner of the state, by the Pennsylvania border. But he was the only person I met at ODNR who had ever seen one," said Bob.

"They certainly do make our lives richer," Ellie remarked, smiling at the charming movements of the cute little creatures.

"That they do," commented Sam, "though I'm guessing that unfortunately the name likely came from the profits people made from them."

Bob and Ellie both enjoyed visiting their new neighbor and observing the martens. Ellie went over nearly every day. Sam was helping her get contacts in the magazine business, so she could freelance, earn a bit of cash.

A week passed, and the marten that had led her to Sam's cabin didn't come to the Kysor's place again. It was almost as if it had purposely seen to it that she met Sam, Ellie thought. Now its job was done. She shook off the thought. I'm going batty, she told herself, up here in the woods, alone most of the time.

The next Tuesday, the snow squalls returned. The coming of spring took its time in the North Country. About two in the afternoon, Ellie heard a frantic series of chatters and eeks above the cabin's front porch.

The little female marten was back, but what was wrong? She jumped from the roof onto the porch railing and flew back and forth, occasionally coming to the door and hesitating before resuming wild movements and vocalizations.

Ellie wondered about the wisdom of putting on boots and jacket and going outside, but curiosity trumped caution. As soon as she stepped out the door, the creature ran toward the trail to Sam's, then back to her again, like a little Lassie, beckoning her to follow.

She hoped the snowstorm wouldn't resume its hurricane-force fury as she ran through the woods following the marten's lead. She did have her phone and compass, but they were pretty useless in a whiteout. She probably should learn to use the GPS, she admitted.

But the little creature knew its way through the white and drifted and blowing snow. Soon they were in Sam's clearing, the marten running right up to the house, and through the front door, which stood open.

Uh, oh, thought Ellie as she realized the seriousness of the situation inside the cabin. Sam sat on his sofa, a rifle equipped with a silencer pointed at his head. A man with a knitted Harley hat pulled down to his eyes, stringy hair extending over his shoulders, face twisted into a grimace, had apparently been about to shoot the old man when she had walked in, complicating the situation.

"Who's this," he demanded of Sam.

"Ellie, run!" exclaimed Sam, as he kicked the shin of the man with the gun.

The man flinched, but didn't fall, aiming the rifle toward Ellie, instead.

"Now I got two bodies to deal with," lamented the Harley guy.

"Who are you?" Ellie managed to croak.

"Who am I? I'm just somebody who was minding my own business when your friend here, had to stick his nose in where it didn't belong."

One of the poacher guys, Ellie surmised. Must have figured Sam was onto them. Maybe Sam fired shots at them and the threat intended to discourage, had the opposite effect, enraging this man to the point of attacking Sam.

Were his accomplices nearby, or was he alone? Could she somehow distract him so she or Sam could grab the gun like the heroes do on television?

"I know you got a stash of cash somewhere around here, old man. Never trusted banks. Got your retirement fund in the mattress or some such place. You hand it over, and I might let you live, or the girl at least. How about it? You got one minute, before I let you have it."

Sam pointed to a small metal box on the floor under his computer table, covered by a ragged blanket. "There. Under the blanket. It's all I got. In that fireproof box."

The Harley man gave them a warning look, then reached sideways under the table, with his left hand, keeping the gun pointed as directly at Ellie as possible.

In the next moment he emitted a bloodcurdling scream, as a small dervish with teeth flashed with swift fury toward his arm, fangs landing in the skin of his left wrist. The furry little marten clung on, as the man waved his arm in an attempt to shake her off.

He dropped the gun and began to flail at the creature, which was definitely getting the best of him. Ellie ran to grab the weapon but the man managed to take hold of her arm, crushing her wrist in a viselike grip. Just then, three male martens ran in through the open door. One jumped to the man's right wrist, the others attacked his ankles, effectively disabling him. Sam reached his own gun, grabbing it from the wall and aiming with intent to pull the trigger.

Ellie, never a fan of violence, implored him to wait. She kicked the Harley man's gun away and ran to grab it, now that she was free thanks to the surprise attack. The animals were so swift the Harley man had no chance of escape. Ellie dialed 911, thankful for a spot of strong service, even in the deep woods.

Sam and Ellie each held a gun on the man until the Piscataquis County Sheriff's department came. As the cruisers pulled in, the female marten returned to its den behind the box that, Sam later told Ellie, actually held no cash. It was a spot where the marten liked to sleep, curled within the part of the blanket that was draped onto the floor. The trio of ninja martens exited the open door just as the lawmen entered, nearly tripping them.

Everything about the story was perplexing to Bob, when Ellie and Sam shared it with him later that evening. He was already amazed that the typically shy creatures seemed content to live so close to humans. That they would actually enter a residence, and appear to protect the humans against an intruder, as pets often do, seemed improbable, yet that's what apparently occurred. He was unspeakably thankful that it had.

The Harley man, Kenny Darlington, had the scars to prove it. Misfortune being a fan of company, Kenny was compelled to turn his buddies in. They soon joined him in jail. The team had been bullying residents in remote locations across the northern wilderness, but had until that day, eluded arrest.

Sam had taken shots at Kenny's vehicle the last two nights the group had pulled off the road below his house. They hadn't succeeded in bagging any prey in the area as of yet, but had spotted more creatures there than anyplace else they'd hunted. Something special about the site attracted the animals, yet protected them from capture.

Kenny had heard Sam kept his life savings in the cabin. He'd intended to discover the loot, and then get rid of Sam. If only that girl and those crazy creatures hadn't shown up.

Two months later, Bob and Ellie stepped into an enchanting scene when they entered Sam's clearing. Mimsy rested in the roots of the maple, at the entrance to her den, surrounded by six little ones. The tiny creatures writhed in the dappled sunshine beneath the tree's delicate, emerging leaves.

Ellie could never have never imagined, when they'd moved to Maine, that she would be saved from murder by a marten and receive career assistance from an old man living in the wild forest.

Opportunity knocks in the most unexpected settings sometimes. The move to the wilderness was turning out to be a stepping-stone on the path to a new career. Spring beckoned like a second honeymoon, filled with promise.

"Now this is what I call a richness," she remarked to Sam and her husband, as they basked in the warmth of the sun and watched the little family cavort in the clearing.

Three-time winner of the Derringer Award for Best Short Story, Earl Staggs also writes novels, including Justified Action. When a book starts with a man taking the afternoon off, flying to Texas, blowing up a couple of cars (that's before things get busy), it's a guaranteed good read.

As a group name, a gaggle of geese caught his interest. He added conflict (and very loud sounds) by introducing a tribe of goats to the geese.

A Gaggle of Geese and a Tribe of Goats
by Earl Staggs

On Saturday morning, I opened my eyes and focused on the clock radio on the nightstand beside the bed. Ten minutes after eight. I vaguely remembered my husband Lilburn leaving sometime ago for his weekly golf outing with his pals. That meant I could sleep as late as I wanted to. After twenty years on the Fort Worth police force and the last five years as sheriff of Watango county, I'd gotten accustomed to getting up at six o'clock five days a week, putting on my uniform, and being on the job by seven. But Saturday and Sunday mornings, I could be as lazy and spoiled as I wanted to be. I closed my eyes, wiggled into the most comfortable position I could find, and began drifting into blessed sleep.

But then, the phone rang.

I swung my feet to the floor and reached over to my cell phone on the nightstand. I recognized the number on Caller ID. The sheriff's department. I answered with a drowsy "Hello" in the middle of a yawn.

"Sorry to bother you, Mollie, but I figured you'd want to know right away," my dispatcher, Grace, said. "Millard Hamilton was found shot dead in his home this morning. Bubba's there now and Doc Spradley's on his way."

Thirty minutes later, I was in my uniform, in my SUV, and on my way to Hamilton's house. When I accepted the job of sheriff, I was told there had not been a killing in Watango County in the last twenty years. That was one of the things I liked about the job. I'd worked enough homicides in Fort Worth to last me a lifetime. Watango is one of the smallest counties in Texas. Life here is rural, quiet, and peaceful. Murder doesn't happen here.

But it had.

Millard Hamilton was one of many African Americans in the county who, like his father and grandfather, was a rose farmer. He was well-known and well-liked by everyone.

By everyone except Evangeline Harper.

There was a long-standing feud between the two seventy-something-year-olds, but no one knew for sure why they hated each other. Most figured it was because Evangeline was also a rose grower, and the two of them had a hot competition every year for the ten thousand dollar prize for Best New Variety of Rose.

Shortly after I moved here, I learned growing roses is a hell of a lot of hard work, and those who do it in East Texas take great pride in what they do. Tyler, a town just southeast of here, calls itself the Rose Capital of the World. Something about the weather and soil around here makes it a natural for growing roses. Apparently, it's also for great for harboring old feuds.

People in town still talked about the stand-off between Evangeline and Millard a few months ago. I wasn't there, but I heard about it. It seems they both pulled up in front of the hardware store at the same time, and there was only one parking spot left. They both aimed for it and had to stop just short of a collision. Then the story goes they just sat there, staring daggers, each waiting for the other to back off. Some said they sat there like that for an hour. It was probably less, but stories grow. Still, it must have been quite a sight. An old white lady and an old black man sitting there in a staring contest, each trying to intimidate the other. Evangeline finally gave up and, shaking her fist and shouting a few choice remarks about Millard in particular, took off.

And came straight to my office.

Evangeline is a large woman, maybe an inch under six feet tall and built solid and strong as an oak tree. She stomped into my office shouting, "Mollie, if you don't do something about that man, I'm going to shoot him."

"Now, Evangeline," I said in my calmest voice, "you know darn well you can't shoot someone."

"You wouldn't say that if you knew what he's done."

"What has he done now, Evangeline?"

"Goats. That's what he's done now."

"Goats?"

"Yes, goats. He's gone into the goat business. He bought a couple hundred of the damn things, and he intends to sell goat's milk and cheese."

"A lot of people raise goats, Evangeline. There's a large market for their milk and cheese."

"I know that, but a lot of people don't put their goat pens right on the property line between his place and mine. They're ugly noisemakers, that's what they are. Have you ever heard a screaming goat?"

"No, I can't say I recall ever hearing one."

"Trust me, Mollie, if you heard it, you'd recall it. They let out a godawful sound like a human screaming. It's like living next door to a bunch of people being tortured. They do it day and night, non-stop. He put that pen smack between his place and mine, right next to where I keep my flock of geese. It's driving them crazy. And it's costing me money. Geese don't lay eggs when they're upset, and that a big part of my business. Mollie, you've got to do something about that herd of goats before I go crazy and shoot him."

"It's a tribe."

"What is?"

"A group of goats is called a tribe, not a herd. Just like your geese are called a gaggle of geese, not a flock."

Evangeline crossed her arms over her chest and stuck out her chin. "How in the hell do you know that?"

"I do a lot of crossword puzzles."

"Good for you. Well, I don't care what they're called. If you don't do something about this, you're going to have a dead farmer on your hands."

"Now you listen to me, Evangeline. I'll talk to Millard about the noise problem, but don't you go getting yourself in a lot of trouble by doing something crazy."

I visited Millard that afternoon and heard the screaming goats for myself. Evangeline was right. It sounded like a crowd of people being tortured. Millard explained that his goats were making a lot of noise because they were in a new environment. Once they were used to their new home, it would stop. He must have been right because I never heard another word about it.

Still, I couldn't get it out of my mind. Evangeline threatened to kill Millard and now he was dead. Damn!

When I entered Millard's house, my chief deputy, Bubba Williams, motioned me into the kitchen. Two other deputies were going through the house looking for anything that might tell us what happened there. Millard lay face down on the floor, in his pajamas, with a bullet hole in the back of his head. One of Millard's employees found him when he came to work at seven o'clock.

I glanced out the back window of Millard's kitchen and saw Evangeline Harper walking slowly toward the barn with her arms wrapped around herself and her head bowed.

I talked with Bubba and Doc Spradley for another minute or two about what needed to be done, then went out the back door. Evangeline gave me a wave of her hand for me to keep coming, and walked into the barn. When I stepped inside, she stood in the center of the barn with fire in her eyes.

"Well, do you see it?" she said.

I looked around. Bags of goat feed, a few bales of hay, farm tools hanging here and there. "Uh, see what?"

"Millard's tractor."

"No, I don't see a tractor." Four tractors had been stolen in the county over the last three months and I was no closer to arresting the thieves than I was after the first one. Farm tractors sold for good money on the black market and, unlike cars, were almost impossible to trace.

"Well, at least you ain't blind," she said. "That's something. They stole all them other tractors and now they took Millard's and killed him over it. What are you going to do about it?"

"Wait a minute," I said. "We can't say for sure if it was the same people. This doesn't fit the pattern. All the other robberies took place when nobody was home and no one was ever hurt."

"Millard wasn't supposed to be home either," she said. "This is Saturday."

"Okay," I said, "what does Saturday have to do with it?"

"On Saturdays, Millard leaves home at 4 a.m. to deliver roses to his customers in Dallas and Fort Worth. Everybody knows that." She gave me the look teachers give little girls who lose their homework.

"Not everybody. I didn't know it. But if that's true, why was he home today?"

"He was sick. Been down with the flu for three days and hired Caleb Simpson to do his deliveries for him. That's why he was home today and that's why he got killed. He saw someone taking his tractor and they shot him." She took a hands-on-hips stance. "Now, what are you going to do about it?"

We held a staring contest for a few seconds. She was waiting for an answer. I couldn't think of a single one she would like, so I gave her the safest one, the one cops always fall back on. "We're going to do everything possible to find the person who did this."

She gave me more of the hard stare, then rolled her eyes in disgust and brushed past me and out of the barn.

Which is exactly what I would do if a cop said that to me.

"Wait up," I called after her. "I've got some things I'd like to ask you about this."

She didn't even slow down. "I got things to do," was all she said as she walked out of the barn and turned toward her own place.

I had some things to ask her, all right. Like why she was there at Millard's house in the first place. And how she knew so much about Millard's delivery schedule and his being sick when the two of them hated each other so much. The big question, of course, was did she make good on her threat to shoot Millard? And was talking about the missing tractor just to steer me in the wrong direction?

I could see Millard's goats from the barnyard and they were not making any noise.

When I went back to the house, a small crowd had gathered outside by then. News travels fast in a small town. Cars and trucks were parked along the road and a dozen or so people milled around the front yard. A couple more were perched on the steps leading up to the porch. Old Mrs. Crudder sat on the porch swing, fanning herself with one of those folding paper fans from Johnson's Funeral Home. People would soon add another of those fans to their collection. While I stood on the porch, Doc Spradley finished his preliminary exam and followed the stretcher carrying Millard's body to a Johnson's hearse.

My deputies were busy too. Bubba had set up a folding table and chairs on the front porch and was taking statements from everyone he could grab. Some of them were Millard's employees. Others were neighbors and friends.

As I walked toward the house, a man stepped out of the crowd and blocked my path. I'd seen him around a few times but couldn't think of his name.

"Excuse me, Sheriff," he said. He was tall and heavy-set, dressed in jeans and a dark tee shirt and had thick dark hair under a Dallas Cowboys ball cap. "I'm Jason Hardcastle. I live down the road a little ways, and I heard some here say Millard Hamilton's been killed. Any idea who did it?"

"No, we're just getting into our investigation. It's too soon to know anything."

"Damn shame," he said. He reached up to his cap and repositioned it on his head. "He was a good man. Hard to think a man can be shot to death in his pajamas in his own kitchen."

"Yes, it is, Mr. Hardcastle. Now if you'll excuse me, I have to get to work."

"Sure thing, ma'am."

He stepped back and I went to the porch. Mr. Hardcastle was right. It was hard to think about. Not so hard in big cities, but in a small farming community, it struck especially hard.

I helped Bubba take statements from Millard's employees and friends. There wasn't much to take. No one saw or heard anything unusual and no one heard a shot.

Driving to my office, I thought about the unpleasant task ahead of me. Notifying the next of kin. I had never seen or heard of any of Millard's relatives, but that didn't mean there weren't any. Willis Pickett would probably know. He handled legal matters for most everyone in the county.

I had to pass right by his office, so I stopped in. Luckily, he was there. He'd already heard the news about Millard, of course. His wife's best friend lived close to Millard's farm and was there at the farmhouse earlier. She made a few phone calls to spread the word. The people she called made a few calls and… well, that's how new gets shared in small towns.

"I've been expecting you, Sheriff," he said from behind his massive walnut desk. He must have liked walnut. The walls of his office and the chair he offered me with a wave of his hand were walnut. Even his three-piece suit matched the color. He was a large, jowly man in his sixties with thick bushes of gray hair around his ears and even bushier gray eyebrows. "Terrible news about Millard," he said. He was a good man and he'll be missed."

"I'm sure he will, Mr. Pickett. My problem now is I need to know if he had any relatives. I'm guessing you made up his will, and I was hoping you'd know who his next of kin would be. We need to notify someone about his death."

Mr. Pickett smiled and looked at me for a moment. Then he opened a desk drawer and brought out a file. "Fortunately, that's all taken care of, Sheriff. Millard made it very clear in his will what was to become of his remains and his worldly possessions." He opened the file folder on his desk and lifted a few pages. "He had no family. His parents passed on when he was very young and he had no siblings. There may be some cousins and what-have-you somewhere, but none that could be considered close family. Millard made it clear his remains were to be cremated and the ashes spread over his property. He lived every day of his life on that place as had his parents and grandparents before him."

"Then that's taken care of," I said. "But that still leaves his estate. His farm and business should be worth something and I imagine he had some money put away."

Pickett looked up at me over the desk and another smile formed on his face. "I suppose I can tell you, Sheriff, in your official capacity. Hamilton's personal worth, including savings and a few investments he made over the years, will amount to somewhere in the neighborhood of two million dollars."

I'm sure my surprise was written all over me. He continued to smile and seemed to enjoy it.

"That brings us to the big question, doesn't it?" he said. "The matter of who will inherit that estate."

I nodded, still a bit shocked at the amount.

"Millard left everything he had, part and parcel, to Miss Evangeline Harper."

That took all the wind out of my sails and Pickett knew it. He was really enjoying himself now.

"Does that surprise you, Sheriff?"

"Well, of course it does, Mr. Pickett. Everyone knows they didn't get along and that's putting it mildly. Does Evangeline know?"

He closed the file folder and put it back in his desk. "As a matter of fact, I was on the phone with her just before you came in."

After a moment, I asked, "When was that will made up?"

"Originally? Some forty years ago."

"And it's never been changed all these years?"

"No major changes. Millard came in at least once a year to update it. The last time was only two months ago."

"Two months ago? Now I'm really curious. Maybe you can explain to me..."

He held up a hand to stop me. "Sheriff, I can tell you what I've already told you because of the office you hold, but anything beyond that, I must retain as client confidentiality. You understand, I'm sure."

I assured him I understood and thanked him. I left his office reeling from he'd told me. Why would Millard leave everything to Evangeline, of all people?

When I got together with Bubba in our conference room back at the office, it didn't take long for us to agree we had practically nothing to tell us who killed Millard. All we knew was he was shot with a .22 rifle. No one we interviewed heard or saw anything that would help. Our tech was still out there gathering fingerprints, but we didn't have high hopes for that. Millard had twelve employees and they were all inside the house frequently. Besides, gathering the prints and checking for their owners would be a long, slow process.

"I have to admit, Mollie," Bubba said. "This thing really has all of us shook up. This kind of thing happens in movies and on TV, not here in Watango. I still can't believe someone I knew was shot dead in his own home." Bubba turned toward the window and stared out. "In his pajamas, for Pete's sake."

"I know what you mean, Bubba. I thought I left all that behind me when I retired from Fort Worth PD." I went to the counter and poured a cup of coffee. On the way back to the table, something he'd said stuck with me.

"Bubba," I said as I sat down at the table, "you mentioned Millard was in his pajamas. Before I got there this morning, did anyone go in the house?"

"Just Doc Spradley. I made sure no one else did."

"Did you talk to anyone at the scene about the position or condition of Millard's body?"

"Absolutely not. I may not be a big city cop who handles a lot of killings, but I know the drill. Why?"

"A man named Jason Hardcastle approached me in the yard. He said something about Millard being shot in his kitchen in his pajamas. I'm wondering how he knew that."

"Mollie, I saw him there, and I guarantee he did not go in the house, and I didn't say anything to him."

"Bubba, how much do you know about Mr. Hardcastle?"

"Hardly anything. He's only been around here maybe six months or so. I know he lives in that trailer park a couple miles down the road from Millard's place, but that's about it."

"Bubba, I think we need to find out all we can about Mr. Hardcastle."

"I'm on it, Mollie." Bubba sprang to life and almost ran out of the conference room. I knew where he was going. He was a whiz with the computer and knew how to find anything about anybody if they've ever crossed paths with the law.

Bubba was back in thirty minutes. "Guess what, Mollie. Our Mister Hardcastle has quite a history. When he was twenty-five, he did five years in Oklahoma for forging checks. In his thirties, he did ten years in Arkansas for car theft. In between, he served time for breaking and entering. Back in March, the farm he inherited from his parents was seized by the bank for non-payment of his mortgage, and that's when he moved here. And guess what else. He drives a big black GMC truck with plenty of horses to move a big tractor."

"Bubba, I don't think going from car theft to tractor theft is a big leap, do you?"

"No, I don't. I think we should get a search warrant for his place and see if we can find Millard's tractor."

"Didn't you say he lived in a trailer park? Be kinda hard to hide a tractor there. He hasn't had time to move it very far. Where was that farm he inherited from his folks? Maybe if it's still vacant, he stashed it there."

Bubba checked his notes. "Good idea, Mollie. The farm is in Caddo County, only about twenty miles from here. Shouldn't be hard to check it out."

"I have a friend in the Caddo sheriff's office. I'll give her a call."

My friend, Jill Towers, said she would see what she could find out about the Hardcastle farm. She called me back an hour later to tell me the farm was still standing and still vacant. She said she would meet us near there later and help check it out.

———————

Bubba and I met up with Jill a few minutes past eight o'clock that evening and rode in my SUV to the Hardcastle farm. The farmhouse sat about a hundred yards off the road, surrounded by a thick stand of oak trees. The trees allowed us to get within fifty feet of the house without being seen. We left the car and walked the rest of the way. The big farmhouse was dark, but behind it was a barn with lights on inside. Beside the barn sat a big black pickup truck. Bubba assured me it was a GMC.

We split up. Jill moved twenty feet to my left. Bubba went to the right and volunteered to sneak up to the barn and see if he could see anything inside through a window in the side.

Bubba looked inside and threw us a thumbs up, his signal the missing tractor was there. Our plan was to get close enough to tell whoever was inside to come out with their hands on the air.

Before we could do that, the barn door flew open and Jason Hardcastle stepped outside. We could see the tractor, covered with tarps, loaded on a flatbed trailer behind him.

"I don't know who you are," he shouted, "but if you don't get away from here, I'll blow your heads off.

He held a small rifle in his hands. It looked like a .22. The murder weapon.

"Jason," I called out, "This is Sheriff Goodall from Watango County. Beside me is Deputy Jill Tyler from the Caddo County sheriff's office. We need you to put down your weapon and lock your hands behind your head. You're under arrest for the murder of Millard Hamilton."

"No way," he shouted back. "I ain't going to prison again." He raised the rifle to his shoulder and pointed it straight at me.

"Yes, you are, Jason," I said. "You may have to go to a hospital first. You can use that little pea-shooter if you want, but you're not going to do much damage with it. Now, my deputy is over there beside the barn with a 30-30 Winchester, and he's the best shot in the county. If you don't put that weapon down, I'm going to let him put a round in your gut. It won't kill you, but you're going to be in one hell of a lot of pain. What's it going to be? You have just three seconds to make up your mind."

He thought about it for only two seconds, then dropped his rifle and raised his hands.

After we had him handcuffed and stowed in the back of my SUV, Bubba said. "Gee, Mollie, you didn't tell me to bring my Winchester."

Jill and Bubba and I had a good laugh. Jason Hardcastle didn't seem to think it was funny.

———————

The next morning, I drove out to Evangeline's house. She was sitting on her porch. I walked up and sat on the chair beside hers. She already knew about the arrest of Jason Hardcastle. She didn't even look at me. I suddenly realized she looked different. I'd never seen her without that strong chin of hers stuck out and her fiery eyes piercing into everyone in range. She even looked smaller than I remembered her. It was as if someone had let the air out of her body.

"Evangeline," I said, "I talked to Wilson Pickett. He told me about Millard's will."

"So?" she said. Even her voice had weakened now. It was almost a whisper.

"So, I know he left everything to you. You and Millard must have been very close at one time."

I waited.

"Close?" she finally said. "You might say that. We almost got married."

She looked over at me then. I saw a moist haze over her eyes.

Not sure what to say, I came up with, "Things are so different now. I can imagine how it was back then for an interracial couple…"

She looked at me now with a hint of the old fire in her eyes. "Interracial! Dammit, Mollie, you don't know me very well, do you? Hell, that would never stop me. Millard either. We'd planned to march right into the County Office Building and get married, and we didn't give a damn what anybody thought or said about it."

I felt like I'd been lashed with a whip. "Sorry. I just thought—."

"Oh," she said, softening again. "I guess it's normal to think that. But we really didn't give a damn about it. We were going ahead with it anyway until we had a big blowup.'

I hoped she would go on but she didn't. I had to ask. "What happened?"

She looked away for a moment, and then turned back to me with a little smile. She looked almost embarrassed to say it.

"It was all about where we were going to live. Millard wanted me to sell my place and move to his. Can you believe it? My family worked this place for more than two hundred years. There's no way on God's green earth I could ever sell it and live somewhere else." She laughed then, a nervous little laugh, and I joined her.

"We had a real big fight over it," she went on after a bit. "One thing led to another and before you know it, we both said some stuff we shouldn't have said."

"And that led to all the bitterness all these years?"

"It sure did. We were a couple of mule-headed, stubborn fools."

"Evangeline, I don't know what to say. In spite of that, though, he still left everything he had to you, including his farm and his goats."

She gave that little laugh again. "Yeah, how about that. I wound up with all those damned goats after all."

We sat in silence for a few moments before she asked, "You remember that run-in I had with Millard at the hardware store a while back?"

"Yes, I heard about it."

"Well, that evening, there was a knock on my door and there stood Millard. You could've knocked me over with a feather duster. First, he stood there just looking at me with a big scowl on his face and I didn't know what the hell to say or do. Then he smiled. Oh, that smile of his, Mollie, you should've seen it. It lit up the whole county. Turned me to butter right there on the spot. Then he laughed and I laughed and all those years just floated away like they never happened. He came in and we talked and giggled like a couple of school kids on a first date. Before you knew it, we were seeing each other every day. He'd come to my place, I'd go to his."

"It's too bad you two didn't work things out a long time ago."

"Awwww," she said. "I know now, it never would have worked out. We were both so stuck in our ways and too darned strong-willed. We'd never have stayed together back then. Sometimes, Mollie, it takes a lot of years to soften the edges of people. I know that now and so did Millard. We had us a great few weeks, though, before he…"

Her voice weakened and trailed off.

"I'm glad you had that time together, Evangeline," I said. "I mean that."

She touched her hand to mine. "Thanks, Mollie. That's the way life is. You take what you can get and be thankful for it."

We said goodbye then and she hugged me. As I walked to my car, she said, "The problem now is, what the hell am I going to do with all those dammed goats?"

I didn't have an answer for her, but she worked it out for herself. A couple weeks later, she hired someone to run Millard's farm for her. The first thing she had them do was move the goat pen far away from her geese.

A week after that, she dropped off a box at my office. Inside were three gallons of goat's milk and six-dozen goose eggs. I've always liked goat's milk, but I wasn't sure what to do with those eggs. Fortunately, my husband is a self-taught master chef, and I came to love the delicious creme brûlée, pudding and fresh pasta he came up with.

Marianne Wilski Strong taught literature and has published over forty mystery short stories, including series set in Ancient Greece and another in Northeastern Pennsylvania.

She grew up listening to her coal miner uncles tell stories of tragedies and rescues, breakers and doorboys, and canaries warning of cave-ins or deadly gas in Pennsylvania. Remembering their detailed maps of the mines, with tunnels branching right and left, led to her story, impossible without the help of canaries.

The Canaries in the Coal Mine
by Marianne Strong

"There it is," Stephen said, pointing to a black hole in the side of the hill. "That's where we go in."

"Are you sure?" Mike asked.

"Yes. My father described it perfectly lots of times. This is how the miners escaped after the cave-in. He always said he wished he could have gone back in to save more of the men, but it was too late."

"So some of the miners are still in there?"

"Their skeletons, yeah."

Stephen looked up and met Mike's eyes. "My father said the mine was really dangerous. Do we go in or not?"

Mike stared at the entrance. "We go. If the money is in there, we have to get it. My mom needs the reward for my brother's doctor bills. And your family needs money too, after your Dad died."

Stephen nodded. "Okay, then we need to do this before somebody else does. I know the guys next door to us are talking about it."

"Okay," Mike said. "Let's go get the stuff."

At the mom and pop hardware store, Ray, the cashier, looked at the rope, shovels, and picks Stephen and Mike loaded onto the counter. "What are you boys planning to do with all this stuff?" he asked.

Both boys stayed silent for a minute. "We're planning to build a treehouse," Mike said. "With a rope ladder," he added.

The cashier gestured to the shovels and picks. "You don't need these to build a treehouse."

"But," Stephen said. "We need them for digging the stakes for the birdhouse and the doghouse."

Ray shrugged and began ringing up the tools.

"Wait a minute," Stephen said. He went back to the shelves and returned with some miners' hats equipped with lights.

Ray picked up one and eyed the boys. "What the hell are you going to do with these?"

Stephen shrugged. "Stay in the treehouse at night."

The cashier frowned. "You kids aren't planning to go into that old mine, are you?"

Mike cleared his throat. "Why would we do that?"

Stephen kicked Mike's ankle. "Of course not," he said. "Everybody knows that mine was dangerous."

"That's right," Ray said. "And if you heard any silly tales about the Central Bank robbers hiding the money in that mine when the police were on their trail, you can forget about it. Anyway, one of the robbers escaped from prison recently. Even if the money's in the mine, he's probably coming back for it. He'll shoot anybody who goes near the mine." Ray flashed a big toothy grin. "Get it? Besides, if the robber doesn't get the intruders, a cave-in or a rockslide will. So, stay out of that mine."

The boys nodded. They loaded their tools into a wagon and dragged it to Stephen's home.

"What the hell are you two doing?" one of the men from the neighboring porch demanded.

"We're going to build a treehouse," Stephen said

"That so," the man said, snapping the top off his beer can.

The boys stashed their tools behind the garage.

"We go tomorrow," Stephen said. "We gotta get in that mine as soon as we can."

They shook hands on it. Mike walked out to the street, ignoring the two men on the porch.

———••———

At the mine at one o'clock the next morning, Mike and Stephen put on their hardhats and their boots.

"Okay, so here's the plan," Stephen said. "I stand watch while you cut a hole in the wire over the entrance. If I see anybody, I whistle. You get away from the opening as fast as you can, and we pretend we're digging for Indian arrowheads."

"Right," Mike said. "And once I cut the wire, I whistle for you. I get into the tunnel and you follow."

"Yeah," Stephen said. "And I pull the wire back into place so no one notices that it's been cut."

Mike nodded. They secured shovels and picks on the hooks around their belts.

"Look," Stephen pointed to a yellow bird settling onto the branch of an elm. "My dad took care of the canaries in the mine. He fed them and freed them when he could. He said they still breed here. He told me they use the trees in the summer and the mine in the winter. The mine stays warmer than the outside."

Mike nodded, then held up the wire cutters. "Okay, ready?"

They clasped hands. "Ready," Stephen said.

At the mine opening, Mike crouched and snipped the wire. Then he pushed it in and up to prevent it from snagging on his clothes. He jutted his legs into the tunnel and whistled for Stephen. Then he heard it. Whoosh! Whoosh!.

Stephen's legs poked in next to Mike's. "Did you hear that?" Stephen whispered.

"Yeah," Mike said. "Wind, maybe?"

"I don't think…" Stephen gasped. "Duck."

Both boys flattened out.

Canaries flew up from the tunnel and fluttered about their heads. The boys covered their heads until the birds flew out of the mine.

Mike switched on his miner's light.

The tunnel lit up for about twenty feet.

"It doesn't look too steep once we get past the first ten feet," Stephen said.

"Right," Mike said, sliding forward. Around him, dirt and rocks bounced and rattled down the tunnel but he held steady, anchored by the cleats of his boots dug into the ground. He inched his way further down the tunnel and waited for Stephen. In a few moments, Stephen slid to a stop by him.

The light from their hats gleamed on the blue-black anthracite coal.

"Okay," Stephen said. "We have to find the door to the main mine shaft. That's where my father worked when he was a door-boy."

"What's a doorboy?"

"A boy who had to sit by the doors that opened into the deeper tunnels. He had to make sure the door didn't get stuck when the miners opened and closed it to bring out the coal. If anything happened that door had to be open or the miners couldn't escape."

The boys began to slide forward, inch by inch.

Stephen stopped abruptly and looked up at the roof of the tunnel. "Hear it?" he said.

"Yeah. Sounds like someone groaning."

"Not someone. Something. The timbers holding up the tunnel are moving."

Mike looked up. "What do we do?"

"Nothing. Just hold still until it stops."

"What if it doesn't stop?"

"Then we get out of here fast or the tunnel might crash down on us."

Both boys sat perfectly still. Some dirt fell on their heads and a few rocks rolled by their feet.

Finally, the groaning stopped.

But Mike heard something else. "Did you hear that? Something snapping?" He shifted round to the opening of the tunnel.

"See anything?" Stephen asked.

"Too far away. Maybe a shadow. A tree branch?"

"Okay," Stephen said. "Let's go." He slipped ahead of Mike.

They made some progress, then stopped again and listened to the crackling and groaning. Mike swung his light around. The coal seams flashed. "Look," he said. "There."

"I see it," Stephen said. The tunnel split, right and left.

"How do we know which way to go?" Mike asked.

"We don't. We'll have to pick a way and hope we pick the right one. Otherwise we'll have to go back out."

"Okay, right or left?" Mike asked.

Stephen shrugged. He was about to go left when the fluttering began. He ducked his head as three canaries flew up from the right tunnel. "Okay," Stephen said, pumping his arms up and down. "Those canaries know this mine. I bet they stick to the main tunnel. So, we go right."

They slide forward.

A rumbling started. Rocks and dirt slid down from the tunnel above them.

"Ouch," Stephen yelped.

"What started that?" Mike asked. "Maybe somebody else is in here with us. The robber?"

They sat still and listened.

"Well," Stephen said, "if the robber is in here, we can't go back up. We have to go forward."

"Okay, the quicker, the better."

They slid forward.

A high-pitched squeaking and a low rumble rose up from the left.

"Jeez, now what?" Mike asked.

Stephen swung his light to a low side tunnel. "Rats," he cried out. "Rats."

They stared in horror at the glowing beady eyes rushing upward toward them. Rats. Hundreds of them, heading right for them. The rats would soon be on them, biting, scratching.

Then, the fluttering began again. An opera of canaries flew over them and straight into the tunnel of rats, their wings fluttering against the tunnel arch, beating, beating. They wheeled and flew over the boys' heads again.

Mike and Stephen stared as dirt and rocks spewed down from the tunnel's roof. In seconds, the tunnel entrance had disappeared behind a mound of rock and dirt. The noise of the racing rats stopped.

Mike heard Stephen coughing. "You okay, Stephen?"

"Yeah, but I swallowed a ton of dust."

"Well," Mike said. "that's better than being run over by a thousand rats. Our luck is holding out."

"Not luck. Dad's canaries."

They descended another twenty feet.

Stephen felt the floor of the tunnel slope down sharply. "Mike, it's getting pretty steep here. We'll have to dig in our heels."

"Stephen, you hear that?"

They sat still, listening to what sounded like huffing or blowing.

"Mike, what do you think it is?"

"I don't know. It sounds as if somebody else is in this tunnel." Mike turned and flashed his light upward. He saw nothing but the blue-black glow of the coal seams. "I don't see anybody or anything."

"Well, we have to go forward. We should be near the main tunnel. That's probably where the robbers left the money. Far enough down, but not too far. We have to really watch the walls now. Maybe the robbers left marks of some sort." Stephen wiped more coal dust from his eyes, then moved forward, then stopped. "Oh no," he said. "Not again."

"Please don't tell me more rats."

"Not rats. Another fork in the tunnel."

"Rats," Mike said. "I mean damn. So we have to guess again?"

"Let me go in to the right just a little way. That tunnel doesn't look very high. If it gets lower, it isn't the main tunnel."

Mike waited. He heard Stephen gasp.

"Stephen," he yelled. The name echoed up and down the tunnels.

Stephen came scurrying out of the right tunnel, like a crab.

"What's wrong?" Mike yelled.

"Somebody's in there!"

"Who? What's he doing?"

"He isn't doing anything. He's dead."

"A miner?"

"No," Stephen said. He took several deep breaths. "This guy didn't die in here years ago. I felt... I mean... I grabbed his leg. I didn't mean to, but I did. He's cold and stiff."

"The robber," Mike said. "It must be. Maybe he came in to get the money. Maybe he got stuck and died in here."

"Maybe," Stephen said. "Or maybe the other robber escaped too and killed him. Maybe the money's gone."

"Let's go back," Mike said.

"No. Wait. I see it. Dad's door to the main tunnel. C'mon. We have to at least try." He scrambled forward.

Mike followed.

Stephen pushed the door with his feet. "It's opened, Mike. It's opened. Help me push."

Mike slid next to Stephen.

"When I say 'go,' we push. Okay?"

"Okay."

"Go."

The door creaked, groaned, scraped over the tunnel floor. Then it came open with a jerk.

Mike raked his flashlight over the tunnel. "Look. There. See it."

"X," Stephen whispered. "Still white. The robbers' mark."

They scrambled to the X.

"We really found it," Mike whispered.

They stared at the metal box tucked into a hole dug at the bottom of the tunnel wall.

"Get it, Mike."

Mike slid to the wall, lay his flashlight on the ground, reached in, and slowly pulled the box out. "It's locked," he told Stephen.

"Then the money's there. The other robber didn't get it."

"No," Mike said. "But if he killed the robber in the tunnel, then why didn't he take the money?"

"I don't know. Let's get out of here." Stephen turned and stared into the face of a man.

"You didn't think you get away with doing this, did you?" The man grinned. Stephen's flashlight picked out the man's big chin, crooked white teeth, and glinted on the black gun he held. "I knew when you bought all that equipment at the hardware store you were planning to come in the mine. I sat here all morning, just waiting for you."

"Why didn't you stop us then?"

"I almost did. But then I figured I'd let you idiots lead the way and get crushed if the roof fell in." He chuckled. "Besides, I figured if I got rid of the two of you in the mine, nobody'd ever find you. You two are gonna rot in here. Now throw me the flashlights."

Stephen and Mike looked at each other. "Better do it," Mike whispered.

They tossed the flashlights.

"You killed him, didn't you? One of the robbers."

"No, I did."

The cashier swung round, dropping the flashlights. They rattled down the tunnel. Stephen grabbed them. He raised one and stared into the face of his neighbor.

"We can divide the money," the cashier said.

"No, we can't," the neighbor replied.

Stephen slid closer to the door. With his right arm, he pushed just a bit against it, hoping Mike had noticed.

The cashier raised his gun.

Mike shifted closer to Stephen.

The neighbor fired. The crack vibrated in the tunnel. Rocks and dirt flew from the ceiling and walls. The cashier slumped over.

"Throw that box up here," the neighbor ordered.

Mike stared down at the box in his hand, the box that would help his brother live.

"Throw it."

A fluttering, beating sound echoed down the tunnel. Bursts of yellow flashed in and out, up and around the neighbor's head, his eyes, his ears. He flailed, yelling and groaning. More beating and fluttering. The tunnel filled with canaries.

The neighbor fell onto his back, turned over and began crawling up the tunnel.

Suddenly, a grinding, rumbling noise filled the tunnel. More canaries flew down, beating against the ceiling. They flew over the neighbor, through the door and past Mike and Stephen.

"It's a rock slide," Stephen yelled. "Get back, Mike. We have to hold the door."

Mike scrambled down. Stephen grabbed the door and slammed it shut. "Jam your feet against it," he yelled.

They could hear the screams of the neighbor through the sliding, grinding, bumping sound of the dirt and rock. The door jerked and groaned as rocks beat against it.

Then the mine fell silent as the dust settled

"It's over," Mike whispered. He could barely breathe.

They sat still.

"We can't get out," Mike said.

"We have to try. Let's use our picks to break some boards from the door. Then maybe we can dig our way out."

They sat still, afraid moving might send the rock slide down on them.

The fluttering, beating sound began.

Stephen whirled, raising his flashlight. Just below, canaries chirped and sang, fluttering down beyond the light, up again, then down.

"Come on, Mike," Stephen yelled.

The boys scrambled down, following the canaries.

Stephen saw it first. "Look, Mike." He pointed at the dim circle of light on the tunnel floor.

Mike trained his flashlight where Stephen pointed. "It's a shaft," he breathed. "A shaft and a ladder. A metal ladder."

"You're lighter than me, Mike. Start up. I'll be right behind you. If you slip, I can lean against you and keep you from falling."

Tucking the box into his waistband, Mike stepped onto the first rung, and then pulled himself up to the second, the third, the fourth. When he reached the ninth, the ladder shook. The boys hung on, waiting for the ladder to steady.

"Okay," Mike said. "The next rungs look rusty. I'm going slower." He put one foot on the first of the rusty rungs. He took a deep breath, then pulled himself up. The rung held. He did the same twice more. The next rung broke. He lurched against the side of the shaft. Dirt covered his head and face. He spat out grit. He blinked again and again. His eyes watered. Slowly, the dirt washed out.

"You okay, Mike?"

"Yeah, rung broke. Watch out for it."

Canaries fluttered around the boys, then flew up.

"I'm going up," Mike said. He hoisted himself onto the next rung. It held. He climbed ten rungs. He could see the light of the sun and feel its warmth. He moved up, tossed away branches that lay across the opening, heaved the box out, and scrambled over the top. He turned and pulled Stephen up and out.

Both boys lay, stretched on the ground, drinking in the light and air.

The canaries chirped and fluttered overhead.

A week later, the boys climbed to the mine entrance. The police had removed the bodies and placed heavy wiring over the entrance and the shaft.

"Well," Stephen said, "no one else will get into the mine."

Mike looked at the birds in the trees. "Except your father's canaries."

Damien McKeating was born and a short time after that, developed a love of fantasy and the supernatural. His published stories include modernized Irish mythology and sci-fi adventures for young readers. He writes daily and is currently the oldest he has ever been.

Writing Spiderwebs was a love affair between a locked location, a closed circle of suspects, and an amateur sleuth. Is it possible to kill someone without laying a hand on them? Yes.

Spiderwebs

by Damien Mckeating

It was raining the night Michael Fitzpatrick died. It was raining the morning his body was found. The rain drummed against the windows as Jessica Wright left her room in the Three Oaks Guest House. She saw the Fitzpatrick family clustered in the corridor, facing a young woman called Sally, who Jessica recognized from a room down the hall.

"I'll sort out the details," Sally said with some authority. "Please, it's best if you leave this to me for now."

"Detective, he's my husband and I should be able to go into his room." Annabelle Fitzpatrick said. She was a short and slender woman, but well-turned out, and with an intimidating, icy composure.

"We can come back later," said a young man, her son, Michael.

A younger daughter, Ruby, stood next to him, her eyes red and ringed black from both tears and sleeplessness. "It won't bring him back," she said.

"Mrs Fitzpatrick," Sally said and left the sentence hanging.

Annabelle glowered. "I'll make some calls and begin to organize his affairs," she said. "If I'm allowed to do that?" She glared at Sally before leading her children away.

"Has something happened?" Jessica asked as the family left.

"There was an incident. Mister Fitzpatrick died during the night. His wife wanted to see him but I've told her we should wait for the coroner. Only, with the rain…"

"No one's getting in or out," Jessica said. The torrential rain and flooding had closed the roads, leaving the guesthouse isolated and ruining everyone's plans and holidays.

Sally opened the door to the room and Jessica followed her inside.

"You shouldn't be here," Sally said.

"I'm not ancient but I'm no spring chicken: I've seen a dead body before. Besides, you look like you could use a little friendly support."

"Well, don't touch anything."

Michael Fitzpatrick lay in bed. His face was stuck in a rictus of pain, his mouth open, his eyes wide, his hands twisted around the bed sheets.

On the nightstand stood a collection of medicine bottles and a dog-eared paperback book about the industrial revolution in the north of England. The medicine bottles were arranged in a neat line, all of their labels facing out, except one. Jessica picked up the out-of-place bottle and recognized it as the same blood-thinning medicine her husband had used.

"A heart attack?" she suggested. She shook the bottle and it was empty.

"You said you wouldn't touch anything," Sally said. She was staring at the bed, her face pale. "He looks terrified."

"Wouldn't you be?"

"If he ran out of medication that might explain what happened."

Jessica clucked her tongue but said nothing. A wisp of a cobweb drifted in the air and caught her eye. One end was attached to the ceiling and it looked like it had been broken away

166

from the top of the wardrobe. A chair had been dragged over to the wardrobe, making it impossible to open the door.

"Unusual place for a chair," Jessica said.

"What?" Sally pulled her gaze away from the body. "The chair? That is odd. Look, you can see the marks in the carpet where it should be. And this…" She pointed at a dressing table next to the chair. A lamp sat on top of it, the shade broken. Remnants of the broken glass could be seen under the chair.

"Curious," Jessica said.

"Odd bloke," Sally conceded. She turned her attention back to Jessica. "You really shouldn't be here. I'll be fine, thank you. I've already made the call."

Jessica moved to leave and noticed a smudge on the door handle. She reached out and scraped off a bit with her finger.

"What is it?" Sally said.

"Make-up, if I'm not mistaken. Some kind of foundation."

"I'm sticking by what I said: Mister Fitzpatrick was an odd bloke."

Jessica hesitated at the doorway. For some twenty-five years she had been a piano teacher and, like a discordant note in a concerto, something about the room was *wrong*.

"It's my experience," Jessica said, "that people with serious medical conditions don't let themselves run out of medication."

"Perhaps he was due to get some more and the flood stopped him."

"Even so, you should consider the possibility that something more untoward occurred here."

"Are you suggesting murder?"

Jessica raised an eyebrow. "Something to consider."

"But everyone here would be a suspect."

"With no way to leave," Jessica said. She left Sally alone to think it over and went down to find breakfast.

Over eggs and toast, Jessica watched the rain trickle down the window. She found its arrhythmic tapping a welcome distraction as, by habit she tried to hear a regular beat in its downpour.

Across the room Sally was talking to the owners of the guesthouse. She hoped the detective wasn't wasting her energies. The owners were victims too. They now owned a guesthouse that had been the site of a murder.

After breakfast, she made her way back upstairs and met the maid on her rounds. She was about Jessica's age and there was a no-nonsense bustle to her as she went around each room.

"Excuse me, miss?" Jessica offered the question.

"Maggie," the woman replied. "Well, Margaret, but call me Maggie."

"Do you mind, I was wondering, was it you who had the misfortune to find that poor man this morning."

"Mister Fitzpatrick? Oh Lord, no. He was a very private man. Insisted that no one enter his room, not even to clean, until he'd checked out."

That explained the cobwebs, Jessica thought. "An unusual man," she said aloud.

"I've seen stranger," Maggie replied and nodded towards the room she was cleaning. "This one has got a line of horse chestnuts on her window." She carried out a wastepaper bin from the room and emptied it into the bag strapped to her cleaning cart. Jessica watched a cascade of small, white pills tumble out amidst a collection of crumpled tissues.

She watched Maggie take the bin back into the room.

"Whose room is that?" Jessica asked.

"Mrs. Fitzpatrick," Maggie replied without hesitation.

"They had separate rooms," Jessica realized. She was embarrassed she hadn't made the connection sooner.

"Oh, yes. Trouble in paradise there," Maggie said, and waggled her eyebrows.

Jessica recognized a soul in desperate need of gossip. "Do you think so?" She prompted.

"As sure as eggs is eggs. They wouldn't have lasted the year, you mark my words. Cold as a Highland winter, those two. I saw them talking, well, I say talking, more like arguing, but she had this look on her face like she'd just smelled something rotten."

"What were they arguing about?" Jessica joined in the gossip, leaning forward to hear what Maggie had to say.

"She was rattling on about him signing something or other. Be best for both of them, she kept saying. She kept on even when I walked right past her. Full of airs and graces, that one."

"I had no idea."

"If he hadn't had heart attack, I wouldn't have put it past her to do him in, if you don't mind me saying."

"Quite shocking," Jessica showed the appropriate levels of surprise and intrigue. "You take care of yourself now," she wished Maggie well and went back to her own room.

She felt like she had something more now. Not just a single note, but a chord, ringing out bright and clear. Yes, to her mind a mystery was very much music—they both followed a pattern. Now she just had to find the next step in the progression.

There was a lounge at the rear of the guesthouse. It over-looked the gardens and had an upright piano. Jessica sat at the piano and let her fingers move through familiar patterns, hop-ping between songs and genres as the mood took her. The ram-bling musicality occupied the noisy part of her brain, allowing her thoughts to move freely.

The rain had stopped at last. Glittering buds of water hung suspended from leaves and plants that had been drenched over the subsequent days. Annabelle Fitzpatrick and her son, Matthew, were making the most of the dry spell and were walking in the garden. They stood close together, heads bent towards each other in earnest conversation.

"Lovely playing," a voice said.

Jessica turned. It was Oliver, another guest who had been marooned in the deluge. He was an affable and rotund man. He reminded her of a travelling salesman and she imagined he had a briefcase full of samples of carpets, or ladies' stockings, or encyclopedias.

"Years of practice," Jessica replied.

"I never had the ear for it. Or the fingers for that matter," Oliver waved his heavy hand at her. "My family tends towards the big side." He sat down near to her, his breathing labored. "What do you think about this bad business?"

"It's a terrible shame for the family," Jessica said diplomatically.

"We're all suspects, you know. I've never been a suspect before. It's terribly exciting."

"I'm not sure you are now."

"What?"

"A suspect."

"I'm not?"

"You're a very sound sleeper." She saw his confusion and continued. "I heard you snoring last night. I can vouch that you never left your room."

Oliver blushed. "My apologies. One of the many drawbacks to carrying a little extra weight. They say he was poisoned you know. That's a woman's thing, isn't it, poisoning someone? Isn't that what they say?"

"Who said he was poisoned?"

"Oh, just idle chatter. Was my snoring really that bad?"

"It was quite profound."

He shook his head. "It took me forever to fall asleep, too. I was up chatting with the lad," he gestured out of the window towards Matthew. "We were trading stories and he was telling me about the ghost on the first floor."

"Ghost? This is the first I've heard of it."

"Well," Oliver got comfortable, recognizing he had an audience. "There was a young woman who stayed at the guest house one night. A night much like these; dark and full of bad weather. She was meeting her lover. They were going to elope."

"I didn't think that was something people did anymore."

"Oh, this was a few years ago. Perhaps it was still de rigueur back then. Well, she's waiting for her gentleman to come, to leave his wife and run away with her. The hours tick by, and it's a dark and lonely night. No word comes. It gets darker and lonelier. She begins to doubt herself, wonders what she has to offer over the settled and comfortable life her gentleman is supposed to be leaving behind."

"Go on," Jessica encouraged.

"He never comes. In the small hours, when the night is darkest and loneliest, she is overcome by despair. Standing on the first floor landing, she hurls herself out of the window and onto the patio, just here," Oliver gestured towards the paving slabs just beyond the bay doors. "That's not even the tragic part."

"No?"

"Oh no. She couldn't know, of course; there was no way for news to travel that fast back then. There had been a car accident in the night. The driver had lost control on the flooded roads. He'd gone straight into a tree, his body thrown from the car."

"Her gentleman," Jessica joined in with the reveal.

"Her gentleman," Oliver agreed. "They say the young woman can still be seen upstairs, walking the landing, or you can hear her footfalls pacing back and forth as she comes to her despairing, final decision." Oliver sat back with a broad smile. "There. Couldn't sleep for ages with that going around in my head. Every creak of the floorboards set my heart to racing."

"It's a good story and you tell it wonderfully."

"You're not a believer?"

"I believe in the things I can prove."

"I've too much of the romantic in me. Perhaps it was a similar fright that did for Mr. Fitzpatrick, and not poison after all. Matthew said his father had a passion for macabre stories. Perhaps he'd have been pleased to have a starring role in one."

"I'm sure he'd have been happier with a different outcome."

Oliver looked embarrassed. "Sorry. Apologies. I got carried away with myself."

Jessica noticed Annabelle and Matthew still talking in the garden. She thought about the strand of cobweb floating by the wardrobe, and what other strands might be woven around it. "If you'll excuse me," she stood up, "I think I'll go and see how the young lady is bearing up."

She left Oliver to his ghostly musings.

———————

As she approached Ruby Fitzpatrick's room, Jessica hesitated. She heard low voices; a murmured conversation that spoke of secret dealings. She took a few steps closer and her finely tuned ears began to follow the cadence and rhythm of the sounds and she realized she was listening to one person talking.

She knocked.

"Yes?" a quiet voice replied.

"I'm sorry to bother you, I just wanted to make sure you were holding up. It's Jessica Wright. I have a room just down the hall."

A moment later the door opened. Ruby greeted Jessica with a smile, but her face was still marred by tears and lack of sleep.

"Please, come in."

"I wasn't sure if you already had a visitor. I heard you talking," Jessica said as she stepped into the room. She glanced around. The bed was made, clothes packed away, the window open a crack to let a fresh breeze air the room.

"Practicing my lines," Ruby said. "It helps to distract me. If I focus on them, then I'm not thinking about…" She trailed off and drew in a shaky breath.

"I don't mean to pry," Jessica reached out and stroked her arm. She felt a twinge of guilt at the lie. She had every intention of prying. "The lines you were rehearsing, are you an actress?"

"Yes," Ruby said, caught between pride and modesty. "Trying to be, at least. It's tough out there. You have to develop a bit of a thick skin. I thought I was quite tough until… I hate remembering it." She shook her head as if she could dislodge the thoughts.

Jessica studied her. The young woman was deeply affected by her father's death, that was clear. It was a marked difference to the widow and son, who appeared to have faced it with a grim practicality.

"The theatre is wonderful, isn't it," Jessica said, hoping to direct the conversation to more cheerful topics.

"Oh, yes. I've always loved it. A costume and a little make-up and you can transform yourself. It's like living dozens of different lives in one lifetime."

"I performed a little myself. Nothing like you. I'm a piano player and I played in a burlesque show for a time."

Ruby stared. "You?"

"Not as a performer," Jessica smiled. "Strictly just the music."

"They say burlesque is just stripping made respectable," Ruby joked.

"I have no problem with people taking their clothes off, if it's their free choice. It's when people's choices are taken away that I object." The comment was pointed and she watched the young woman's reaction carefully.

"It's just so difficult," she said. She stood by the window and stared out over the dripping garden.

"What is?"

"Just trying to survive. Father was always so supportive. He always said I had talent." Ruby shook her head. She dabbed at the tears rolling down her cheeks. "I didn't think I could cry any-more."

"Grief surprises us," Jessica said. "Even years later, you can never be sure when it will hit you." She reached out and gave Ruby's shoulder a supportive squeeze. "Still, chin up, as they say. I'll be around if there's anything I can do for you."

"Thank you. I just... I just can't wait to leave."

Jessica went to leave. "Just a thought, are you afraid of spiders, at all?"

"Spiders?" Ruby smiled in surprise. "Well, no, not really. No more than anyone else."

"I didn't think so," Jessica smiled in return and left before the confused young woman could respond.

173

Sally's room was a mess. Clothes were strewn over the chair, a suitcase was propped up in a corner, and a damp towel hung over the door to the en-suite. Jessica tried to not let her distaste show.

"If it was foul play, like you suggest," Sally said, "then my money's on the son, Matthew. He's already admitted he was in debt and that his father had refused to help him. A few people have described how cold they were with each other but there's no evidence he had anything to do with it. You can't *make* someone have a heart attack. A pathology report will sort it out."

"I've been thinking about the spiderweb," Jessica said.

Sally frowned. "The what?"

"The spiderweb."

"What spiderweb?"

"On top of Mister Fitzpatrick's wardrobe there was a broken spiderweb. He had instructed staff not to clean his room for the duration of his stay. He put something there and then removed it recently."

"So?"

"What do people keep on top of their wardrobes?"

"My wardrobe is jammed with clothes, boxes and shoes from top to bottom."

"I'm not surprised. I'd suggest that most people, when staying in a place such as this, might unpack and then put their suitcase on top of the wardrobe."

"I don't see how this is relevant. As soon as someone else gets here, we'll sort this out."

Jessica looked Sally up and down. As patiently as she could, she laid out her thoughts. "There was something in the suitcase. Something he wanted to see or something the murderer wanted to see."

"The weather's broken and water levels are dropping. Someone will be here soon. I'm on holiday, just like you."

"Would you indulge me? Let's see what's in the suitcase."

Sally hesitated. She bit at her lower lip, realized what she was doing and frowned at herself. "You've got no business in this… Fine. One quick look."

They went back to Michael Fitzpatrick's room. With nowhere else to store it, the body still lay on the bed, a white sheet draped over it. Decay had not yet started to taint the room.

"It's not there," Sally said, pointing at the wardrobe.

"No." Jessica thought for a moment, looking at the chair that had been moved. Michael Fitzpatrick was a tall man who could easily reach the top of his wardrobe. Someone else had used the chair.

Jessica knelt and looked under the bed. "It's here," she said.

"So you were wrong."

Jessica slid the suitcase out. Behind it was a pair of polished black shoes, shoved to the middle, pushed by the suitcase.

"He was an orderly man," Jessica said and pointed to the neatly arranged medicine bottles. "Doesn't it strike you as odd he would jam this under the bed, knocking his shoes out of easy reach?"

"Who knows why he did it?" Sally flipped open the suitcase. "Empty," she said.

Jessica looked inside and nodded. "I thought as much."

"Then what are we doing here?"

"Confirming my thoughts."

"Some might call this wasting police time."

"If you're on holiday, can it technically still be wasting police time?"

Sally slapped shut the suitcase. "I don't want to hear any more about this."

Jessica pointed at the strand of spiderweb that still floated from the ceiling. "A web has been woven. I'm simply following the strands to see what I find."

"It's usually a fly," Sally quipped, looked at the figure on the bed, and had the good grace to flush with embarrassment. She sighed and rubbed at her face with her hands. "All right," she said. "Out with it. Tell me what you think happened."

"All in due time. I have another strand I need to follow first."

"One that will lead to a spider?"

Jessica smiled. "Absolutely, *detective*."

Sarah looked at her through narrowed eyes. "What does that mean?"

"You're not a detective at all, are you?" Jessica accused.

Sarah blanched. "How? No, don't say anything. Have you told anyone?"

"I've not said a word. If I'm being entirely honest, it was a bit of a guess, but an educated one. You are police but you're not a detective."

"I'm a constable. I told Mrs. Fitzpatrick I was a police officer and she called me a detective. I thought it best not to contradict her. Sometimes a bit of authority can go a long way. Don't say anything. I'll hand the case over as soon as the local constabulary arrive."

"My lips are sealed. But make sure you're at the evening meal tonight. I may need to borrow some of your authority."

———————

Jessica found Maggie sitting in a cozy nook in a cozy room. In the morning it served as the breakfast room. Maggie occupied a choice spot by the bay window. It offered a wide view of the front of the guesthouse, looking down a tree-lined driveway towards a high hawthorn hedgerow that blocked any view of the road. A break in the clouds let a stream of sunlight through the window. It beamed down towards the table, illuminating the crossword puzzle Maggie studied while she sipped her coffee.

"At last," Maggie said and nodded towards the outside world. "We can stop building that boat and rounding up animals. Thank goodness. I'm too old to repopulate the world."

Jessica paused for a beat. The conversation had not started how she had imagined. She rallied, took the seat opposite Maggie and cast a glance over the crossword puzzle.

"Don't say a word," Maggie said. "I'll solve this on my own."

"A sentiment I heartily approve of," Jessica replied with a smile. "I did have a quick question for you, if you can spare me a moment."

Maggie looked intrigued. "What is it?"

"It's about the ghost upstairs."

"The what?" Maggie started to laugh until she saw how serious Jessica was. "Are you pulling my leg?"

"I heard a story." Jessica related the ghostly tale as succinctly as she could.

"What a load of rot," Maggie snorted.

"You don't believe it?"

"Well, of course I don't. That sort of nonsense is fine for them young fools what want to go around believing crystals have powers and all sorts, but I've seen a thing or two and I'll tell you this. The real world is a lot stranger than this supernatural stuff."

"Oh, I agree. More importantly, I wanted to know if you already knew the story."

"Never heard it before. No one's ever mentioned a ghost and I've never seen one; and I've been here every hour of every day at some point or another. Got stuck here Christmas Day once, when we had that bad snow that year."

"Curious how these stories start," Jessica mused.

"People with too much time on their hands."

"Thank you. I'll leave you to your puzzle."

Jessica went back to her room and put her thoughts in order.

The residents of the guesthouse gathered in the dining room that evening. It was good fortune that the house had been well stocked before the flood left them stranded. They had, in truth, not suffered much in the way of hardship. Had it not been for Michael Fitzpatrick's death, their stay would have been unremarkable.

Jessica sat alone. Sally was at the table next to her, and Oliver the next one over. They had exchanged pleasantries and fallen into a comfortable silence. Sally tried to catch Jessica's attention with significant glances but Jessica refused to be drawn until she was ready.

The Fitzpatricks sat together. Annabelle was reserved and aloof, her spine erect, her dark hair pinned back, and her dress immaculate. Matthew lounged. He slouched in his chair, toyed with his cutlery and made idle chatter that no one else in his family saw fit to rise to. Ruby was as quiet as her mother, her gaze downcast, her hands resting on the table, as still and as quiet as a spider in its web.

The turn of phrase gave Jessica a moment of sadness. She saw no wickedness in the young woman, truly, but the truth had to be revealed.

Jessica stood up and went to stand by the Fitzpatricks' table. Annabelle and Matthew stared at her, but Ruby only looked from under her eyelashes.

"It's time to tell the truth," Jessica said. She held Ruby's gaze.

"My family would like to be alone," Annabelle said.

"I still can't be certain if you meant for him to die, although I have my suspicions."

Ruby looked down, tears rolling down her cheeks. Annabelle glowered, her lips pressed into a tight, white line. Matthew stood, indignation large on his face.

"Now listen," he started to say.

"Yes; listen," Jessica commanded. "Michael Fitzpatrick died last night of an apparent heart attack. I think some of us here know differently. At the very worst, we are talking about murder." Jessica began to pace the room. She had everyone's attention. No one made a move to stop her.

"Mister Fitzpatrick was very orderly man; I saw that from the way his medicine bottles were arranged, all except for one… his heart medication. Someone tampered with it and removed the tablets. Then was the chair next to the wardrobe, the smashed lamp and the broken spiderweb. Someone had been through his belongings. But to what purpose? Perhaps to remove divorce papers?" She looked at Annabelle.

"What are you suggesting?" Annabelle responded, but her voice was faint.

"Last night Matthew spun a tale to his father and Oliver," Jessica said. "One about a ghostly woman haunting the guest house. It was nonsense. No one here has ever heard this story. Matthew tried to suggest his father enjoyed macabre stories, but the book on his bedside table suggests otherwise. However, the story did serve to put his father in a certain state of mind. Either before or after, Matthew brought Ruby in on his little joke. Using stage make-up, some of which was left on the door handle, she made herself up into a spectral woman and paid her father a visit. The resulting shock was too much for his heart and he died." Jessica paused for a moment. "The rest hinges on one simple question. Was this a practical joke gone wrong, or a premeditated murder?"

"He wasn't meant to die," Ruby wailed. "It was just a joke."

"Ruby," her mother hissed.

Jessica nodded. "I thought as much. When you saw what had happened, you panicked. Mrs. Fitzpatrick was afraid their forthcoming divorce proceedings would be seen as evidence of wanting her husband dead. She removed the divorce papers, the ones they were overheard arguing about, from his suitcase." She turned to Annabelle. "The spider on the wardrobe frightened you, causing you to knock over the lamp and break it."

"You have no evidence to even suggest such a thing," Annabelle fumed.

"Incidentally, the horse chestnuts you keep on your windowsill are an old wife's tale. Spiders are not bothered by them at all. You emptied your husband's medication, perhaps thinking it would look like it had run out and brought on an attack."

"He wasn't meant to die," Ruby repeated.

"Maybe he was," Jessica said, her gaze firmly on Matthew. "An early inheritance would certainly solve your debt problems."

"This is all hearsay and nonsense," Matthew replied. "We did nothing wrong."

"But you did," Jessica said. "Ruby has already told us: at the very least, you watched while a man died and did nothing. You attempted to cover it up for your own gain."

Sally stood up. "And that is definitely not nothing."

Ruby looked up at her brother. "I'm sorry. It's just too much. I can't sleep… I can't think… It was an accident, wasn't it?"

"Stop talking," Matthew said. "We'll be speaking to our lawyer," he said to Sally.

"I'd expect so." Sally glanced at Jessica. "So not one, but three spiders. A veritable gaggle of them."

"A cluster, actually," Jessica corrected her. "And a tangled web of deceit."

The door to the dining room opened. Maggie wheeled in a tray filled with food. She stopped and looked around at the assembled figures, sensing the tension in the room.

"Did I miss something?" she asked.

Jessica left early the next morning. The local police had arrived first thing, along with a coroner. The Fitzpatricks had stared daggers at her, except for Ruby, who Jessica fancied had looked rather relieved.

As she waited for a taxi to take her away. a glimmer of light caught her eye. On the front porch was a spiderweb. Caught in the early morning sunlight, the web glistened. In one corner she saw the spider, ever-patient and watchful. Jessica wondered, did flies feel trapped or comforted by the eight arms that held them?

She cast the maudlin thought aside as her taxi arrived, went home, and left the tangled web of the Three Oaks Guest House behind her.

C.A. Fehmel is a daytime librarian, nighttime writer, and leader of the pack for her motley crew critique group, Writers Under the Arch. They thrive on rejection, publication, and chocolate.

At the zoo's primate house, she saw an orangutan who sat next to the glass that fronted the cage. She put her hand against the glass and the orangutan mirrored her move. Since then, humane treatment of animals has been both a conundrum and inspiration.

Cell Break
by Cindy Fehmel

The enemy held young Hector down. They yelled and shrieked at each other, but Hector's cries were worse. He called for his mother. He pled for his freedom. The enemy didn't understand, but desperation transcends language. My heart felt squeezed. "Let him go!" I bellowed.

The enemy agents glanced at me and then continued shouting at each other. A decision was made—an unpopular one since their chittering continued. The tall one stabbed Hector with a needle. Hector's cry pierced through our cacophony before falling silent. Shuddering, shuddering, his limbs jumped on the rectangular, silver table.

The mothers keened out of sympathy and grief. The stabber took her needle and swaggered in the pretentious way of lions. I was enraged but helpless.

The enemy agents left save one, she of the brown hair. She put Hector in his cell. His glazed eyes stared at her. She watched him through the bars. He continued to shake. The brown-haired one opened Hector's cell again. We watched her as she watched him. She grasped him gently and pulled him out.

Would she set him on the rectangular silver table? Would she hold him down so his limbs wouldn't jump? Instead she clutched him to her chest, like a mother and an offspring, like an older sister to a sibling. This was a new sort of behavior. The brown-haired one stroked Hector with tenderness. He gazed at her with empty eyes. His shaking slowed. Eventually, he went limp. He wasn't sleeping or dead. She put him back in his cell.

The following day, the brown-haired one acted like all the rest. The routine of the prison continued. We had our orders and did our work. The enemy shuffled white rectangles filled with squiggly lines, forced us to match one to another, and then talked amongst themselves. If they were pleased, we would receive extra rations.

It wasn't until the next time the brown-haired one was alone with us, she took Hector from his cell again. He wasn't well. He still shook. I worried he might die. There had been others who'd given up hope, and they'd wither. She cradled him. Hector sighed, but otherwise didn't respond. She spoke to him in her language. I spoke to him in ours. The brown-haired one carried him closer to my cell.

"Don't give up hope. You have to be strong for your mother, your aunt, your brothers," I said.

His eyes didn't have their usual warmth. We were losing Hector. I felt the enemy agent knew it too. She cradled him for a long while. Once he slept and she put him back in his cell, she came to mine. I am the leader. How she knew this, is a mystery.

She had a large white square with black drawings. We did this work often, but never in the cellblock before. There were cylinders, a sphere, and even a pyramid. But beyond the shapes, I couldn't understand.

She gave me things to smell. Odd things. Things I hadn't smelled before. There was something red and round. She took a bite to prove that it was safe to eat. Then she gave me a piece. There were odd plants. Some small brown ovals she kept repeating were "nuts."

Finally, she took one of the green bags from her pocket. I moved to the back of my cell. No telling what she had in the pocket. It could be a weapon. It could be a needle. Instead it was waste from another of my people. I smelled it. I didn't know why she shared this with me. It had something to do with the white square, but I didn't understand. She took an odd thing from her pocket. After touching it with her finger, she showed me pictures. Unlike the white squares, these pictures moved.

The next time she was the main guard, she did the smell test again. She showed me the white square and the moving pictures. I watched, confused, but focused. Then she put all the smelled items in a bag and laid it by my cell. She opened all the other cells. We were free. She came to my cell and opened the barred door. She went to the door to the cellblock and peered beyond the clear square. She pushed and propped it open!

I called to my family, my brethren. They leapt from their cells onto the floor! I went for Hector and pulled him onto my back where he clung to me. The females called to each other. I shouted over them. "Follow me. We escape."

"Detective O'Brien and Officer Daniels." The policemen showed their badges through the locked research facility's reception window. The head scientist, Dr. Jeanie Hynes, was called up front and they were buzzed inside.

Jeanie introduced herself and led them back toward her office. "Thank you for coming so quickly."

The policemen took seats across from her. O'Brien leaned forward to speak but Daniels beat him to it. "Well, we've seen the movies. We need to cut the zombie apocalypse off at the pass." His smile was snaggle-toothed.

Jeanie leaned back with a scowl. "There is nothing wrong our research subjects. They haven't been given any diseases or infections."

"Forgive my... colleague, Doctor Hynes. He's a rookie and will wait outside for the remainder of our visit."

O'Brien's scalding glance sent Daniels out into the hall.

"Our test subjects aren't dangerous. They're rhesus macaques, quite harmless, unless threatened," Jeanie said. "In India macaques live in human communities in relative harmony."

O'Brien nodded. He dug the notepad out of his suit jacket. "How exactly did they escape? I circled the building before I entered and you have cameras and alarms on every door."

"I don't know. It's unbelievable. The macaques left by way of the front door. We have that on the security camera." She offered him the disc in a paper envelope. He took it and put it in his pocket. "What time was this?"

Jeanie's face crumpled. "Friday evening."

"So you're monkeys have been gone over forty-eight hours?"

"Yes. You don't search for a missing person before twenty-four, right?" Her lame joke limped over the punch line.

A smile didn't crack O'Brien's face. "These aren't people. They're wild animals."

"They aren't really wild. They won't attack unless threatened. They've been acclimated to humans. They may be able to be lured back to captivity with food. We give them treats when they respond to tasks."

"Retrieving the monkeys is another department's trouble, ma'am. My concern is how they got loose."

Jeanie fidgeted and took a file folder from her side of the desk and thrust it toward the detective. "These are copies of all the protests we've received. None of them are from legitimate animal rights companies. World Wildlife Federation is aware we aren't testing animals in any way that would harm them. These are from outlier radical organizations. They'd be just the type to break in here."

"Was there a sign of a break in? I didn't notice any of the doors being marred."

Jeannie dropped her eyes. "No."

"You didn't keep the animals locked up? In cages or crates?"

"We did, but we treated them humanely. Not like some cosmetic companies."

"How did they get out of their cages? Would these radical organizations have been able to break them out?"

184

She toyed with her earrings and messed with her dark auburn hair.

"I don't know. It could've been just one was left open, by mistake. The monkeys may have figured out how to open the others by watching us. Some of them have been here a long time."

O'Brien had Jeanie walk him through the small facility. It was less than four thousand square feet. The housing was limited to twenty test subjects. This facility had hit its maximum. All the stainless steel cages were empty now. They looked relatively clean. "Has anything been touched or removed since you noted the disappearance?"

"No, the policeman on the phone said not to. That it was a… a crime scene." Jeanie teared up. O'Brien turned away.

The detective noticed the place didn't stink of urine or worse. There were crumbs of some sort of food and some brown goo he suspected was left over from bananas. Several bunches hung in another room. Enormous dust-bunnies of monkey hair lay in the cages and around the floor, but he considered that normal. If anything it seemed too clean. Daniels had followed them on the tour, and for once kept his trap shut.

"Daniels," O'Brien said, "Have CSI check for prints on the cages and the locks to see if any show up of non-employees. Then check through this file of protest letters to see if we have anything on any of these people breaking into research facilities."

"Yes, Boss." Daniels tucked the file folder under his arm and started typing into his phone.

O'Brien turned to Jeanie and had her explain how the locks worked. They were push button number codes. "I'll need to speak to all of your employees immediately." This was an inside job.

———— ·•· ————

The facility only had five employees to care for twenty monkeys. A custodian came from the university proper twice a week to empty the trash and sweep the floors, but he wasn't allowed in the research area or anywhere near the animals. The employee who had been scheduled that evening had an alibi of seven pounds and three ounces and an entire obstetrics ward of witnesses.

When her water broke unexpectedly, she called her husband and locked the facility. She'd texted her colleagues Friday around 8:30, so they knew she was leaving. Her movements were caught on the security cameras, right up until the time her alarmed husband struggled to get her into the back seat before driving erratically off campus.

Jeanie Hynes claimed she had been out of town and she assumed one of the other employees would fill in to check on the research subjects while she was away. "I'm sure they settled it among themselves."

O'Brien made a note to check on her alibi and asked her for specifics. Then he went back to what happened on the night in question.

"No one is on the security cameras. None of the alarms went off. If someone came in the rear employee door, they parked out of range of the camera. To get in unnoticed, they would've had to sneak in behind the dumpster. There is a dead spot there if they could get that close." O'Brien grumbled. "Did any of the inner door alarms go off?"

"We don't have alarms on the inner doors, just the exits," Jeannie said. "But it doesn't make sense. If someone wanted to free the test subjects, they'd know we'll just get another twenty. Why traumatize twice as many animals? It would just make it worse."

O'Brien's head went up. "Traumatize? I thought you said your research was humane?"

"It is. Compared to a lot of medical and commercial research, these are the luckiest monkeys around, but they still are taken from their homes. They're still separated from each other. That's traumatic."

O'Brien knew what it was to be ambivalent about your job. Dr. Hynes' concern for the animals seemed genuine.

O'Brien used her office to interrogate the other employees. Daniels sat in to take notes. First was Lara Bucharin, a Russian émigré. She had dark hair and Ava Gardner eyes. O'Brien liked the way she emphasized the first syllable of his title with her heavy accent.

"I can't tell you anything, Detective. Except I had nothing to do with the missing monkeys. I do as I am told. I do it for science, Detective," Lara said without prompting.

"You don't think it was some radical animal rights group?" O'Brien asked.

"How could they get in? They don't know the code, Detective. You must believe me. I am cooperating!"

"Do you know how anyone could get in and out without being seen on the security cameras?"

Lara's shrug was like a convulsion. "I don't know, Detective. I couldn't get in without being on the security camera. I know it watches me. I have nothing to hide."

O'Brien knew the security camera had caught Lara Bucharin outside the back entrance smoking several times. She didn't seem to care and was far more relaxed on the security discs than she was sitting before him and Daniels. Bucharin had no alibi. She'd only been in the U.S. for eighteen months. She lived alone. She had no relatives or friends. She said she spent the entire holiday weekend at home alone.

"She seems pretty nervous. My money's on her," Daniel's said once Lara left.

"It's a good thing you don't get paid much then. Her green card is expired. She's worried we'll tell ICE. Her agitation may not have anything to do with this case. And why would she bring that kind of attention to herself? On the other hand, when I spoke to the dean of this department this morning, he showed me this complaint letter."

O'Brien handed Daniels the photocopy of the complaint.

Daniels did a low whistle. "Bucharin ratted out her boss for inhumane treatment. Sounds like the cosmetic companies putting lipstick on pigs aren't the only evil entities."

O'Brien ignored his remark. "Also on her statement to get the visa to enter the country, Bucharin said she was a biologist who strongly objected to the treatment of test subjects in her mother country."

"So it is her!" Daniels said.

"It's too soon to tell," O'Brien said. "Call the next one in."

Lara Bucharin was followed by Sally Carter, who was as cool a customer as Lara was a hot mess. Her brunette hair was pulled back in a tight bun and she did everything with a professional air.

"Can you tell us where you were Friday night and if anyone saw you?" O'Brien asked.

"I was at home watching movies alone."

"Could anyone vouch for you? Maybe a neighbor who heard the TV in the apartment next door?"

"I don't know."

"What movie did you watch?"

"Titanic."

O'Brien nodded. "Can you think of any reason someone would release the monkeys in this facility?"

"No."

All her answers were short and to the point. Maybe a little too practiced, O'Brien thought. Though if she was planning to release the monkeys, she would've had a better alibi planned.

"Are you concerned about what could happen if the citizens are attacked if the monkeys get spooked."

"These research subjects aren't infected with diseases. They're harmless."

"Ms. Hynes seemed to think the monkeys might get violent if threatened or think they're being threatened, and some citizens may panic if they see a group… a mass… a bunch of twenty monkeys."

Sally's expression was that of a good bluffer holding a full house. O'Brien was disgruntled. He glanced back at Daniels. "Find the collective noun for monkeys."

Daniels googled away.

O'Brien saw Sally's jaw tighten.

"It's a barrel," Sally said. "A barrel of monkeys like they all belong in a circus."

Sally was dismissed. All the employees were asked to wait until O'Brien's interrogations were over. However, there wasn't much work without their research subjects. "Call the last one in."

Kyle Jenkins sauntered in and collapsed in a chair instead of sat in it. O'Brien was direct. "Mr. Jenkins where were you last Friday and can anyone vouch for you?"

"I was at Orbit racking up the points."

"I don't know where that is or what that means."

"Pinball, Jack. It's a pinball joint and I am bad-ass."

"Did anyone see you?"

"Everybody saw me. I scored thirty-three million on Lu-lu-Bells."

"Cool!" Daniels said.

O'Brien sighed. "Do you have any idea who would want to release the monkeys from this facility?"

"No idea, man. That's screwed up. Though the bitches were all upset when we had to tranq Hector. They don't even like it when we withhold treats if the macaques misbehave."

Kyle said bitches emphasizing the second syllable. O'Brien disliked that as much as he enjoyed Lara Bucharin emphasizing the first syllable of his title. "You mean your colleagues?"

"Yeah, my girls."

O'Brien heard Daniels snicker. He ignored it. "Tell me about 'tranqing' Hector."

"He's a little guy. Born in captivity. He kept freaking, you know, so like we tranqed him so he'd chill." Kyle gnawed at pinky-nail with a ferocity that belied his casual attitude.

"You weren't upset by this?"

"I'm a grad student. I just put my hours in and keep my head down. Big ass primates, that's what I'm into. Apes... gorillas, that's what I'm talking about."

"And tranqing a big primate, that wouldn't upset you?"

"Hell, no. Those things could take your head off, man. If you're trying to get a radio tracker on them or some research material, they better be out and I mean totally."

O'Brien dismissed Kyle. Daniels said HQ texted him no outsider prints had been found on the cages and that campus security verified there were no suspicious vehicles on the facility lot. That all corresponded to an inside job.

"Who do you like for this? I still think it's the Russian or maybe the head of the facility, Dr. Hynes," Daniels said.

O'Brien turned to him. "Why would she? What's her motive?"

"She could get away with it. Maybe she'll get more funding if the University thinks radicals have targeted the facility."

"Why not Mr. Jenkins? He could've easily played pinball before or after releasing the monkeys."

"Nah, he's cool."

"A little too cool. His demeanor was over the top. I wonder if he always talks like a surf bum. Do a background check on all the employees and see if they were in animal rights organizations prior to working here. And see if we can get a search warrant for their cars. Those monkeys had to be transported somewhere if they haven't been seen."

O'Brien picked up the phone on Dr. Hynes' desk. "Give me a few minutes and send Sally Carter back in here."

O'Brien called the dean again and asked if what Dr. Hynes had said was true about getting another twenty rhesus macaques. The dean wasn't as optimistic as the head scientist. The cost of primates for research was astronomical and the missing barrel full of monkeys was negative publicity for the university. Besides, they'd learned about all they'd expected for the study already. Grant money was tight for future projects and unlikely to materialize.

Hanging up the phone, O'Brien nodded to himself. If Jeanie Hynes had a crisis of conscience she might still be a suspect. Then he went to the door and found Sally Carter waiting.

Sally returned to the seat across the desk. O'Brien leaned forward. "Did you release the monkeys from this facility?"

She leaned forward too. She looked directly into O'Brien's eyes. "No."

O'Brien leaned back. He scanned her employment evaluation. She had very high marks. "What's your specialty, Ms. Carter?"

"Behavioral psychology."

"So you would know most guilty parties look away or falter when lying."

"Yes. However, you must be aware that despite our best efforts, there would always be a 'tell'. Do you think you could lie effectively when asked a direct question?"

O'Brien stared at her over his cheaters. He leaned forward again. "Yes," he lied in a firm tone.

He knew she was guilty. The tell had been when she was angered over the collective noun for monkeys. Whether or not the tranquilizer had pushed her to make the decision, O'Brien couldn't be certain. What he was sure about was that she was methodical and meticulous. They'd never be able to prove anything. Perhaps the reason she didn't have an alibi is that she took advantage of her colleague's early delivery.

"Where do you think these monkeys are now?" O'Brien asked.

"No idea." Sally was back to short answers.

We covered a lot of ground. I thought at first, I'd been caught, but Hector, who rode on my back, had bitten me. A loud noise scared him. He didn't mean to bite.

We went in the direction the brown-haired one pointed. They often pointed when they wanted us in the cell cubes or on the silver rectangles. We traveled in the dark and then I saw them. They rose before us, huge cylinders like on the white square. I knew this meant something.

It wasn't until I found many trees with the red round objects I realized the smells were to lead me to my people. We ate the red round things. Water was harder to come by. Food was in all sorts of places. Big cylinders, huge cubes. We found water in a large square pond, but it tasted bitter. Maybe it would hurt us.

We traveled on. We hid from the enemy and ran from large wild beasts that travelled at amazing speed in straight lines one right after another, like elephants cross the land during migration. When I found rows and rows of trees with the small brown food-type objects the brown-haired one called nuts, I knew we were on the right path. The enemy, a stranger, chased us away. Escape was difficult that day.

For a while, we were lost. Then at the top of a hill I saw the pyramid. We loped toward it. In the valley far below I saw the big sphere up in the sky. We went into the valley and we searched for food and our brethren.

I couldn't find our kind until a strong wind came and I smelled them. We traveled a long distance. Finally, a large screen of silver diamonds rose before us, and one of our tribe watched from beyond it.

With a gesture, the rest of my people clung to the foliage of trees. A long bough brought me closer to my tribesman. I sat up at my full height. "I am the descendant of kings. I have brought my people to claim sanctuary."

"Welcome. Welcome. This is a safe place."

"Are you are trapped inside?"

"This place is safe. There are trees. There are our cousins and our kind. The enemy provides us food."

"Water? Do they have safe water?"

"Yes, yes!"

As he answered, two of the enemy came from a large rectangle. They stopped. One dropped a small cylinder. "Look, there's a monkey outside the sanctuary."

"You mean one got away?"

"No, I don't think he's one of ours."

I didn't know what their chittering was all about. I drew back, ready to flee.

"No. Stay. They won't hurt you here," my tribesman said.

I waited. We needed water. We needed it soon. The cylinder the enemy dropped contained water. I could smell it.

One of the sanctuary people spoke into a small rectangular box. An enemy agent came running. The other agents spoke to this new addition with deference. I assumed this female was in charge.

"Look there's a monkey outside," one of the enemy agents said. "He was chittering away to Bobby here on our side of the fence."

Their leader said, "Those may be the ones from the university facility."

"It's just him. Maybe he was somebody's pet," the enemy agent said.

Their leader shook her head. "No, there are several out there in the trees behind him. Look more closely. I bet he's in charge of this barrel of monkeys."

"Should we let them in?"

"We *should* report it. They were doing behavioral research, teaching them colors and shapes. If we let them in, we could lose our funding.

The sanctuary volunteers were dumbfounded. "So we let them go?"

The sanctuary boss thought for a moment. She observed the monkeys beyond the chain-link fence. "They must be thirsty. Lead them around to the east end of the sanctuary by carrying buckets of water. There are trees on that side, but the steep grade leading down to the highway means no one will ever build there. They could make a home in those trees. That way we could help them without actually breaking any rules."

One of the volunteers glanced at her boss and then back at the outside monkeys. "Will they stay if they're not contained?"

The sanctuary boss nodded. "If we feed and water them. Those monkeys know what's out there. It's no circus."

Weeks later, Sally Carter kept her sunglasses on while getting out of her car. She also wore a baseball cap she'd bought for the occasion, though she was a sports atheist. It had taken her less time to get here than it had the other times. Now she used the highway. She slammed the car door and snickered to herself. Daniels had found a quick sketch she'd made of the water treatment plant, the odd church on the hill shaped like a pyramid, and the bulbous water tower for this town that was within a mile of the sanctuary. The policeman had been thorough enough to find it wedged between the seat and the gearshift, but had made some smug quip about women drivers needing landmarks and tossed it into the backseat.

Sally walked through the sanctuary, apprehensive. She looked at the primates in the large enclosures with trees and toys and fresh air. After touring the place twice she was on her third stroll around when she noticed activity in the trees beyond the far back fence. She cast a look behind her. No employees in sight. She jogged toward the fence. There they were, maybe not in their natural habitat, but better than the sterile cages of the facility. Most of them kept to the foliage. A relieved sigh escaped her.

Sally turned to leave, but heard a cry somewhere from high in the trees. She looked back. She waved. Clinging to one of the female macaques was Hector, looking healthy, looking safe.

Linda Kay Hardie is an avid reader, writer, freelance editor, speaker and author of the children's picture book Louie Larkey and the Bad Dream Patrol. Linda teaches composition and humanities at the University of Nevada, Reno, to unwilling students.

When she saw a photo of a light fixture that looked jellyfish, she got lost in the Research Zone (similar to but scarier than the Twilight Zone). Unable to waste good research, she wrote this story.

Smack

by Linda Kay Hardie

Jellyfish are great. Don't you think so? I fell in love with them at an exhibit in the Monterey Bay Aquarium. Pulsating canopies with trailing tentacles, gliding through the water. Beautiful and fascinating. They're in every ocean in the world. And wonderful names: *Moon Jelly, Lion's Mane, Cannonball, Mauve Stinger.* The Box Jellyfish is actually cube shaped. Really! Some are so small you could fit three or four of them on your thumbnail, but the Lion's Mane is eight feet in diameter and 150 feet long. Jellyfish are older than the dinosaurs. They've been around maybe as long as 700 million years. There's even one species that is said to be immortal. Did you know the adult phase—the jellyfish we're used to seeing—is called a *Medusa?*

Ma'am, please. We need you to tell us what happened.

Yes, I know. Sorry.

I guess I was in a bad mood this morning. I thought I was feeling pretty good at first, but I guess I really wasn't, because Chuck said so.

"What's wrong?" he asked me.

"Uh. I don't know," I said.

195

"You look upset."

"I thought I felt fine."

"No, you definitely look upset. What's wrong?"

"I don't know."

I was definitely in a bad mood. I contemplated going back to bed, but I had to fix our breakfast, feed the cats, and clean the litter boxes. The dishwasher needed emptying, and I had to roll the garbage can and recycle bin out to the curb. I didn't have any classes on campus, but I had to grade papers. No wonder I was feeling bad. But it all had to be done, and there was no one else to do it. And I hoped to find the time somewhere to do some writing, even though I'm not very good.

How did you get the black eye, ma'am?

Oh, he didn't mean it.

Who didn't mean it?

Chuck. He was really sorry. It was mostly my fault. Kind of an accident. He was hungry, and I'd gotten busy with the laundry. There was just so much of it that I got behind and was late making lunch. He didn't mean to hit me, but his blood sugar was low, and that makes him impulsive and cranky. And he was sorry afterward. I was folding my jellyfish kitchen towels, the ones I got at the Monterey Bay Aquarium, and I lost track of time.

Did you know that jellyfish pulsate to move through the water, expanding and contracting their bells to push water behind or beneath them? They're so beautiful. Oh! Do you know what a group of jellyfish is called? That's not rhetorical; it's a real question.

Uh. A school? A swarm?

Good guess! There are several names for a group of jellyfish, and swarm is the boring one. Before I got into jellyfish, I didn't have any idea what they were called. I thought maybe it was a sandwich of jellies. Or a salad of jellies.

A salad, ma'am?

Have you ever seen a molded Jell-O salad? That looks a lot like a jellyfish, jiggling and pulsating. Besides swarms, there are blooms of jellyfish, which are very large, invasive groups of jellyfish. Those are dangerous. Climate change, overfishing—these things are thought to cause blooms. Jellyfish are better at surviving in extra-warm, low-oxygen conditions than most ocean life. The blooms can even tear fishing nets. They can mess up cooling equipment for power plants, and they once caused a blackout in the Philippines and damaged the Diablo Canyon Power Plant in San Luis Obispo.

But my favorite name for a group of jellyfish is a smack. I'm not sure how they got that name, although an apocryphal story says a nun in the fifteenth century wrote a book that included collective nouns for many sea animals, and she invented the name.

Another source I found says a smack of jellyfish is a descriptive name, invented by writers, that you could get smacked by the jellyfish's tentacles, which sting. I like the story about Dame Juliana Berners better. A noblewoman and prioress writing a book about naming collections of sea animals. She came up with a battery of barracuda, a shiver of sharks, and a turmoil of porpoises.

Ma'am. You're off topic again. We need you to finish your statement.

Right. I'm sorry.

I don't know what was different about today. I got the housework done not long after lunch, and I started grading papers. I'd gotten behind, so I had two classes' worth of English papers and one for Core Humanities. Essays take forever, at least for me. I'm glad English comp classes are smaller, only about twenty students each, but humanities clock in around thirty students per. I hadn't gotten very far when Chuck came into my office to talk to me. Today was one of those days when Chuck needed lots of attention. I tried to get him to let me finish the set of papers I was working on, but he wanted to talk about his day. Not that there was much to talk about. He'd been working at home, just like me, so I already knew what he'd been doing. He's a computer tech, has his own business, and he was fixing someone's fried computer. He wanted to tell me all the technical details of it and how he heroically figured out how to fix the unfixable.

"Honey, that's great, but I really need to get these papers graded. Can we talk about this in about an hour? I'll be at a stopping point," I said.

As usual, he ignored me and kept talking. So I put my pencil down and tried to pay attention. When he was growing up, he could never please his father, so he likes to tell me about his accomplishments. He's been working since he was fifteen. His father wanted him to go to college and he did, but he was expected to work full-time and pay his own way, so he wasn't able to finish. Besides, Chuck had already been working with computers for so long he knew more about the hands-on stuff than the professors.

When he took a breath, I said, "Why don't you follow me to the kitchen, and I'll start dinner?"

"Dammit, why do you always interrupt me? Geez, can't I even talk about my day without you blabbing on?" he said. He shot me a really dirty look.

But he did follow me, then once I started to chop vegetables, he realized it was news time, so he went to the living room to turn on the local station. It was too late to stop working on dinner, since I'd already started slicing the potatoes and couldn't leave them or they'd get brown, so I was kinda annoyed that he'd abandoned me again, but that's life. Once I'd gotten the meatloaf and scalloped potatoes into the oven, I went back to my papers. I had fifty minutes to grade more.

Chuck showed up just as I was getting into the next paper. He started talking again about how he'd fixed that computer. By the time he ran out of things to say, it was time for *Jeopardy* on TV, and he wanted me to watch it with him. It was nearly time for dinner to come out of the oven anyway.

I hoped Chuck would get an emergency call over the weekend to fix someone's crashed computer. Maybe I could get my papers done then. Of course, he would probably want me to go with him to watch him work. He always said he wanted to spend time with me. But he also wants me to do the driving. I get tired of doing all the driving, but what are ya gonna do? That's life.

I just wish Chuck could let me know he enjoys what I've cooked once in a while, but he only seems to notice food when he's unhappy with it. He wolfed down the scalloped potatoes and ate most of the meatloaf before he started to complain.

"What's this crap? Where's the vegetable? Why didn't we have a salad or something?" he said.

"I thought you liked my meatloaf," I said. Dinner started to feel like a bowling ball in my stomach.

"Meatloaf? I thought it was dog food," he said.

I smiled, thinking he was joking, because it's always important to recognize his jokes, but then he jumped down my throat.

"What's that smirk? Do you think it's funny to serve me this garbage?

I didn't know how to answer. I hate fighting with Chuck, because I can never win. I never seem to know what's going on. I just don't know what he wants me to say.

Why don't you say what you feel?

How can I know what I feel if I don't know what he wants to hear?

I said, "I'm sorry. I didn't mean to smile. I thought you liked my meatloaf."

"No. I don't like dog food," he said.

Suddenly I was scared. I had no idea where this was going, but it didn't feel like it would be anywhere good.

Speaking of nothing good, no one seems to know how many people are killed each year by jellyfish. The only numbers I've ever been able to find are that they kill twenty to forty people a year in the Philippines. Boy, the Philippines have big problems with jellyfish, don't they? Their tentacles are poisonous, you know. Jellyfish, I mean, not the Philippines. That's what makes them sting. Actually—technically—jellyfish are venomous, not poisonous.

What's the difference?

Poisonous means that if you eat it, you get sick or die. Venomous means if it stings or bites you, you get sick or die. So frogs can be poisonous, but snakes and spiders and jellyfish are venomous.

And the tentacles of jellyfish don't have stingers like bees. They actually have little harpoons they can shoot at you. Isn't that weird? And cool? Maybe you've heard that you should use urine to calm the sting of a jellyfish, but that will only make it worse, because hormones or something in the urine makes more of the little harpoons release their venom. Use vinegar. I think maybe it's in Australia where beaches have emergency stashes of vinegar for jellyfish stings. Some jellyfish can kill you.

Please, ma'am, I hate to keep nagging you, but the medical examiner has pronounced your husband dead and is removing the body. We'd like to get the rest of your statement. How did you get those bruises on your throat?

Yes. I'm sorry, officer.

Chuck was more agitated than usual, than I'd ever seen him. He started shouting at me. "You and your precious master's degree. You think you're so smart, don't you?"

I didn't know what to say. I just stared at him.

"Answer me when I speak to you!"

"No?" I didn't think any answer would be correct. I was right.

He stood up, dumping his plate onto the floor. "Why can't we have real food around here? We should have steak and baked potatoes once in a while. Meat and potatoes, not always these stupid casseroles and stuff."

Houdini appeared out of nowhere to start nibbling on the meatloaf on the carpet. The ketchup was really going to stain the beige carpet. Chuck liked neutral colors for the house. Our carpet was beige, the couch was light brown with darker brown patterns, and the chairs were off-white. It was all so hard to keep clean. I really wished for a bit of color somewhere, but for some reason he never explained, Chuck wanted everything neutral.

Chuck moved faster than I'd ever seen him move. My plate got dumped onto the floor, too. He almost stepped on Houdini.

"Watch out!" I said before he grabbed my throat.

It escalated so fast, it's kind of a blur.

One minute Chuck's got his hands on my throat and the next he's threatening my cats.

"You never do anything for me," he shouted into my face. "You think you're so smart, with your master's degree and your college job. All you care about is your job and your damn cats. They need to go, one way or another."

He shoved me to the floor.

Gypsy had come into the living room to see what the ruckus was all about. Chuck grabbed her by the scruff of her neck.

People think it's okay, because the mama cat picks up her tiny kittens that way. But an adult cat shouldn't be held like that, even a small cat like Gypsy. Chuck knew this. I realized he didn't care.

"Chuck, put her down," I said. I stood up. I was very calm. This was too much.

"Make me," he sneered, and turned his back on me, still holding Gypsy.

I grabbed the nearest weapon, which turned out to be Chuck's jellyfish paperweight. Three inches wide, seven inches tall, an elongated ovoid with a flat base. Chuck was so proud of that thing you'd think he gave birth to it himself. He wouldn't let me get one at the aquarium. All I was allowed to get were the jellyfish kitchen towels. He never let me touch that paperweight, but I found it fit my hand beautifully.

"Chuck!"

He turned when I shouted his name.

"Put that down, bitch," he said.

I ignored him. He took a step toward me. Gypsy squirmed out of his grasp and darted away. I was already swinging, and I smacked him in the side of the head, in the temple, with the paperweight.

It sounded like the time I dropped the watermelon on the driveway. Kind of a thud-squoosh.

And that's when you called 911, ma'am?

First, I chased down Gypsy to make sure she was okay. She was. Then I called.

Isn't it amazing? A smack of jellyfish saved my clowder of cats, my kindle of kitties. Aren't jellyfish great?

Helen O'Neill lives in South East London, spending her days project managing and her evenings, writing. She's been published in the UK and the US and is currently working on her first novel.

The Park Pack is inspired by the dogs and humans she met in a park close to her home. In typical fashion, everyone knows all the dogs by name, but none of the people. And isn't that just how it should be?

The Park Pack
by Helen O'Neill

The path through the woods was littered with orange leaves and horse chestnut shells. Bailey, my miniature schnauzer, doesn't like the prickles on his paws, so I picked him up and carried him. He wiped his muddy beard against my face to let me know he appreciated the lift, then wiggled to get free as soon as the prickles had cleared, leaving my jacket smelling of wet dog and my hands covered in woodland muck. I searched the bottom of my satchel for a tissue to clean up with and pulled out a roll of poo bags along with it. They unraveled all around me.

Bailey ran ahead, his grey tail swinging as he paused to push his nose into every bush and pile of leaves he passed. I followed him on his walk, returned crumpled poo bags to my satchel and smiled as we rounded the corner. Bailey rushed to join the circle of other dogs all looking up at a woman in faded jeans and a navy wax jacket. She was the Piped Piper of the park; her pockets were always full of treats.

Dogs of all shapes and sizes would leave their owners to worship at her boots. She stood under an ancient oak tree, believed to have been planted by the young Earl when he inherited the estate hundreds of years before. Its gnarled branches twisted up to the sky with a trunk so wide, generations of children and dogs had worn a shallow moat around it from their races. That day it sheltered a cluster of dogs, all sitting and staring at the Pied Piper, pleading, with puppy dog eyes to convince her they were starved and forgotten. Bailey knew the rules to that game. He gently raised his paw and watched her hand as it left her pocket to toss each dog a biscuit in turn. Most caught them mid-flight, but Ruby, the Piped Piper's own Labrador clamped her mouth shut, completely missing the treat and then frantically searched for it in the leaves before one of the more coordinated dogs could get it.

I'd prefer the woman didn't feed Bailey. He struggles with recall, or rather I struggle with his recall so I'm often forced to bribe him back from an adventure. The previous week he had managed to cross the shallow river that separates the lower field from the hill up to the old mansion. He had a wonderful time, pushing his nose through the undergrowth on the other side for nearly half an hour before I was able to convince him the treat in my hand was more desirable than whatever he smelled. I'd wondered what it was, but I thought it best not to know.

A big bulldog lumbered over and bumped Bailey aside to join the semi-circle. Bruce was a block of muscle and a face of slobber, but his heart was gentle, and he was careful around the younger pups. Bailey and Bruce had been friends since we started coming to the park. I'd got to know his owner, a tall slim man, one of those people who always seem to be impeccably dressed regardless of the weather, no muddy paw prints on his jeans.

While Bruce waited for his treat and the others realized there was a chance to earn another, our little pack of humans clustered in the damp, under a canopy of branches and chatted about the important news of the day. There was a rumor that the park we loved and enjoyed through the seasons was going to be re-developed. The estate had been donated to the community a century ago by the wealthy landowner who had died under mysterious circumstances. He left funds in his will to employ a grounds-man for maintenance and instructed the land should be open to the public. His magnificent house rested at the top of the hill, abandoned, looking down on the landscaped gardens, fields and woodland, its paint cracked, and windows boarded up. Dog walk-ers, cyclists and families kept the estate alive but it was a large space in an urban area, and the council saw it as an opportunity to generate extra funds.

A man made his way over to us and tussled the fur of his German shepherd, Max, who was in the circle. He was ex-army, tall as he was broad and covered in tattoos. He always had a tan and despite the cold, he wore a pair of combat shorts and a t-shirt, his only concession to the season being his brown-leather hiking boots. Max and his owner were always at the park. The rest of us had our routines and could generally be relied upon to meet up at about the same time on the same days each week, but you could almost guarantee that you'd meet Max every-time you were there, roaming the park from sunrise to sunset, rain, snow or blistering heat. I got the impression something had happened to the army veteran, but he never talked about it. We all assumed his rehabilitation centered around the companionship of the gentle Max and spending his days outdoors. Max adored him and while he would gladly claim his treat, it wasn't long before he returned to his companion's side, ever watchful, ever loyal.

It was the Veteran who had first shared the news about the development. He had talked to the groundsman who had men-tioned there had been "suits" around, taking measurements and pictures. Since then there had been further sightings of people who had no place in our park, but no official news. I guessed we were safe for a little while yet.

We stood with our four dogs, feeling the sun on our faces as it broke through the clouds and crept through the canopy; the Piped Piper, the Impeccable Man, Veteran, and me, and our dogs playing or sniffing in the undergrowth. Our casual chat was inter-rupted as a young woman ran towards us, holding her phone up as she approached,

"Have you seen Jack?" she asked, and I looked at the picture of an adored Yorkie, his head tipped to the side and tinsel around his neck. "He ran off and I can't find him."

We confirmed we'd not seen Jack and took the young wom-an's number. I plugged in "*Jack's Human*" to my phone, telling her that we would head out around the park to look for him. We all knew the feeling of fear when you lose sight of your dog and they don't come when called. We'd all heard the stories of beloved pets who had been found wandering along the side of the railway or worse still, those that had been presumed stolen and never seen again. We were a friendly community and looked out for each other's furry friends. We separated to start the search, with promises to let each other know when Jack had been found. It never occurred to me that he wouldn't be.

I latched Bailey onto his lead, much to his disdain. He tolerated lead walks, but much preferred to amble along at his own pace, taking detours, taking his own good time. We headed up the path to the right, the Piped Piper and Ruby went left, the Impeccable Man and Bruce, the path behind, and the Veteran and Max wove their way through the undergrowth, following paths only they knew.

Our route took us toward the old mansion, and although I was focused on the search, I was, as always, taken aback by the beauty of the old building. I could imagine the owner welcoming visitors up the long gravel pathway, now overgrown with weeds. The giant wooden doors would have been wide open, letting out the light from the latest party. Guests would enter, sparkling in their finery. It's still magnificent, but time has taken its toll, with rotted windowsills and ivy climbing untamed up the walls.

Bailey pulled on his lead, which wasn't like him. He seemed keen to search the raised flowerbed to our side. The groundsman still maintained small areas such as this. The beds were tidy, facing a row of benches where people could sit and enjoy the seasons.

My phone vibrated in my satchel and I pulled it out to read the message,

"No sign in the lower field."

That was good news. The lower field was where the fence to the train tracks was and we were always complaining to the council to fix it. The metal chains designed to keep children from venturing over there were often broken, either by the children themselves or by the foxes that buried underneath.

Bailey tugged at me again, impatient to continue the search, so, with a guilty look over my shoulder I placed my boot on the edge of the raised flowerbed and we ascended. I'd never normally let him pull me off the tracks in this way, but I'd also never forgive myself if I didn't search this part of the park and Jack was later found there. We made our way through the dirt path between the flowers. I pulled my elbows in tight to avoid pricking myself on the rose bushes and it wasn't too long before we emerged at the top, through a gap in the hedge.

I'd never been in that part of the grounds before. These were the old allotments, set up during the war to help with the effort. Plots had been laid out in equal areas for different types of vegetables but it was many years since they had been used. All that remained were a few stone markers pressed into the ground, presumably to indicate who owned the plot. The plots themselves were overgrown with an assortment of wild flowers and grasses, as if the space itself were remembering the fallen.

Bailey tugged and I followed. We were soon standing in the middle of the space, protected on three sides by an old stone wall. I searched the area and was rewarded by the slightest swish in the corner of my eye, a tail, from a little dog who was on an adventure.

We approached carefully. I didn't know Jack and he could have easily been spooked and run away. Bailey wagged his tail and Jack looked up at him, pulling his nose from the mud where he had enjoyed digging a hole. Jack tilted his head to the side in exactly the same pose he had made in the photo. I crouched, called his name and offered him one of the few treats I had hidden in my bag. I ignored the look of disgust from Bailey.

Jack considered. The hole was very enjoyable, but maybe he could get the treat and then get back to his digging. As he thought about it, I leaned forward with my arm outstretched. He made his decision and ran over, sniffed, and then carefully took the treat from my hand. I stroked him and grabbed his collar.

When the young woman answered my call, she was on the other side of the estate, searching the side paths in the woodland. I could hear the soft snapping of twigs beneath her wellingtons as she rushed to where we were. I made myself comfortable, stroking Bailey and Jack to keep them both entertained until she found us.

When she burst through the hedge her cheeks were flushed and she joined me on the ground, scooping Jack up into her arms. Calmer after she had checked Jack for injuries and found none, she explained she was new to the area and this was the first time they had visited the park. Jack was little more than a puppy and was still training. His recall was pretty good, but he had got the scent of something and he'd just run off.

She cried a little, with relief I'm sure. We sat for a while, our waterproof coats tucked under us to protect us from the damp ground. She seemed nice and Jack was a lovely little dog who would fit in well. We did a ring round to let the others know he was safe and then we parted, going back to our lives outside the bubble of the estate.

Autumn turned to winter. In the mornings the muddy fields were frozen, blades of grass coated in crisp white frost that crunched underfoot. The parks fair-weather visitors went into hibernation. They'd return in the spring, but for a few months the estate was just for us. The Veteran conceded long trousers were now required and he even wore a pair of cotton gloves on some of the colder days. On misty mornings, Max would appear through the fog, his majestic form quite imposing, especially if you didn't know him. I wrapped up warm to go to the park, two pairs of socks, thermal base layer, normal long-sleeved top, fleece, coat and padded gloves. Even my wellies were insulated. I'd learned the hard way how cold your toes get on a winter's day without this investment.

Jack's owner, the Young Woman, became part of our group and I saw her most weekends. She'd rung the dog walker the Pied Piper had recommended, so Jack visited the park when she was at work too. He wasn't afraid now that he knew the layout and would often decide which route they would take on a given day. We shared stories of our dog's adventures. They seemed to enjoy visiting the other side of the river and although Bailey normally preferred to keep his feet dry, there was something there that was so enticing it called him over on more than one occasion. We'd also found the allotment area had a draw. Even Max had decided to explore its hidden walls.

On New Year's Day, it was bright and sunny. You could see your breath in front of you as the world woke up to its resolutions. My new flask, a Christmas present, was filled with coffee, ready to take with me. I clipped on Bailey's lead. We always enjoyed watching the New Year walkers going for their exercise, full of good intentions to get fit and breathe fresh air to clear their heads from the celebrations of the night before. These visiting walkers would enter the park by the main gate, in their jeans and trainers and pick their way across the puddles and through the mud.

Some would be cross when an excited young pup jumped up to say hello, to check if their hands were in their pockets because they were holding treats. They didn't know the rules in the park and looked at us with distrust when we smiled and said good morning. They weren't used to people they didn't know speaking to them. Their responses ranged from a half smile to completely ignoring us as if they were passing someone they used to know but didn't want to acknowledge.

As Bailey and I reached the gate, I saw someone had clipped a lost poster to the railings and I stopped to take a look, to note the number on the poster in case I saw the missing dog on our route around the park. The poster had been printed in color and I was shocked to see that it was showing a picture of Bruce, the Impeccable Man's bulldog.

The Veteran, on the other side of the main field, wore a light sweatshirt and a pair of combat trousers, Max gliding by his side. Some of the visitors diverted from their course to avoid the pair, judging, with a glance, the breed of dog and the bulk of the man. Bailey and I did the opposite and crossed the field to join them, to share our walk and to ask after Bruce. The Veteran nodded a good morning as we approached and Bailey ran ahead raising his nose to Max in greeting.

"Have you heard anything?" I asked and he shook his head. Bruce had been missing since the day before and the few people that had still been in the park before dusk had spent the last of the daylight searching for him. The Impeccable Man had returned at sunrise to put up posters. He and his family had spent New Year's Eve printing, as well posting on every social media platform they could find, asking for help. His eight-year-old son was with him today, handing out flyers to visitors, hoping the increased footfall the estate got on this day would work in their favor.

Bailey and Max suddenly left our group and ran forward towards the entrance to the woodland area. Here the path narrowed and turned from stone to wood-chip. They trotted past a couple who froze at the sight of Max approaching, fear in their eyes as the beautiful beast came near and then brushed past.

As expected, the Piped Piper was standing just inside the entrance to the woods. Max and Bailey took up their positions in front of her, sitting and waiting. There were no other dogs with her today and the absence included Ruby. The Pied Piper tossed a treat to Bailey and Max and then reached out her hands to the Veteran who took hold of them gently.

"I can't find her." She was nearing tears. "She never leaves me and then she just ran off when I was chatting to one of the visitors. I can't lose her, I just can't."

We split up. Now there were two of our park family missing and around six hours of daylight left. Bruce had already been out overnight, so we could only hope he had been able to keep warm.

"I've done the circuit once already today," the Veteran said, "so they must be either off the main paths or…" he didn't have to say it, they had been stolen, every owner's worst nightmare.

"I'll take the far side of the river and the allotment." I said. I was the only one of us in wellies so it would be easiest for me to wade through.

"I'll take the mansion and make my way there from the other direction," said the Veteran. He instinctively took hold of the Pied Pipers hand. "You can come with me." She was in no state to search alone.

This time Bailey didn't resist when I clipped on his lead. It was like he understood that this time was different, this wasn't a puppy on an adventure, these were mature well-trained dogs that never left their humans and we needed to find them.

When we reached the river, the banks were slippery and Bailey's paws were quickly coated in muddy socks. It was lucky that it hadn't rained recently, and the water flowed gently over the gravel bed, making our way across easy enough. Bailey scrambled up the root network that made up the steep bank on the other side. I dropped his lead to pull myself up, not caring that my leather gloves got dirty.

On the other side, the plateau was covered in ivy and moss. We began a methodical search, Bailey sniffing while I swept my feet from side to side, gently, in case I came across a clue to one of the missing dogs. When we had searched the area, we made our way out onto the field where we approached every tree, searching around it, every bush, searching inside it. We zigzagged across the field until we eventually made our way to the base of the driveway leading up to the mansion. Bailey tugged. He had the scent of something and once again I let him pull me up onto the raised flowerbed, through the hedge and into the walled allotment.

The corner where little Jack has been digging all those months ago was hidden behind long grass. I pushed it aside and discovered a pile of earth surrounding a hole and held my breath with hope that maybe this was the answer to the mystery. The naughty dogs had been digging for freedom. My hope grew when I realized the size of the hole and more importantly, there was a bright red collar, Ruby's collar, resting on the earth mound. Bailey tugged to get free, to follow his friends no doubt, but there was no way I was going to let him.

Instead, I plunged my knees into the cold earth and stuck my head into the chamber calling out for Ruby and Bruce. Moments later a mud-covered flat face appeared, shining black eyes looking back at me. Bruce wiggled out and bumped against me, nearly knocking me over. I rustled his head and told him how much worry he'd given us. He snorted mud out of his nose to let me know he understood.

As I rang the Impeccable Man, a golden face popped up, flecked with dirt. Ruby wriggled her way out and shook her long coat to free herself from the soil and leaves attached to it. I made another call, and sat on the ground with Bailey's lead under me to secure him, my hands free to hold the two mischievous dogs.

When the Pied Piper ran to us, she stumbled, and then hugged Ruby tight, not bothering about how muddy she was. Max and the Veteran followed and stood a safe way back watching the scene. The Impeccable Man and his son were next, the boy breaking away from his father to embrace Bruce, letting Bruce lick tears of joy from his face.

When the reunions had finished, and everyone had caught their breath, the Veteran crouched and looked into the hole.

"There must be something down there if the dogs are so keen to explore."

Max was flat alongside him, his chin resting on the entrance, his nose searching for possibilities.

"Go on then boy, fetch." The Veteran gave Max permission and the large dog squeezed himself into the space. Minutes ticked by but when he returned, he held something in his mouth. He looked up at the Veteran and waited for the command.

"Drop." Max opened his mouth and out fell a small stone. The Veteran bent to retrieve it, wiped it clean and held it up to the light.

"Diamond?" he said. Max had returned to the hole and we repeated the process. Stone after stone was brought back, until morning become afternoon and there was a little pile of sparkling rocks on the leafy floor.

I emptied my satchel into my pockets and we filled it with the precious cargo. We left the allotment and made our way back to the main park. Jack came running over and jumped up to my bag to sniff it before taking his place at the Piped Piper's feet.

We filled the Young Woman in on our excitement. She invited us back to her flat, just a few minutes' walk from the park so we could discuss what to do next.

The flat was warm. The floor covered in towels to catch the mud from winter walks, the sofa covered in throws because Jack preferred it to his bed. The Young Woman filled two large bowls with water and placed them alongside Jack's smaller bowl.

The dogs drank, then found a place to rest. Bailey borrowed one of Jack's toys and took it out to the hallway to see if it would squeak. Max rested by the Veteran, sitting just on the edge of his feet. Jack jumped up to what was clearly his spot on the sofa. The Young Woman made us all tea and gave all of the dogs a treat or two, and then we began to discuss what to do about our find.

The stones were the property of the estate. We all agreed, we should really hand them in, but we could also use them to save our park, couldn't we? We had to think and act with care. The Young Woman clicked on her laptop and researched what she could of the law, finding it to be unhelpfully vague. In the end we decided. We would speak to the groundsman. He was the only person that knew the estate better than we did. We would hand the stones to him and let him decide how they should be used.

On New Year's Day, the sun was setting when we arrived. The small house had been converted from one of the estate's outbuildings. The Veteran knocked and we all clustered round waiting for it to open. The groundsman welcomed us but with a confused look on his face, not expecting a visit from these five friends of the land he cherished.

We explained what we had found. He was overjoyed at the news. Although his family had never lived in the mansion, he was the last living descendent of the late Earl. He loved the grounds and had dedicated his life to maintaining them for the use of the community, just as his grandfather wanted. He'd heard legends of treasure, of course, but then all old families had these myths. He'd never believed it.

I opened the bag so he could see for himself. The Piped Piper caught him as he stumbled in shock.

It is a beautiful winter's day. The air is crisp and you can see your breath in front of you as you walk. As I enter the park, I see the familiar sight of the Veteran patrolling the borders of the fields, making sure the new fences along the railway line are secure. His maroon park uniform is as distinctive as the large German shepherd who accompanies him.

I let Bailey off the lead and he runs to the corner where the Pied Piper has set up a marquee for visitors to purchase treats for their dogs, asking only for a small donation to benefit the estate. Bailey joins the row of dogs waiting patiently for their owners to catch up and provide them with their biscuit.

Jack is playing with another terrier in the middle of the field. He's found a little friend the same age and it's lovely to see the young ones run off their energy. The Young Woman is standing to the side, chatting with the Impeccable Man. His son is playing with the dogs, running one way, then the next. They will sleep well tonight.

Not much has changed since we found the stones. The developments were called off. The groundsman asked the Veteran to help him with the upkeep of the park. The mansion has been re-opened. We all dedicate some of our free time to help bring it back to life. The jewels we found are not enough to restore it completely, but we are taking a room at a time and giving each a new purpose. The ground floor now has a coffee shop and a room where local children can come and do crafts. The attic has been transformed into an artist's studio. The groundsman runs a weekly tour of the estate, telling the story of the grandeur of its past and how our dogs solved the mystery of the missing jewels.

New people come and go. Some stay and find their own routine, slotting into our community. New pups join the park pack. I watch the seasons change, see the bluebells coat the woodland floor, the horse chestnut shells drop in the autumn. Bailey still doesn't like their prickles on his paws. I go to retrieve him from the Pied Piper.

Shielia Rizer's had jobs from retail clerk to reading and writing tutor. Retirement has allowed her to spend quality time with the people living in her head. Along with her short stories, there's a novel in its second incarnation.

She says the gift for the fourth day of Christmas is four colly—definitely not—calling birds. Discovering a group of blackbirds is called a cloud, she found the alliteration and ensuing inspiration irresistible and shared.

A Cloud of Colly Birds
by Shielia Rizer

They sat in the last of a row of eight identical booths. On the wall beside them hung a framed calligraphic rendering of eleven lines from Wendell Berry's poem *The Handing Down.* The woman with her back to the kitchen access looked up and focused on the description of swifts in the night sky, *"the black flight of swifts."*

At 11:15 a.m., in the crowded sanctuary of the First Baptist Church, she had read those words—had read aloud the entirety of the poem's seventh section titled, *The Heaviness of His Wisdom.*

At 11:55 a.m. her companion had sung the song whose lyrics adorned a space beside the third booth. McCartney. *The White Album.* Blackbird.

These two black on white pieces and the other blackbird themed expressions that were exhibited in the Four and Twenty were the result of the loving craftsmanship of Ula Lorenson, Cousin Ula… Ula with the large dark eyes and the long raven-colored hair… Ula who loved to explain—when occasionally a visitor would mistakenly interpret the sign hanging from a pole above the entrance to the gray stone building to be a declaration of the establishment's operating hours—that the *Four and Twenty* painted in black script on the oaken dodecagon was a reference to the number of blackbirds that had reportedly serenaded the king when they were released from a pie.

For three generations this eatery occupied the space catty-cornered from Graham's pharmacy and directly across Poplar Street from Calton Ridge's city hall. From the July day in 1925 when Jace Lorenson had launched the Four and Twenty, it had served as an unofficial extension of that government edifice. The city fathers often congregated there to discuss civic difficulties and to devise plans to deal with those problems.

Jace's wife, Hannah, had suggested the name for their business. She loved the songs of the blackbirds who claimed as their territory the woods behind the Lorenson's log cabin home. Jace was glad of the cabin's location—between the woods and the restaurant—when the time came that Hannah left the kitchen of the Four and Twenty and began the raising of their son. and then another son.

In 1973, Jace retired and handed over the running of the Four and Twenty to his sons. Logan and Asher were then twenty-six and twenty-seven years old respectively. They had recently come back to Calton Ridge after eight years in the United States Marine Corps, years that included meritorious service for which each of them was awarded the Bronze Star Medal.

On the day of their return to Calton Ridge, Poplar Street was decked in flags and balloons and bunting of red, white, and blue. Speeches were made by local dignitaries, and joyful tears shed by family, friends, and sweethearts. The high school marching band played Sousa's *Semper Fidelis*, and Logan and Asher humbly expressed their gratitude for the welcoming ceremony and got on with their lives. It was only to each other that they ever spoke concerning their meritorious service.

It pleased them to be able to grant to their parents the next thirty years in which to survey the many trails through the Calton Woods and the many volumes on the bookshelves of the Lorenson home. As time passed, Jace and Hannah were accompanied on their explorations by their three granddaughters.

Logan's twins, Anna and Norrie, and their cousin Ula, Asher's only child, were fascinated by and devoted to Grams and Grandpa. Even after the girls became valued part-time employees of the Four and Twenty, the teenagers made time to spend with their grandparents a scheduling priority. This remained the case after the girls enrolled in the nearby University of Kentucky at Calton Ridge—a land grant institution established in 1867.

Along with their liberal arts curriculum, they studied business management, nutrition, and, at Grams' suggestion, ornithology.

Following their graduation the young women spent 2002 and 2003 in visiting eleven of Europe's sovereignties and forty-nine of America's United States. After this Grand Tour they entered into an extended internship and then a partnership in a business that seemed more a member of the family than an enterprise.

In 2010 the culinary mantel was passed on to the trio; the brothers, with their pipes and their books and a copper-haired water spaniel named Francis spent most of the afternoons of their retirement alternately in two of the rockers on Logan's front porch or in the two recliners beside the fireplace in Ashton's den. From *them indoors* there was never any complaint about their men being underfoot.

Since the emergence of the Four and Twenty on that July morning in 1925, Calton Ridge had grown from a small, friendly farming district into a thriving—and still friendly—destination for people on holiday. Every season had its lures. There was a profusion of Kentucky wildflowers in the spring, and the cool waters of Lake Estelle in the summer. By early September the reds, oranges, purples, and yellows of the northern hills were ablaze along Calton Ridge. December and January's temperatures often teased with the promise of snow and perhaps a frozen pond.

"No matter the time of the year, people will always flock to the Four and Twenty," Hannah Lorenson had been fond of saying.

In 2013 this was still true.

There still was no twenty-four hour service under the cousins' management, but the doors were open—hours posted—

every day of the year. On Easter, Thanksgiving, and Christmas a brunch was served for travelers, local residents who preferred not to cook, and those having no one with whom to share a holiday meal.

That day, that December Friday, the doors of the Four and Twenty were closed and the windows were dark.

In their booth, Anna and Norrie felt the eeriness of the absence of movement and the dearth of sound around them. Each was loath to speak of the thing that occupied her total consciousness. Neither had truly consented to the brittle fact of their loss. Perhaps their silence could hold off that awful moment of actual acceptance.

Looking across the table and into her sister's eyes—into her own eyes—Norrie discerned the images that were churning in their green depths and felt the need to activate some sensory switch that would put an end to the relentless replay.

Fingers of sunlight brushed away the last vestiges of dove gray and slate blue. Bundled against the biting morning air, they pulled the blackbird wagon to the feeder behind the house into which they had settled after taking over the handling of the Four and Twenty.

Grams had begun the tradition of the blackbird wagon. Three days a week she would haul a load of wild bird seed, or berries and fruits to the high, wide, fifteen-foot perch. Recently, Norrie had introduced a new item on the avian menu. She developed a vegetarian suet comprised of vegetable shortening, peanut butter, oats, corn meal and bird seed.

Combining the ingredients took a good deal of time, as their repurposed industrial mixer could process only eight quarts at a time. Once blended, the mixture was poured into foot square, stainless steel baking pans and placed in the twenty-five year old chest freezer that sat in the garage beside the bags of seeds. After several hours the suet bricks were ready to be distributed. The recipe had been an immediate success with the appreciative, if somewhat impatient, diners.

On that morning as Ula and her cousins passed the holly and hawthorns that created a hedge several yards before the feeder, they heard what they recognized as a territory alarm coming from the woods. Something had frightened the flock.

A loud wha-shing pierced the birds' call, and a cloud of ebony feathered creatures deserted their shelter and filled the sky.

"Somebody's shooting at our birds," Anna exploded.

"Get down!"

She and Norrie landed hard onto the rimy ground beside Ula.

Ula.

Blood.

Ula and blood.

There was a red stream cutting across the pink and green stripes of Ula's favorite sweater.

Anna pulled her phone from her hip pocket and summoned help.

Glancing over her sister's shoulder, Norrie saw the kitchen door swing open to admit their mâitre d into the dining room. Truth Rosenberg approached their booth and slid onto the bench beside Anna, reaching across the table to touch Norrie's hand, resting on the table.

"Is it okay for the crew to begin setting up the buffet?"

Anna checked her watch, nodded and said, "Truth, thank you again for keeping things running these past two weeks."

Truth hugged her, treating Anna to the coconut and hibiscus fragrances drifting from her multitude of dense, shining curls.

"You might not have noticed that I took down the piece over the fifth booth. I thought it might upset the family and Nick. I brought in the sketch Ula made for me to replace it."

"You were right," Norrie said.

The twins could quote all of Ula's creations. The one Truth had removed was the first verse of Tennyson's *The Blackbird.*

O blackbird! sing me something well:

While all the neighbors shoot thee round,

I keep smooth plats of fruitful ground

Where thou may'st warble, eat and dwell.

"So, I'll send out the food and take up my station by the back door."

Invitations to this afternoon's observance had been hand-delivered to twenty friends. Each person had been instructed to use the rear entrance and present their black-on-ivory cards. No unexpected faces would make their way past Truth.

She stood and started away.

"Oh, I almost forgot to mention that there will be one extra person. You'll recognize her. It's Dr. Moore from the university."

Truth tucked her chin and stared at the sisters through her thick lashes.

"Red hair and big gray eyes?"

"That's her," Anna said. "I don't know how she found out about our plan for today. She may have heard someone at UKCR mention it. She called this morning and offered to join us in her capacity as a psychiatrist, in case anyone needed to talk. I was taken completely off-guard. I couldn't think of a civil way to say 'no.'"

"She comes for lunch every Wednesday," Truth told them. "I noticed the day because it's when *The Bosses* take some time off."

"And the day," Norrie wistfully added, "when Nick would have lunch with Ula before their hikes through Calton Woods."

They were momentarily silent in honor of those Wednesdays.

"Maybe she's just trying to make friends," Truth speculated. "She never has a companion for her meals. I'll introduce her around the room."

Those gathered in the dining room that afternoon were the sorts of people that you wanted near you in hard times. Members of the staff, who rose occasionally to check the buffet or refill a glass, were among them.

Truth was seated between Anna and Nick Whitman. Nick and the three cousins had known one another since kindergarten. He and Ula had been looking forward to a wedding in the not-too-distant future. This was still the case for Anna and her high school sweetheart, Frank Andrews. Both ceremonies would have taken place on the day that Norrie and her best beloved, Kay Dunn, could legally join them in their walk down the aisle.

The pact between the three couples was common knowledge among Calton Ridge's citizenry. Any number of teenage females had notebooks filled with future great novels based on their story.

Truth studied the man beside her. The usually bright eyes were dull with a pain underscored by dark circles. His shaggy hair did little to disguise the hollows that had formed in his cheeks during the last two weeks.

Anna leaned forward and spoke around Truth.

"Nick, what do you know about Arlene Moore?"

His answer was preceded by a heavy sigh of disinterest.

"She hasn't been at UKCR for long... maybe six months. She's filling the space left when Jeff Collins unexpectedly retired. I have heard colleagues mention that she tries too hard... to fit in and force friendships. I hadn't thought to ask why she's here."

"She called and offered her professional shoulder for anyone who needed to talk... or, I suppose, to cry."

"I have a great respect for her profession," Nick said, *"I ain't that lonely yet."*

It was one of Ula's favorite songs. She had liked the words and the echo of a twang in Dwight Yoakam's voice.

Ula's music was playing now.

In the center of the floor, there was always left open, a space that would have accommodated five of the Four and Twenty's round tables. Ula had been of the opinion that you never knew when somebody might take a notion to Tennessee waltz in the middle of lunch hour.

Roger Miller had just gotten into Kris's song about a worthless kind of freedom when Sheriff Rod Williams stopped behind Norrie's chair and tapped her on the shoulder. Smiling up at him, she left her seat and followed him to the dance floor.

Losing herself in the comfort of his arms, as she had done through four years of sock hops and gala fetes at Calton Ridge High School, she was surprised by his opening words.

"I appreciate your letting me be here today, Norrie."

He gave the fingers of her right hand the gentlest embrace.

"Why wouldn't we want you with us?"

He hesitated; she allowed him the time and space to pull together his reply.

"For starters, I haven't done much towards finding the person who... did this to Ula."

"Rod, everybody in Calton Ridge knows that you've had almost nothing to go on. No tracks, no shell casing. Even the dogs that the State Troopers brought in spent hours following two different scents in two different directions and found nothing. All you have is…"

All he had was the bullet that Dr. Sands had removed from Ula's body.

"I suppose I could call for everyone to surrender their rifles for testing."

He grunted, and she felt the back and forth motion of his head.

"Which would be pointless, because the guilty person is probably in possession of an unregistered weapon. Norrie, it was Ula. What possible motivation could there be? I keep going in circles. I was almost ready to listen to an idea that that professor from UKCR was talking about."

"Arlene Moore?"

"Yeah. She came by the station last week to see if she could be of any help. I explained that we didn't even have anything to start building a profile from. I could tell that she didn't want to bring it up, but she mentioned the fact that sometimes a jilted lover can turn violent. She and I knew that she was trying to not accuse Nick. Hell, Norrie, she might as well have suggested that I would do something vicious to get back at you."

Neither of them spoke, letting Dolly and Porter sing the bittersweet tale about *a picture that I carry*.

The group around her table was discussing that year's movie about Jackie Robinson when Rod returned her to the seat beside her best beloved.

"You're a lucky lady," he said to person who had left him with just little things to remember.

At ten o'clock, Asher and Monica announced their intention to leave. Slowly, after their departure, the room emptied. Anna and Norrie helped their staff to clean up and ready the place for morning.

When the only task remaining was that of returning the cooking utensils to their hooks above the work island, Anna said that she and Norrie would finish. With hugs and soft words the crew left the twins to their kitchen and their memories.

"When we finish here," Norrie said, "I suppose who should try to save that botched batch of suet."

They had been working early that morning on a new supply of suet bricks. Distracted, they had both added 1½ cups of oil to the ingredients in the stainless steel mixing bowl.

"I think that we can just use a bigger bowl and balance out what we already have with some more dry ingredients," Norrie suggested.

Anna reached towards the drying rack to retrieve a large copper-bottomed sauté pan.

"We may as well…"

She was interrupted by a knock.

Anna shot a questioning look at her sister and went to glance through the small rectangle of glass towards the top of the heavy metal door.

"It's Arlene Moore," she said.

Norrie joined her sister as Anna unlocked the door and admitted the professor.

"I'm glad that I caught you here," she said as she pulled her bright red, ankle length coat more tightly around her. "I wouldn't have wanted to bother you once you were home."

"Actually we were heading out at this very moment," Anna smiled.

She was in no mood for any more company or conversation this evening. No doubt Norrie was also ready for the sanctuary of the cabin.

"I won't keep you for long. I just wanted to thank you again for inviting me to the memorial. I haven't been very successful in my attempts to get to know people in town or at the college. You'd think that someone who studies people would be better at making friends. It's going to be so important that people accept me as one of them when… well, you know."

Anna looked from her sister to their unwanted visitor.

"What are you talking about?"

"My first week here, I overheard two of my students talking about the arrangement that the six of you have… had. It was hard for me to accept that it was the truth. There was something totally medieval about it. But when I asked around—casually—people confirmed what the girls had been saying. Don't misunderstand me. I see nothing wrong with gay marriage… but to involve normal people in some quest for your equality seemed a bit unfair."

Norrie interrupted the rambling.

"Arlene, I don't think that we owe you any explanations or defenses, but you might be interested in knowing that our pledge was Nick's idea. I suppose that you've noticed that he is one of the normal people."

"Yes. I've certainly noticed."

The blue eyes gleamed as an actual smile surged through the muscles of her face.

"And now that I know it was his idea, it all makes sense," she said in a high delighted squeal.

Maybe to you, Anna thought.

"Nick is such a kind person," the psychiatrist explained to them. "You were all just teenagers when he became entangled with Ula. When he was old enough to realize his mistake, he had to find a way to delay having to hurt her."

She paused and looked from one to the other.

"I suppose then," she finally picked up the completely loose thread, "that I've done things in the wrong order."

She focused on Norrie as a troubled expression took hold of her features.

"I should have begun with you, but I thought if you were out of the way, he might actually marry her. But now, I suppose he would have been forced to tell her the truth. I'm really sorry."

She paused and seemed to be considering her next word or her next move.

"There was no need to kill her. If you were gone… I mean that since I wasn't a part of the pledge, it wouldn't apply to Nick and me. Would it?"

For several moments she seemed lost in her thoughts.

"And now," she sighed," I've said too much, and I'll have to get rid of both of you. If you told Nick, he might not understand."

This person had killed their cousin and now was expressing her regrets at having to do away with them as well.

Anna reached for her sister's hand and eased her to a position in front of the draining rack.

"Do you think that we're going to just march into the field and let you pick us off?"

"And anyway," Norrie came up with some fast improvisation, "if the two of us died in the same way as Ula and then you and Nick got together... Sheriff Williams might get suspicious and reopen the case."

The once and future killer inclined her head towards her potential victims.

The smile had receded, but now flooded back across her visage.

"There's that freezer in the garage. I've heard that you use it when you make your bird food. When they find your bodies in a day or two, I'll tell people that I had spoken with you before I left and that I was worried about your moods."

There was another pause followed by a sigh.

"Do you think that the sheriff would believe it was a suicide pact? Everyone knows how close the three of you were."

Anna wasn't prepared to travel any further down this particular rabbit hole.

"We are not going out to the garage and climb into a deep freeze."

Arlene Moore's hand slid into the pocket of her beautiful red coat and came out with a fist full of black metal.

It wasn't a rifle, but Anna felt pretty sure that it could do a lot of damage. She tightened the grip on her twin's fingers. With her free hand she felt behind her for the heavy pan that had not been hung back in its accustomed spot.

"I won't speak for you, Norrie, but if I'm going to die, I'd just as soon do it here in a warm building."

"Are the pair of you going to be difficult?"

Anna jerked her head towards the back door; the movement temporarily distracted Moore, and Anna clutched the shining utensil and swung hard at the hand holding the gun. The mad woman groaned and went down on her knees, cradling the injured fingers as the gun slid across the floor.

The twins made their way around the work island and out the back door. Halfway down the bricked path to the cabin, they became aware of the footsteps behind them.

Was there the chance that she might have recovered her weapon and could possibly summon the strength to fire at them?

"Keys, in my jacket pocket," Norrie gasped. "Back in the kitchen." She veered off of the path and towards the garage, which was seldom locked. The sound of Moore's high-heeled boots came on behind them.

They managed to hoist up the door, and Anna was pulling her cell phone from the pocket of her slacks when their pursuer reached them.

She raised the gun. It was clutched in both hands.

"Now I'll have to come up with another way to explain your deaths."

The tone held more petulance than anger.

Norrie wondered when that *click* had sounded inside of Arlene Moore's head and why nobody had heard it.

"Arlene, what if we just promise never to tell?"

Anna had always admired her sister's powers of imagination. Norrie continued.

"Why take a chance on being arrested and ruining all the plans you've made? Who'd take care of Nick if they put you in jail?"

Arlene Moore cocked her head to one side and narrowed her eyes. Concentrating seemed to be growing more difficult for her.

"What if you got mad at me one day and told?"

"We'd never do that," Norrie continued to distract and stall her opponent.

Scanning the garage for a tool that she could use as a weapon or a shield, Anna's gaze lit upon the eight-quart bowl sitting beside the mixer. Lunging, she grabbed it and slung its contents to the floor in front of Arlene as she took a step closer to her prey.

Her feet made contact with the extra oily mixture and the crazed woman screamed as she went down hard, face first into the slimy mess.

The sisters ran from the garage. They veered around the hedge and dashed towards the woods. Just before they reached the safety of the sheltering trees, they heard her fire again. They both dropped to the ground and began crawling slowly towards the woods.

There was another shot, and then there came a loud grunt as she either tripped or slid and fell.

Anna and Norrie stood and ran the last few yards and into the woods.

There was moment of silence followed by a rustling far above their heads. One blackbird gave out the alarm… then another… then the whole cloud was exploding with the cry.

Then the wings, like hundreds of squares of ebony paper being crushed and crumpled, as the dark bodies rose and then dove toward the unexpected nocturnal odor. Food.

Norrie's mind filled with the final verse of the nursery rhyme.

The maid was in the garden hanging up the clothes
Along came a blackbird

"Your face," Norrie screamed into the night. "Cover your face."

Sisters Mary Ann Davidson and Diane Davidson live in Ketchum, Idaho and Vienna, Virginia respectively. Hikers, bikers, and surfers, the sisters share a concern for the conservation and restoration of the environment—and a darker side with a secret desire for revenge as necessary.

The thought-provoking How to Clone a Mammoth by Beth Shapiro and The Song of the Dodo by David Quammen inspired the dodo aspect of their story—and maybe Jurassic Park?

An Extinction of Dodos

by Maddi Davidson

The chick's attack on its shell succeeded in opening a small hole through which I espied its beak. My worst fears were confirmed: my boyfriend had cheated on me.

I should have known by the size of the egg. The sixteen-inch, ground-dwelling Nicobar pigeon typically produces but a single, one-ounce egg per clutch. This egg was nearly three times that size and the largest I'd seen in my eight years of breeding them.

Desperate to hide the emerging creature before dawn broke and my staff arrived, I broke the cardinal rule of bird breeding and moved the egg, nest, and parents. Transporting them to a seldom-used quarantine building was not without difficulty. During breeding season, birds become territorial and despite my long sleeves and safety gloves, mama Kliou's pecking and clawing left deep scratches. Once the pigeons were ensconced in their new location, I ensured their safety from prying eyes by blocking their access to the outdoor cage, unplugging the closed-circuit television, and locking the door.

One of my bird keepers wandered by while I was tacking up a "Keep Out" sign. I told her to pass the word that the egg was taking longer to hatch than normal, the parents were agitated, and

I'd attend to their care and feeding. My obsession with Nicobars being well known, this last instruction would surprise no one. Finally, drenched with sweat from my exertions in the sauna of a Floridian August day, I slipped into my office, sat down with a sweet iced tea—it was too early for anything stronger—and brooded.

I had met my boyfriend Nathan Davies, an evolutionary biologist, at an international conference on avian biology in Vancouver, BC. Nathan was part of an Oxford research team that had extracted bits of DNA from a dodo skeleton and scientifically proven that the closest living relative to that extinct bird was the Nicobar pigeon. As bird curator for the South Florida Conservation Park, I'm responsible for over two hundred species, including several breeding pairs of Nicobars. Professional courtesy and the fact that Nathan was cute in a nerdish way led me to introduce myself after the presentation. We clicked and were inseparable for the remainder of the conference. Six months later Nathan secured a position as an associate professor of molecular biology with Naples University and moved in with me.

Inexorably, I'm drawn to men who share my passion for the preservation and restoration of the environment. My first live-in boyfriend, Charles, pursued a Ph.D. in biology by studying the implications of crocodile preservation on the ecosystem of Namibia's Caprivi Strip. According to Charles, Caprivi was more beautiful than Eden. Unfortunately for him, it was also more dangerous: he inadvertently joined the food chain, courtesy of his cherished crocodiles. My second love, Eric, was born to wealth, his father having made barrels of money in the oil business. To atone for his sire's rapacious exploitation of the earth's resources, Eric gave both his soul and inheritance to Greenpeace. One of a dozen activists who illegally boarded a Royal Dutch Shell ship heading to the arctic for offshore drilling, poor Eric fell overboard in the midst of retching. Greenpeace recognized his sacrifice by naming a lifeboat in his honor.

Nathan, in contrast, was not a risk seeker; his sole experience in a dangerous locale was the Pirates of the Caribbean ride at Disneyland Paris. However, he was just as committed to preserving the environment as my previous eco-beaus, often railing about mankind's annihilation of wildlife by citing the extinction of twenty or more significant species just in the last quarter century. Nathan endeared himself by being particularly attentive to my beloved Nicobar pigeons, visiting them so often at the park that they recognized him and would call when he approached.

Found on small islands and coastal regions in the South Pacific, a Nicobar is the most beautiful of all pigeons—fact, not opinion. Its iridescent green, blue-toned, and copper feathers shimmer as it moves, suggestive of the lustrous northern lights. The bird also sports a small, tungsten-gray head and short, stark-white tail. What the Nicobar pigeon unequivocally does not possess is a large, dodoesque beak like that of the soon-to-be-hatchling in the quarantine hut.

Six weeks earlier in the midst of a rant about another Hawaiian songbird being declared extinct, Nathan proposed that the world should mount an effort to resurrect extinct species. I knew he'd had too much to drink and I suspected he was high on cocaine, but foolishly I tried to reason with him.

"You know de-extinction is not practical. First, we can't extract enough intact DNA from what remains of these creatures. Second, we don't know the dietary or environmental needs of the long-gone species. We might inadvertently place existing species at a greater risk of extinction. Think of the scientists planning to implant mammoth skeletal DNA into elephants who are in the midst of their own extinction battle. Even were the scientists to be successful, the result wouldn't be a mammoth but a mammophant, an entirely new creature."

"Forget the wooly mammoth, babe," Nathan responded. "We've got something better: I managed to liberate a little dodo DNA from my work at Oxford. You, me, and your Nicobar pigeons are gonna bring back the dodos!"

I felt like I'd been cold-cocked. "You can't do this! You'll end up in jail and the theft of the DNA will become obvious once you announce your intent."

"I welcome the media spotlight, the bigger the better. Think of the paid speaking opportunities that will come out of this. The mega book deals. We'll be rich. They won't dare prosecute me," Nathan sniggered. "The collective noun will have to be changed from 'an extinction' of dodos to 'a Davies' of dodos. Our careers will be made!"

"But more animals will become extinct. Don't you see that if you're successful, a torrent of money will flow into de-extinction efforts for all sorts of—"

"I'm counting on it."

"—species, crippling efforts to preserve what we have left. It will be a disaster for our environment!"

"Au contraire: there will be more money for everyone. We'll be able to fund the extraction of DNA from other extinct species, maybe resurrect the passenger pigeon. You and me, babe, will be revered as the founders of the Enviro-age!"

I threw him out.

At least, I tried. He was too drunk to leave that night. I ordered him and his hangover out the next morning, but returned late that evening to find a contrite Nathan waiting for me with a candlelight dinner. Blaming the alcohol-drug mix for his ill-conceived scheme, Nathan swore that his intent was always to implant the filched DNA in chickens, barnyard fowl not being on anyone's endangered species list. When he professed his undying love and gave me a diamond-accented, white gold bracelet, I melted.

The dodo-beak hatchling proved I'd been a jackass for believing him. The lying scum must have implanted the DNA in Kliou when I was visiting my sister in Michigan last month. Well, I wasn't going to let my birds be exploited.

In addition to my overall responsibilities for care, enrichment, breeding, and training, I do a lot of manual work in caring for the birds. During the course of the day I plotted my revenge and took frequent breaks from cleaning cages to check on the Nicobars. I also assisted the park veterinarian with Victoria crowned pigeon and a blacksmith plover, both of which were restless during their medical procedures.

By evening I was a filthy, smelly, scratched-up mess and the Nicobar pigeon still had not hatched. However, the physical toil had cleared my mind and I had a plan. Once again ensconced in my office with a cold drink, I called Metik Sengebau, a friend and colleague in the Republic of Palau. Metik's knowledge of the varied fauna of his country was encyclopedic and had been a godsend to my Ph.D. research on endemic birds. We'd corresponded over the years and from time to time he would send me injured birds that could not be returned to the wild. Ironically, one of Kliou's forebears had come from Metik with a broken wing that had never set properly. She'd been a prolific layer and her offspring had been sent to other conservation centers and reintroduced to the islands of Palau.

Since Palau was thirteen hours ahead of Florida, I caught Metik pouring his first cup of coffee. By the time I explained my situation and we discussed what needed to be done, Metik was on his third cup, awake, and ebullient. A cousin to numerous prominent officials in the small country, Metik was confident he could expedite the paperwork necessary to import the birds. My fight with the bureaucratic jungle, normally a two-month process, would be more challenging. Over the next few hours I called in favors, begged, cooed, wheedled, and promised my first-born—child, not pigeon—and was assured of a two-day turnaround "this one time."

Long days are the norm for me, so Nathan made no comment when I arrived home after ten and went straight to bed. Later he crawled under the covers and stroked my thigh in anticipation of intimacy. I claimed a headache from the heat and humidity, rolled over, and pretended to sleep.

The sun was still below the horizon when I arrived at the park, collected food for the pigeons, and entered the quarantine shed. A small miracle awaited me: a tiny, large-billed Nicobar dodo hybrid with still-wet down. Kliou sang me a little greeting and I slipped into the cage to feed her and life-mate Turturk. Enchanted and absorbed with observing the hatchling, I didn't hear Nathan come in until Turturk squawked.

"Just look at it! That beak! Yessirree!" Nathan was practically dancing with excitement. "No doubt about it, that bird's got dodo. Dear old Oxford Bio Centre is going to be sorry they let me go! Just think, thirty-pound dodos walking the earth again!"

I stepped out of the cage, locked the door, and placed myself between Nathan and my birds. "It's not a dodo," I said. "It's an abnormal Nicobar with a small bit of dodo DNA."

"For now. Who knows, we might discover more dodo skeletons with DNA. In the meantime, it's our ticket to fame!" He placed a backpack on the floor, opened it, and removed a measuring tape, notebook, and spare set of work keys I kept at home.

"What the hell are you doing?"

"Taking measurements for the paper I plan to write. Did you save the shell?"

Keys in hand Nathan brushed by me, intent on opening the cage door.

"No!" I threw my arms around his neck and pulled him back. He grabbed my arms and twisted around, freeing himself from my grip. I was flung against the wall.

Dazed, I became aware that Nathan was in the cage and the pigeons were squawking. I struggled to my feet, but was too late.

Perhaps Kliou remembered the indignities Nathan had inflicted upon her while implanting the modified genes. Or perhaps it was instinctual, a mother protecting her offspring. In any event, she flew at Nathan's face. He flung out both arms and batted the large bird away. She shifted her attack, pecking at Nathan's feet and ankles. While trying to jump out of her way, Nathan slipped on the copious bird poop and fell. He crawled out of the cage and took refuge against a wall, knees pulled up to his chest and arms covering his head. He swore a blue streak, including phrases I'd never heard before.

Not wanting Kliou to be hurt, I intervened, herding her back into the cage where Turturk and the hatchling cowered. Keys retrieved and cage door locked, I turned to Nathan.

"Get out. Get out now!"

Moaning about his sprained ankle, bruised knee, and cuts from Kliou's assault, Nathan staggered to his feet, grabbed the backpack, and limped away. I fed the birds the rest of their food, gave them water, cleaned out the cage, and left. Back at the office

I drafted an email to my staff, explaining Kliou's large egg had produced an underdeveloped embryo. I was concerned about her future viability as a breeding bird and had already located a new home for her and Turturk. Because they were both still stressed from the egg failure, I would accompany them on the journey and would be gone for a few days.

When Nathan arrived home late that afternoon, his belongings were sitting on the driveway in cardboard boxes. I walked out to meet him.

"At great expense, I've had the locks changed on the house, so your keys won't work. Don't even think about trying to see the birds; I have them under guard. If you so much as hint to anyone there are dodo offspring at the park, I'll expose your cocaine habit and label you delusional. By the time anyone listens to you, the birds will be long gone and you'll have no proof. Goodbye, and have a nice life. Or not."

Nathan began his usual protest, with his trademark "Hey babe, c'mon now," but I turned my back and stalked into the house, my hands over my ears. After he'd loaded the boxes and driven off, I jumped in my car and raced back to work. Nathan was no doubt angry, frustrated, and wondering where he would stay for the next night, week, and month. However, when he calmed down and engaged in a few minutes of rational thought he'd realize I had a weak hand. I couldn't move the birds without leaving a paper trail. It was a matter of time before he found them and proclaimed his genius to the world: Davies' dodos, indeed!

A day later I was on my way to Palau, the return of Nathan's bracelet—which raised a few eyebrows—covering most of the airfare. When I arrived I told Metik the whole story of Nathan's meddling. I owed him that. He proposed to introduce Kliou, Turturk and the hatchling into a flock on one of Palau's remote islands to live out their lives in peace. Nonetheless, we both understood that if Kliou or her offspring continued to breed, the odd birds would someday be discovered. I assured Metik that Nathan was out of the picture and the future of the birds was up to the people of Palau. Heck, they might even claim a new species: *caloenas palauan,* perhaps.

Although I would have enjoyed more time on Palau, I stayed but two nights: I had obligations in Florida. On the last, wearying leg home of the forty-two hour journey, I sat next to Dave, a game warden for the Florida Fish and Wildlife Conservation Commission. He was single, funny, cute as a teddy bear, and entertained me with stories about arresting poachers, including a tale of using a robotic deer to catch them. "It's near on midnight and I'm standing next to my jeep having just written up one guy for shooting at my robo-deer when more yahoos in a truck come driving slowly down the road. Their headlights flash on the decoy, the truck comes to a sudden halt, and and two guys in the back of the pickup start blasting away at it. I'm standing right there: dumb as dodos!".

It was a sign: I accepted his invitation to dinner for the following evening.

Arriving home, I shed my scruffy travel clothes, took a long shower, changed into clean clothes, drank three cups of coffee, and drove over to see Nathan.

I got there just as they were lowering him into the ground. I dutifully bowed my head and asked forgiveness for causing pain to the blacksmith plover and a Victoria crowned pigeon; I'd pilfered their sedatives for fentanyl in order to sweeten Nathan's cocaine before I sent him packing. He'd conveniently over-dosed while I was in Palau.

Certain dodos do deserve extinction.

Midwesterner Denise Johnson, Arizona transplant, writes mystery, horror and science fiction. Published in Kings River Life ezine, Determined Hearts: A Frankenstein Anthology, Black Buttons Vol. 3, and Buried, learn more at www. denisehjohnson.com .

A stranger to the rarely seen Desert Sonoran toads, visible only after monsoon storms, she was surprised to learn of their psychedelic yet toxic powers. Toad toxin seemed a perfect combination for a mystery story involving sibling rivalry, greed, jealousy, and murder.

Knotty Inheritance
by Denise Johnson

Sadie arrived at the scene to find the yard cordoned off with police tape. The air was damp, a rarity in the Southwest. The scent of a wet desert always threw her off a bit.

Originally from the Midwest, she was used to the welcoming aroma of wet soil and grass mix common there. Here, the sand mixed with water combination produced a scent more akin to a wet construction site. She scanned the well-to-do neighborhood, as she grabbed hold of her wavy, brown hair and yanked it into an elastic ponytail holder she always wore around her wrist.

Despite the early hour, after two o'clock in the morning, looky loos stood outside their sprawling compounds. No doubt, whispering among themselves on the possibilities surrounding the ambulance and two squad cars that invaded their usually serene neighborhood. A detective for nearly seven years now, Sadie could even imagine their conversations, which were usually sprinkled with comments like, "I knew something was up" and "I never liked them."

The weather had cleared enough that water no longer ran down the roadway, as had been the case earlier in the evening.

Muddy sand covered much of the road and sidewalk leading up to the multilevel house. While rain was beneficial in these drought-ridden parts, Sadie hoped the monsoon hadn't washed away crucial evidence.

"So, what's the story?" Sadie stood next to Hal, a seasoned street cop who chose to remain on the beat rather than kowtow his way up management ranks.

"Not sure. A party broke up around 1:30 and as the family was cleaning up, they discovered their sibling unresponsive." Hal read through his notes. "Sorry, *half sibling*."

"Half?"

"Yeah, her *half-brother* made sure we knew that. Emphasized it several times." Hal flipped his notebook closed.

She liked that he was old school and still used a notebook. Sadie ducked under the yellow caution tape. "Where was the body found?"

"Outside, on the back patio. The place is huge. It's the old Dobbs' place."

Sadie's blank expression prompted him to continue.

"Bill Dobbs. Former Congressman. Died earlier this year."

Sadie nodded. She vaguely recalled hearing the Congressman's name come up during nightly newscasts.

The sprawling front yard was well landscaped, full of backlit desert flora and black river rock. Saguaros, Ocotillos and a variety of Agave, this was easily Sadie's favorite yard she'd encountered yet. It could easily give the city's botanical gardens a run for its money.

"The body still here?" Sadie pushed open one of the very large wooden front doors that was ajar. She noticed a large, metal counterweight on the other side of the door that moved when it opened or closed.

"The things you can do with money." Hal said in a low voice. Sadie winked at him.

Despite Hal's weight, he remained steps ahead as they wound their way methodically through the labyrinth of a house. She never understood why some of the most expensive homes had the worst layouts. This one made no sense to her. Random halls led to the laundry room, what appeared to be a gift wrap/craft room and a workout room. What she could only describe as contemporary wall art, large canvases covered in swaths of bright colors, adorned the halls. Ambient music could be heard, likely piped in via state-of-the-art speakers wired throughout the house.

At last, they made it to what seemed to be the main lower level hallway that led to the kitchen and living room. Sadie paused as she eyed the family seated in the dimly lit living room, assessing the situation before they noticed her. Lou, Hal's partner, stood while questioning the witnesses and taking notes. Despite finding a family member dead in their home, Sadie noticed none appeared terribly distraught.

Hal moved ahead. "The body is this way."

Sadie followed. She noticed Hal had begun walking with a limp and made a mental note to ask him about that. His wife had died a year prior and it seemed to her he needed someone to check in on him from time to time. He mentioned a son once, but they didn't seem close.

They walked into the oversized kitchen where a spread of party food remained on the marble countertops. The biggest prawns she'd ever seen adorned a large bowl of ice. Trendy glassware held colorful drink concoctions while a big fish bowl was filled with colorfully wrapped goodies. As the two exited, they saw the vic's body on the pavers lining the patio between what appeared to be an Olympic-size pool and a large fire pit.

"Name is Meghan Hanlon. Apparently, she is the illegitimate daughter of Dobbs. Lives in Montana where she's a student at Missoula College." Hal flipped a page in his notebook. "Came to light just after he died. Her name came up during the reading of the will."

"Certainly, a motive for murder." Sadie squatted near the corpse. "It doesn't look like rain hit this area. Glad the overhang blocked it." The deceased's jaw was rigid, a sign rigor mortis was setting in. "What did the coroner say?"

"He believes it was cardiac arrest, due to the sudden onset, coupled with her age and no apparent sign of foul play."

Sadie scanned the body. The girl was young, early twenties maybe, dressed in dark blue skinny jeans and a floral Old Navy top. She'd nearly bought the identical top earlier in the week. "What's this?" Careful not to make contact and risk spoliation of the evidence, Sadie pointed her pen towards the corner of the vic's mouth where a white substance had dried. "It looks like saliva. A toxic ingestion?"

Hal shrugged. "Maybe."

Sadie stood. "Let's go in and see how they're doing."

Inside, things were getting heated. While they stood in the hall, Hal passed her a quick diagram identifying the witnesses in the room and where they sat. Mason Dobbs, the deceased Congressman's eldest son, wore a three-piece blue suit. Seated on an oversized tufted brown leather couch, he inched his way forward, frustrated at the line of questioning.

"How many times do I have to tell you that we didn't have anything to do with this?" He motioned to his sisters, seated to his right in two matching tufted leather library chairs.

As Sadie and Hal entered the living room, she motioned to Lou to leave the room. "We understand, Mr. Dobbs. We're just trying to do our jobs."

Out of the corner of her eye, she noticed Hal had retreated into the foyer to speak with his partner.

"Why don't we give you a few moments."

Mason nodded.

Sadie joined the two law enforcement officers back in the hall. She knew Hal was stymied because of his usual tell, rubbing his buzzed head from back to front.

"The officers found an odd substance floating in the pool." Hal paused. "They're taking a sample back to the lab but requested our opinion."

Sadie and Hal returned to the patio. Several moths flitted past, attracted to the outdoor lights. An officer handed a piece of paper, in a protective bag, to Hal.

After a cursory glance, Hal turned toward Sadie. "Man, Old Dobbs would turn in his grave if he knew what was going on in his home now."

Sadie glanced at the paper, apparently an accounting of the party held earlier that evening. There were names with check-marks, and the amount each paid to get in. "They were charging quite a bit for this shindig."

Hal turned the sheet over. "Yeah, it looks like they offered a special multi-course meal. Check out the chef, his name looks familiar."

Sadie didn't recognize the chef's name, then again, that was no surprise given that she wasn't much of a foodie. She pointed to the menu. "Drugs in place of dessert, that's an interesting twist."

Their attention turned to the pool where lights gave the mysterious floating glob an eerie glow.

Hal bent closer to the water's surface to get a better look.

Sadie clicked her tongue. "Do you hear that?"

Hal stood up. "Crickets?"

"No, the other sound. Sonoran toads. They come out at night after big storms to mate and lay their eggs. That's probably what that mysterious glob is."

"A bunch of toads, huh?"

"Knot," Sadie corrected him.

"It's not toads?" Hal sounded puzzled. "You just said it was."

Sadie sighed. "A knot of toads, spelled K-N-O-T."

Seemingly on cue, a few toads jumped out of the shadows, drawn to the lights.

"Man, they're ugly." His confused look reminded her of how often she was on the receiving end of them.

Sadie had to agree. They weren't the most attractive amphibians with their large bulging eyes and bumps that dotted their greenish gray bodies.

The detective and officer stood for a moment, listening to the cacophony of toads and crickets.

"You know, I think we may have a motive." Sadie retreated into the house while Hal trailed behind her.

Back in the living room, things looked to be more tense than before. The siblings were engaged in a heated discussion, though muffled, that ceased abruptly when Hal and Sadie entered the room.

"How much longer will this take?" Mason seemed to have taken on the role of family spokesperson.

Rather than answer, Sadie turned to the youngest Dobbs. "So, Kate, can you tell me how many parties you've hosted here since your father died?"

Kate appeared tired, her long blond curls wilted from the unexpected humidity. "I don't know, maybe five."

Sadie knew if her hunch was correct, she was lying. That meant the number Kate gave her was reduced by five, maybe ten.

"Why do you charge a fee?"

"We offer a luxury experience to an elite group of people." Kate didn't hide the air of contempt she had for regular, non-elite, people as she adjusted her designer skirt.

Sadie noticed Mason and his sister, Jenni, exchange a worried glance.

Kate continued on her high net worth soapbox. "People like us want exclusive events, not parties where bottles of cheap booze and tasteless finger food is passed around by some part-time caterer."

This time Mason was less subtle. "Kate, that's enough. They don't want to hear about it."

"Oh, but we do." Sadie looked toward Jenni.

"What type of drugs were you serving? And remember, even if you don't tell us, our officers are searching your home. We'll bring in a K9 or two to assist."

That was a bit of a white lie. There was only one K9 in their unit.

The siblings exchanged looks with one another but continued to remain silent.

"Hal, want to take a guess?"

Hal nodded. "I'd say marijuana edibles for sure."

"But marijuana is no longer illegal," said Jenni, a bit too quickly.

"We've interviewed some guests who said they heard Mason and Jenni arguing with Meghan." Sadie stared at the trio.

"You know siblings," Kate's laugh trailed off to silence.

"Actually, I don't. I'm an only child." Sadie almost laughed out loud on that white lie.

"It's true, we did argue," Mason admitted. "Meghan wanted to sell the mansion and we were against it."

"Go on."

"She didn't like the parties; they made her uncomfortable. She wanted to split the money from the sale of the house four ways and be done with us." Mason leaned back on the couch, as if spent from the unexpected admission.

"What's the house worth?" Sadie had a hunch it was over a million.

Mason's Adam's apple was noticeable as he swallowed hard. "I don't know, I guess, maybe, over two million," he stammered.

SQUAW, SQUAW!

Sadie couldn't have asked for a better segue.

"What is that? A bird?" Hal looked around the room, searching for the sound.

The siblings remained seated and silent.

"That is the sound of the Sonoran Desert Toad," Sadie said. "One must have come in through the patio doors." She walked around the back of the couch, her lit flash light swinging back and forth. "Would one of you grab it, if it comes out from under the couch?"

"What! No, way!" Kate shrieked. "Those things are dangerous."

Sadie smiled. "Oh, so you are aware they are poisonous?"

Kate nodded.

"You know, I've heard Indians once used the toad's toxins to get to a psychologically altered state. It's similar to LSD."

The screeching toad hopped out from beneath the couch and stopped under the glass coffee table. It was a large one, bigger than a man's hand for sure, Sadie figured. Like a specimen under a microscope, it sat still as if aware it had been caught red-handed in the unfolding sordid family drama.

Mason stood up. "Okay, okay. Yes, the knot of toads was a part of the menu. We hold our parties mostly during monsoon season, because of the toads. They offer a unique high."

Sadie motioned for Mason to continue, only Jenni interrupted him.

"Meghan never heard of the effects. She was pretty square. Had never even done drugs. So, we pushed her to try it. Everyone at the table did. She didn't want to but we held her arms while Mason made her lick it a few times."

Hal's face scrunched in disgust. "We're going to need a list of everyone at the party."

"When did you force Meghan to try it? Was it after the argument she and Mason had?"

Kate and Jenni nodded.

"So, you forced a roughly 110-pound woman to lick a deadly toxic toad a few times?" Sadie shook her head. "That's what likely killed her."

Kate began to sob.

Mason shook his head in disbelief. "We didn't intend for her to die."

"What's going to happen to us?" Jenni asked. Still seated, she and Kate held each other's hands in a tight grip, to console each other.

"We're going to take all three of you to central booking." Hal reached for his cuffs and motioned for his partner to cuff Mason. "You'll be charged with involuntary manslaughter."

Lou read them their rights.

"She was excited to hang out with us. Said she never had siblings and had always wished for some." Kate blurted, as she continued to cry.

"Greed's a bitch." Hal's comment was spot on.

"A quarter of everything is better than nothing," Sadie added, as the officers walked the family out to the waiting patrol cars. She couldn't help but notice some of the looky loos remained outside, talking over the echoing sound of the toads.

*Sandra Murphy, author of From Hay to Eternity: Ten
Tales of Crime and Deception, and stories in The Killer
Wore Cranberry Four, The Eyes of Texas, and The
Extraordinary Book of Amateur Sleuths, lives in St.
Louis.*

*Downwind of breweries, alongside the Mighty Mississippi,
on hot summer days, the aroma of hops ignites imagination,
bringing her imaginary friends to life.*

*Me and Dean combines a love for dogs and a hatred for
poachers and smugglers.*

Me and Dean

by Sandra Murphy

When the phone rang early on a Thursday morning, I felt like
we'd just gotten to bed. I focused a bleary eye on the clock. 1:30
a.m. I was right. About midnight I'd done a face plant on the
pillow, following a ten-hour hunt, chase, capture, and paperwork.
The paperwork was always the hard part.

"Please be a wrong number or drunken butt-dial," I moaned.
I struggled to sit up, looked over to see Dean, wide-awake, alert,
and grinning at the thought of more work. Times like this, it's
hard to like him.

"Up and at 'em. We got a report that a shipment is coming
through. You and Dean ready?" Ralph, my supervisor, sounded
cheery although he'd been awake at least as long as we had.

"Maybe after coffee. Do we have time to get cleaned up?" I
threw the blanket back and stood. I only swayed a little.

"Sure, take a shower, all the time you need. Thirty seconds
enough?" Ralph sneezed. "Damn allergies. There'll be a car out
front for you in three minutes. Be waiting at the curb." The phone
went dead.

"Gear up. Time to work."

Dean grabbed his vest and wiggled into it.

"Getting a little chubby there, Dean. Might be time to lose a pound or two. That didn't used to be so snug."

Dean walked to the door and waited, his back to me. He doesn't like personal remarks, especially about his weight.

I grabbed a pair of comfy black pants and gave them the once-over to see if they were clean or at least clean-enough. They'd do. Sitting on the edge of the bed, I pulled them on without getting tangled in the leg openings. A sports bra and t-shirt came next. I grabbed my official vest and called myself ready to go. Tempting as it was to fall back onto the pillow, I stuffed my feet into running shoes and did a quick bathroom visit. Two minutes, thirty seconds later, Dean and I stood at the curb. I smoothed the ugliness from my bedhead and told Dean, "I'm liable to fall asleep in the car. Wake me up if I start to drool or snore." Headlights came around the corner. I glanced at my watch. Three minutes on the dot.

"Hey Angie. Here, coffee, mocha, four sugars." Edgar was a regular as my driver and knew what it took to keep me going.

"No whip?"

"A whipped cream mustache takes away from your professional look. Or so the director said."

"I thought we were friends."

"There's a full can in the pocket in front of Dean. Already shook it up. Squirt it into your mouth, not the coffee, keeps it off your face. Dean need anything?"

"Probably wants something but not going to get it. He needs a clean palate so the super-sniffer works. He'll get something later."

Dean ignored us and looked out the window.

If we worked in the private sector, Dean's nose would be insured by Lloyds of London. For government work, he was lucky to get a pat on the head. Dean is short, stocky, an outrageous flirt, and friendly to everyone, even the bad guys, mostly smugglers. His charm and non-threatening manner let him get away with stuff that would get most people punched in the nose. Or in Dean's case, snout. Dean's a beagle—and a federal agent.

We're part of the Beagle Brigade, working for U.S. Customs and Border Protection and the United States Public Health Service at entry points to the States. For us, that means airports. Beagles sniff out contraband food and plants passengers bring in. Most of it's accidental. Ask someone if they have food and tired travelers say no. When asked if they have an apple, then they remember. For those who were home for the holidays, there's always a Nonna or Mum who packed "a little snack" for later and slipped it into the luggage. True smugglers are those who try to get past with mangrove roots disguised as restaurant décor, banana leaves for baking, or more gruesome items.

If humans had to search, it would take hours to get through a flight's worth of luggage. Dean walks past suitcases, diaper bags, and people, zeroing in on banned goods. Sitting with one paw up was the signal of a successful search. The innocent think he's cute and the guilty never see it coming until the handcuffs click.

I did a quick change at my locker into my uniform shirt and pants, added the vest and was ready. I'd learned the hard way not to dress at home, and then drink coffee in the car.

"Okay, Ralph, what's the scoop? Dean is perky, I'm exhausted, what are we looking for?" I leaned against the wall, just to keep from toppling over.

"That guy from Tel Aviv, the one we arrested last week, with all the plants and seeds buried under layers of chocolate? He wants a deal. He heard rumors about a shipment coming in but he didn't have much detail. I'm thinking it'll be more of the same. Is Dean up for it?" Ralph leaned back in his chair to look at Dean, snoozing under his desk. "Does he only have two speeds? Working or asleep?"

"Seems like it lately. You just haven't us much play time. His union work rules are better than mine."

"Tank and Joe will be back early next week, Tina and Pete three days after that. You can sleep then. Time for you and Dean to go mingle." Dean was on his feet and headed for the door before Ralph stopped talking.

We had a routine start. A sleepy five-year old wanted her picture taken with Dean after he alerted to the fresh flower in her hair. "He's a very handsome boy but he's not allowed to have his picture taken," I said. We discourage selfies. My voice dropped to a whisper. "He's a super hero. Secret identity. *Shh!*"

She nodded, gave Dean one more kiss on the head, and left her flower behind without any tears.

We continued to patrol the concourses and made regular stops as luggage arrived on the carousels. It was a boring night, finding only a wreath made with live succulents, a batch of homemade tamales, and a bag of oranges.

At four o'clock, Dean got one of his union breaks—a quick trip outside for a breath of fresh air and a potty stop. We went to the break room to meet Tom and Arthur, a Labrador trained to sniff out contraband cash. People would be surprised at the amounts they find. "Time to get back to work. Want to meet here again for the six o'clock break?" I asked. Tom nodded, Arthur, being the agreeable sort, seemed okay with the plan too.

About half an hour later, Dean approached a college age kid who leaned down to pet him. Dean sat and held up one paw and then looked at me to make sure I'd seen it. "Dean thinks you've got a treat for him," I said.

"Might be some crumbs in my pocket. They'd be covered in lint though, nothing you'd want to eat, boy."

"You're right. Dean likes a good peanut butter cookie." Dean still had his foot up but now focused on the kid's jacket. "He seems awfully interested in your pocket. Whatcha got in there?"

One of the great things about Dean is that he's a deep thinker. He figured out he gets a treat for each violation he finds, but for the really big ones, he gets five minutes to play fetch. Any time he has to chase somebody, a rarity, and then it's party time. To increase his odds, he's taught himself to alert to more than the plants and food he was trained for.

The kid shuffled from one foot to the other and cleared his throat a few times. "Nothin'. Look, I gotta catch my plane. I think they're calling it now." He started to back away but Dean blocked him. "Move, dog!"

"See, the thing is, when Dean says there's something in your pocket, he's always right." I took the kid's arm in a firm grip. "Besides, your pocket is wiggling. Hand it over, dude. Dean may be short but I guarantee, you can't outrun him."

I thought the kid was going to break down and cry, right there on the concourse. "It's my hamster, Bob. I'm going home for a week but nobody could take care of him and now I found out I can't take him on the plane. I don't know what to do." He pulled Bob out of his pocket to show me.

Ever curious, Dean stood on his back legs to get a better look. "Bob's not a treat. Don't eat him! Lady, call off your dog!"

In his excitement, the kid stepped back, tripped on his own shoelaces, a duffle bag cushioning his fall. Bob wasn't so lucky. The kid's hand flopped onto the floor and Bob made a run for freedom—right into the path of a beeping golf cart carrying a passenger late for a connecting flight. Bob froze, a one-ounce fuzzy deer in the headlights, unseen by the cart's driver.

"Dean, take it!" I pointed and Dean ran for Bob, sliding out of sight as the cart passed by. Dean's pretty agile but Bob, well, he was out of his element.

"Where is he? Where's Bob? Come here, Bob, come!" The kid seemed confident that Bob had a good recall. I had my doubts.

I heard a little girl squeal, "Eww, the doggie ate a mouse!" Her mom tried to drag her away but she put up quite a fight. People had their cell phones held at Dean height. Passengers think of the dogs as airport greeters and we let them. Smugglers know differently but still think they can outsmart a beagle nose. Dean loves to prove them wrong.

"Dean, quit fooling around and get over here." Dean turned toward me, still grinning like a possum with a persimmon, Bob's little head showing between his teeth. "Give me." Bob popped out into my hand. "Okay everybody, this is Dean and he works here at the airport. This is Bob. He's a hamster. He got scared because he's not allowed on the plane but he's okay, just a little slobbery from dog spit," I grinned. You can always spot a dog lover. They don't think twice about dog spit. "Dean has a soft mouth which means he picked Bob up and saved him from getting hit by the cart but didn't bite him." I miss the clicking sound cameras used to make. Cell phones just don't have that same coolness—but they do get onto social media faster a suitcase can get misrouted to Bangladesh. I had a feeling the Dean and Bob show was going to be viral in minutes. Dean was going to be impossible. Fame goes to his head.

I motioned to Bob's person. "Come with me." I sighed. Why can't kids think ahead? "We'll come up with a plan." We keep cages in the office for this kind of thing. I hoped he could afford the boarding fee with the rescue group that would be Bob's vacation home for the next week.

Bob got squared away, the kid headed to Gate 47 for Seattle, and all was right in Hamster World. My radio crackled, Ralph calling. "Angie, Tel Aviv guy got the date wrong. I think the time zones confused him. Shipment is tomorrow. You and Dean go home, get some rest. I told Tom and Arthur. See you tomorrow."

Edgar waited at the curb. Sleep never sounded so good.

The next day I was rested and as anxious to get back to work as Dean. While we were eating oatmeal and toast, Ralph had called and said the shipment was rumored to arrive in the late afternoon when the airport is the busiest.

"Dean, let's go to the park for a run and then watch the ducks, what do you say? We'll have a little outside time before work. If you're a good boy, we might stop for a veggie burger with the works." Who am I kidding? Dean's always a good boy. An arooo and the scrabble of paws on hardwood was my answer. Dean was ready. I grabbed a bag of frozen peas and we were off.

It's important for a working dog to have time off. To Dean, no vest means off duty. In the park, Dean can pass right by picnics, ice cream trucks, and landscapers planting flowers without so much as a glance. Well, except for popsicles. He has a weakness for blueberry popsicles but we don't get those on workdays. Blue tongues freak passengers out.

We managed a mile-long loop at one end of the park before feeding the ducks. Bread is bad for the pond and ducks. Grapes are good but toxic to dogs who can snarf one up before his person even sees him sniff. I bring frozen peas. They keep me cool as we run, and ducks love them.

By the time we did our mile, the bag of peas had thawed. The ducks rushed to see what snacks were on today's buffet, courtesy of me and Dean. I'd seen the same look on co-workers' faces at the vending machine.

The ducks knew Dean. One was a particular friend. Dean rescued him after he'd fallen through a sewer grate. Mama duck was frantic, squawking, the flight of ducklings crowded around her. Dean's insistence brought the problem to my attention. The park ranger executed a fast but dramatic rescue.

"All gone." I shook the bag to prove it. The ducks did a final check to make sure no peas had escaped, then strolled back to the pond for a carb-burning swim. "There's time for a quick nap," I said. Dean rehydrated and was agreeable about the snooze.

Two hours later, Edgar picked us up, a fortifying mocha in hand. Once Dean and I buckled in, he pulled away from the curb and headed back to the airport. "Rain predicted for later, maybe thunderstorms. What did you tell me about Dean? Does the noise bother him or does the rain dampen the smell of stuff he's looking for?"

"When he's on the job, nothing bothers Dean. He's got a laser-brain, right Bud?" I rubbed the top of his head. "Smugglers use all kinds of things to try to cover the smell of contraband. Foot powder, perfume, stinky stuff. Dean just takes it as a challenge. Rain doesn't dilute the odor, sometimes even intensifies it, due to the humidity."

"Foot powder? What's the deal on that?"

"You know, the kind that's supposed to make sweaty feet tolerable. It's supposed to mask the smell of what they're hiding. It's creative but they underestimate the famous Beagle Nose." I gave Dean one more ear rub. "Ready, dude? It's time to work."

I showed Dean his favorite ball, the one he gets to fetch after a good find. He pulled me into the terminal, anxious to sniff out the first culprit. I barely had time to wave goodbye to Edgar.

It didn't take long, but it wasn't the big shipment we'd heard about, only a florist with exotic orchids. Some passengers get all fake emotional when we confiscate their contraband but this guy's tears were real. Once he confessed how much he'd paid for the black-market plants, I understood. "Dean, just think how many tennis balls and blueberry popsicles he could have bought with that money," I said. We were on our way to the break room for fetch time, Dean weaving between travelers like the lead car in a high-speed chase. "Slow down, I'll give you ten minutes but that has to include a snack." Dean had no comment, just increased his speed.

An hour later, the excitement wore off and we were both bored. "Let's get some air and a potty break," I said. Dean knows where his designated area is and led the way. After a granola bar for me and a sweet potato treat for Dean, we headed for carousel six on the lower level. The plane was due in from Singapore in half an hour. That's a one-stop twenty-hour flight, refueling only. Passengers and luggage checked through to our airport.

Luggage spit off the conveyor and through webbing that reminded me of the car wash, to plop onto the carousel. The area was deserted while passengers declared souvenirs and took a few minutes to stretch their legs. A janitor mopped nearby, catching Dean's eye. Dean is not fond of water unless it's in his dog bowl, too reminiscent of baths.

Well, surely there was another area in need of mopping. I could see the first passengers coming our way. There weren't even any caution signs out to warn of the wet floors. "Hey Dean, let's tell him to do a quick dry mop and move along." Halfway there, a rolling bag the size salesmen use for samples popped out. The janitor dropped the mop, grabbed the bag, and turned to hurry away.

He saw us, veered off course, right over the watery floor, skidding like a pig on ice, gripping the suitcase like his life depended on it. It might have. Smugglers are not a forgiving people. Dean was on the move, dragging me along. I managed to key my mic to alert Ralph we needed reinforcements before we hit the wet area too. Dean's short legs splayed left and right, leaving scribbles in the water before I covered them with running shoe tread marks. I stayed upright but was reminded of an embarrassing attempt at water skiing. We cleared the wet mess and kept running, slip sliding until running over a floor mat dried our feet.

"Federal agents, stop!" Not only did he keep running, but he wove through the arriving passengers to merge with the crowd. I released Dean's leash. "Dean, take the bag!"

I pulled my weapon, stopped, and aimed. Someone in the crowd yelled "Gun!" Our guy looked over his shoulder, banged the suitcase into a man's legs, knocking him down. That guy bowled over a woman and her kid as he fell. Passengers scattered, hid behind potted plants or dropped to the floor to play dead. I wouldn't have another clear shot.

I fired.

Taser probes cause muscles to lock up and his did. He hit the floor with a loud thump, barely heard over his screams. The suitcase went spinning, Dean astraddle of it, biting down on the strap but not letting go, even when it crashed into the side of the escalator.

"Ralph, he's down. Dean's got the bag. Tom and Arthur are here. Send security." I strained to hear over the guy's loud screeching. Geez, he sounded like a barn owl on a mission. "The way he slung that case around, it's not explosive. Dean's alerting and Arthur is not." Because of dye packs in currency, Arthur knows booby-traps too. I ran to Dean. "Are you alright, buddy?"

Dizzy, Dean wobbled a little as he got off his wild ride. "Dude, you really are a super hero." He perked up, shook himself, and strutted in front of the milling passengers who all applauded. I heard the kid who'd been knocked down say, "Mom, did you hear? He's a super hero!" I could visualize Dean's head getting bigger the more compliments he got.

Security has a special container for suspicious luggage, just in case. The container is put into a secure room and scanned. This time we got the all clear but were told something inside the bag was moving. Not only did Dean get to chase, he'd found a big score.

After opening the suitcase, removing all the padding and crap used to disguise the smell—that didn't work—we found what Dean knew all along. "A whole herd of turtles," Ralph said. "Probably endangered species. Exotics."

"A bale."

"A what?" Ralph looked again. "There's a bunch and they are all duct taped together but I'd hardly call them a bale."

"That's what you call a group of turtles, a bale." Ralph gave me that look, the one that said he was sure I was weirder than most people. "I do crossword puzzles. When you give us time off. Gimme a break, it's a portable hobby."

"I'll call turtle rescue and our exotics vet. We've got the get them unstuck as soon as possible. Besides being crammed in there with the guy's dirty socks, glue can give turtles," he paused. "The "bale" of turtles, all kinds of health problems. How many do you think we've got?"

"They're little. Looks like a dozen per tape clod. There's got to be a couple dozen clods. Think this is what the Tel Aviv guy heard about?"

"Tape clod? I'm not even going to ask," Ralph shook his head. "I dunno. They'd be worth a lot to collectors. The eco folks would worry about them getting turned loose and becoming invasive, crowding out the native turtles. I thought we'd be looking at something bigger. Just a gut feeling."

"Dean got to chase the guy so he's got a big reward coming. After that, we'll be back on the concourse and see if you're right. Give us about thirty minutes."

I threw Dean's tennis ball until I thought my arm would fall off. The ball only ricocheted and beaned me twice, a personal best. "Why is it that our breaks wear me out more than work does?" Dean just barked for me to throw the ball again.

Back on the concourse after a snack, and potty break, Dean was on high alert. Success goes to his head, a good thing for us but not for smugglers.

Two long and boring hours later, I was beginning to think the Tel Aviv guy had given us bogus information just to save himself. Granted, smuggled goods are a bad thing and we were here to prevent just that but the thrill of the chase excited me as much as it did Dean. I celebrate with ice cream rather than a tennis ball.

I was just about to suggest a stroll through the boarding gates when Dean froze, mid-step. I almost fell over him. "Dean, you've got to give me a little notice before making abrupt stops or turns. Otherwise, you'll be dragging my lifeless body behind you until the end of the shift." Dean didn't even glance my way, too busy tilting his head from one side to the other, listening rather than sniffing.

He made a U-turn and assumed I would follow. I did, scattering "Excuse me" and "sorry" like confetti. "Dean, what do you see?" The concourse was crowded with disembarking passengers. We were going against the flow. Up ahead, I saw a man pulling a large suitcase on wheels. He was only a few feet away when he entered the men's room. Dean was willing to follow but I was not.

"Dean, we've talked about this. It's okay for you to go in with me but I can't go into the men's restroom with you," I said as I patted him on the shoulder. "We can wait right here if you think there's something we need to check."

I radioed Ralph to let him know what was up. "Dean's zeroed in on a guy, tall, dark hair, dark blue windbreaker which seems kind of odd, given how hot and muggy it is tonight. About forty maybe? Got a wheelie case, dark green." Dean was still focused on the door.

"Ralph is sending Arthur and Tom since they're between checks." Before I could add we'd wait for them, Dean pulled like a sled dog in the Iditarod. Our target was a short, blond guy wearing tan overalls, pushing a dolly with two boxes on it. The wheels sounded squeaky to me. I wondered why Dean had scratched waiting for the first guy.

We made our way past the baggage area and headed for the escalators. I picked Dean up and held him as we rode up to the main floor so he wouldn't get the fur on his feet caught in the treads. He had a good vantage point from that height and kept his eye on our man. We were only about six people behind at that point. I keyed my radio and updated Ralph again. I could see Tom and Arthur headed our way, weaving among the crowd, polite but not stopping to talk. A few feet from the bottom of the escalators was a common area with small tables and chairs, spaced around a low water feature.

I heard the squeaky noise again which was odd since the dolly wasn't moving. Dean let out a rare bark and struggled to get down. The man turned and saw me with Dean and made a misstep, crashing the dolly, boxes, and himself, down the moving stairs, shoving passengers out of the way as he fell.

The boxes must not have been taped very tight because the tape burst and loud noises came from within. Dean ran for them as soon as I set him down. I went after the guy who was stunned and flat on the floor, one pants leg caught in the escalator I yelled, "Everybody hold on!" and hit the emergency stop button. Tom and Arthur were there in seconds, helping riders climb over Overalls Guy.

Any time Dean's out of my sight and on his own, it's anybody's guess what will happen. Today might have been his best stunt ever. When we had our runner cuffed and up on his feet, we heard laughter and calls of "Come see this!" behind us.

There was Dean, aided and abetted by Arthur, herding baby birds. It was hard to tell how many there were because they were pretty speedy, toddling along on webbed feet, aimed right for the water feature. Before Tom and I could reach them, eight chicks, a yellow Lab and a beagle were having the time of their lives in the fountain, much to the delight of the crowd. The chicks dove under water for minutes at a time while the dogs tried to keep track of them.

Ralph pushed his way to us. "I could see on the camera that you were about to start a riot up here. What the hell is making all that noise? Not those little birds?"

"Haven't you ever seen a baby penguin before?" I had to raise my voice to be heard over the racket.

"Sure, penguins are black and white. These birds are brownish and poofy." Ralph shook his head. "Ain't no penguin. Let's round 'em up and get them downstairs. I'll have to call the zoo and the exotics vet. Again."

We were all soaked to the knees before we got the last escapee. People were respectful. No one got mad when Arthur and Dean shook themselves when they got out of the fountain. I heard one kid say, "This is the best trip ever! Can we come here again?"

In the office, the noise was a lot worse. We didn't have the echo of upstairs' high ceilings but the small room contained the sound better. "Dr. Bryan's here. Thank goodness." Ralph had had enough of birds and turtles for one night.

"What you've got here are endangered African penguins. They're not very old." The vet put each in a special cage for transport. "They look healthy, all things considered. They'll look like the penguins you're used to as they get a little older."

"Why are they so loud?" Ralph asked as the cages were headed for the door. "Last time I heard anything like this was at my uncle's farm. He raised mules."

"You got that right. They're called jackass penguins for that very reason." Dr. Bryan laughed. "What was the first thing they saw when the boxes broke?"

"Dean and Arthur, I guess. Tom and I were busy with the escalator, passengers, and smuggler." I turned to Ralph. "Hey, what happened with that first guy Dean spotted?"

"We got him too. He took the suitcase into the restroom to avoid Dean, took the boxes out, transferred them to the other guy." Ralph sneezed. "Damn allergies. It was a good plan. The bathrooms are the only place in the terminal that don't have cameras."

"Hey Doc, why'd you ask what the chicks saw first?" My brain was on a delayed response mode.

"Chicks don't know what they are when they first hatch. I'm guessing these babies were taken before they got to imprint on other penguins. It makes a big difference." He grinned.

It took me a minute. "You mean?"

"Yep, these chicks are going to look like penguins, sound like mules, and think they're dogs, all their lives. Should be interesting to study." He pushed the cart of crates to the door. "Dean and Arthur will have to have visitation rights!"

We sat in the office, exhausted. Dean propped himself up against my knee, Arthur sprawled out on the rug. Either the swim had worn them out or the realization of being foster parents to braying birds had hit home.

"First a herd of, I mean a bale of turtles and now penguins." Ralph leaned back in his chair. "I know you're dying to tell me. What's the name for penguins?"

"What else?" I said. "A waddle of penguins. Seems like a good ending for our shift and the start of our days off, all courtesy of a Brigade of Beagles."

Dean agreed, lifted his head and said, "Arrooo!"

J.B. Toner is the author of Whisper Music and The Shoreless Sea. Toner lives in Massachusetts with his wife, Ellen, and their daughter Ms. Sonya Magdalena Rose. In contrast to writing, he is a black belt in Ohana Kilohana Kenpo-Jujitsu.

The Kindly Dark was inspired by the simple fact crows are awesome. Quick's altercation with the seagulls is based on a real incident involving a single crow and a half dozen larger but not-nearly-so-smart birds.

The Kindly Dark
by J.B. Toner

No bleakness is complete without a crow. A ruined church, a barren moor, a graveyard by a grey and empty sea—without the brooding shadow of a solitary rook, their desolation lacks its full potential. What old forgotten skull could molder properly without the croak and mutter of a murder overhead, the hop and flutter of black wings?

Mind you, we're a merry folk. We glory in the gloom, and this dark world has plenty to spare. But when Fr. McReady installed a new electric light above the rectory door, my favorite eaves were flooded with a bloodless yellow glare. It wouldn't do.

My name is Quick of Lurkwood Murder. We are wise and fast. I've seen sweet summers and bitter winters in the lands around St. Bernadette's. The honor of old age descends upon me now. Life's flight should fall in veiling shade, a crimson leaf on autumn's dusky breeze—not in the dry click of a motion detector. I perched upon the steeple's topmost needle, thinking on these things, when Sharp came gliding by.

"Ho, Quick! What news from the west?"

I made no answer. The cold red sun declined among the mountains.

"You look troubled, Quick. What can I do?"

"Light," I said. "They've made a light beneath my favored rest."

He flapped a bit and cocked his head. "I see no light."

"Fly down and perch there, lad."

"In your rest?"

"It's all right."

He swooped down to the door, beat the air, and swooped up to my spot below the eaves. As he did, that ugly yellow light came on. He squawked with indignation and flew back to the chapel roof.

"Twenty thousand lightnings! There you rest most every night, and have done these many seasons past. It's man's meanness, sheer and clear!"

"Not so, I think. He's a kindly sort, the vicar."

Yes, we know your temperaments. We know your faces. And we can tell each other which of your folk have decent hearts and which of you are cruel. Only two creatures in all of life are cleverer than my people: you, and those oafish dolphins. Only we can fly. We, and the dead.

"Then why, Quick?"

"Like me, the man grows old. I saw him slip and nearly fall several mornings since. The light is no doubt for his safety."

"The man's just a man! Pluck the eyes of his safety, pluck and gulp 'em both."

I shifted from foot to foot, considering. Of course a crow's life comes before a man's—but a crow's convenience? After all, the rectory was his home too, in a way. On the other hand, our life-flight is so much shorter. In a few more seasons I'd be gone, and Fr. McReady could install a hundred lights.

Beyond the west, the blood-orb sank. As darkness rose, the buzzing bulb grew brighter below. "How long does it burn?" Sharp asked.

"An hour. Every time it lights."

He said nothing.

"…it must be destroyed."

Seagulls. Idiot birds. Their chatter woke me early. "Hey look, food! Guys, there's food here! Hey guys, look at the food!" Seven or eight of them in a dirty white ring around the jetsam of some satiated human's breakfast sandwich. I dropped to the earth right in their startled midst.

"Be off, or I'll stuff your holes with your own fat heads."

They scattered, screeching admonitions. "Look out, it's a crow! Hey guys, look out for the crow!"

"Morons." It was a warm, bright day, but my mood was grim. I'd stayed up late to examine that hateful light, and then slept in a hollow pine. The bulb was protected by some manner of metal cage that surpassed my solving abilities. No rook likes to meet the limit of his wit.

The sandwich, however, broke my fast more pleasantly than I had expected. Better still, as I glanced up from snatching down the last morsel, I glimpsed a distant shadow moving through the orange-blue dawn, and caught a faint scent of rain. My spirits kindled.

"Well. If wisdom fails, use speed." An age-old proverb of my kin. "It is time for the shine-star."

I went to the secret place, the ancient place. There by the fallen stone, beneath the rotten root, the shine-star lay hidden. Many times had the leaves of Lurkwood turned since I took it from a dead woman's hand. It was my greatest treasure.

"Gather!" I cawed, rising above the trees. "I, Quick, summon the Murder to meet. Gather!"

The call went out, and swiftly spread. My wing-mates floated through the wood as the welcome storm clouds began to congregate above us. It wasn't long before we had a quorum, nor long before Glint hobbled up the branches to his venerable rest.

"Lurkwood Murder," he rasped. "By the power of the sacred Moon, I call this parliament to order. Who has summoned us together, and for what purpose? Speak!"

We were hatchlings together, Glint and I. Long ago. I was always faster, but he was always smarter. I did not challenge him for the leadership. He was the better choice, and I've never regretted standing down.

"The call was mine," I said. "I seek a boon from the council."

"What boon, friend Quick?"

"The old man of St. Bernadette's has made a light beneath my favored perch. The slightest movement ignites it, and it burns away the hours of my slumber."

"It's true!" cried young Sharp, several branches below. "An affront to our brother, and to all our kind."

"What boon do you ask of the rookery?" Glint demanded.

"I ask this," I said.

And set forth my plan.

There was silence. The spirits of thunder were stirring overhead. A few of our brethren rustled in the trees, ruminating. At last Glint replied: "You ask much, my old friend."

"I offer much."

I ducked my beak beneath my wing and brought forth the shine-star, and a murmur ran through the parliament. Solemnly, I trod the bending twigs to the perch of honor and laid the glimmering stone at Glint's feet.

"Much indeed," he said quietly. "Knock!"

"Here, sir." Knock was as big as a raven, our strongest fighter. An old scar marked his breast, and his left wing was white as bone.

"Will the raptors fly on such a day as this?"

A wry note entered Knock's voice. "Only the boldest and the dumbest."

"Perfect. Ready your team."

"Yes sir."

As he spoke, the first globed raindrop tapped upon the leaves.

———————

Hawks. Accursed birds. They care for nothing but the chase. Their eyes are needles of ice, their talons a death threat. Four of us flew in the vanguard: myself and Knock, and his lieutenants Sharp and Trunk, young and battle-eager. Behind us were half a dozen more tough rooks, flapping grimly as we climbed toward combat.

Knock gave me a sidelong glance as the rain grew heavier. "Quite a plan you've hatched here, Quick."

"My days are going down into the west, my friend. I want to live them out in solace."

"If things go ill, good carrion awaits us both in the shadow-fields of the Moon."

"Truly said."

"No fear," said Sharp. "We can handle those goblins."

"I can handle two!" said Trunk.

"Just keep to the plan, lads," Knock said, his voice loud over the storm.

I pointed with my beak. "There."

A single bird, cruciform, sailed through the wet grey empyrean with never a twitch of those tireless wings. Ancestral dread coiled in my gut. I am a crow of Lurkwood. Fear is for the foolish and the slow.

"You!" I cawed. "You trespass in our nesting grounds."

The bright, keen beak swung toward me. The merciless gaze regarded me. "And if I do?"

"Then murder be upon you!"

No more talk, then. The raptor wheeled and dove, his terrible claws outstretched. We broke formation to the four winds, but his ire was fixed on me. At the crucial instant, I rolled to my back in midair and caught his plunging feet in my own, entangling us. His power and weight were far beyond mine, and we plummeted down toward the spinning treetops.

Knock sprang on the monster's back, shrieking like the gale, and his lieutenants attacked its mighty wings. Lightning blazed. I was upside-down, blinded by the driving rain and the pounding pinions of my foe, but I could sense the earth hurtling to meet us.

Somehow Sharp and Trunk managed to turn the wings, steering our whole grappling quintet in the necessary direction. I clung to the talons as it dragged me through the howling, weeping skies. We were parallel to the ground now, soaring toward the target.

Then the hawk made an impossible barrel roll, flinging my friends clear. Over the shattering thunder, I heard the deep cold voice: "*Die now.*"

Six more of us pounced, weighting our enemy, forcing him downwards, blocking his view. From the corner of my eye, I saw the steeple of St. Bernadette's flash by. I heard Knock's frantic cry: "Now, Quick, now!"

And I ripped myself free just as the hawk smashed Fr. McReady's light.

———————

There were revels that day. We flew and spun and danced our corvine dances. We sang together and retold ageless tales of heroes past. The storm raged and the day waned, and at eventide I went home to my favorite eaves to slumber in the kindly dark.

The night was frosty cold. When I awoke and fluttered down to the windowsill to stretch my wings, I saw patches of ice on the walkway outside the vicar's door. I glanced up at his light: the little cage was dented in, the bulb and fixture cracked beyond repair. I glanced through the window.

Inside Fr. McReady buttoned his coat. On the dresser by his bed, in a nest of blankets, was my injured enemy, the hawk. It stirred in its sleep, and one of its wings flapped crookedly—broken, evidently, in the impact. The old priest set a dish of water by its beak and left the room.

A hawk and a human—they were nothing to me. And yet, one had fought with honor and the other had shown kindness and mercy. Perhaps they deserved more respect than I had given.

As I thought these thoughts, the front door opened and the old man emerged, walking slowly in the predawn gloom. His vision was less keen than mine, and his agility as well; I saw him head straight for an icy patch, and knew he would fall. I croaked a warning and flung myself through the air, landing on the ice just before his foot came down.

He gazed at me with a puzzled smile and said something in the strange liquid tongue of your people. Looking closer, he saw the ice. His smile grew, and he spoke again, and from his pocket he drew a muffin in a napkin. Breaking it in half, he set it on the pavement in front of me. I shuffled and gave a quiet caw of thanks, and he was on his way.

The next morning, we did the same. That evening, I moved a loose stone on which he would have turned his ankle, and he gave me meat. A few days later, the parish handyman removed the broken fixture of the light. And a few weeks after that, the hawk recovered and returned to the distant sky. Neither hawk nor light were seen again.

Since those days, a friendship has grown between myself and McReady—a greater friendship than I ever thought I could forge with one of your kind. And at every funeral Mass, I come and perch by his side. That is why you see me here today. I cannot vouch for certain your soul will reach the Moon but I will travel with you as far as I can. No dying is complete without a crow.

About This Book
The typeface in this book is 11.5 Garamond and Helvetica.
The title font is Black Chancery. It was laid out using Adobe
InDesign software and converted to PDF for uploading to the
printing facility.

About Darkhouse Books
Darkhouse Books is dedicated to publishing entertaining
fiction, primarily in the mystery and science fiction field.
Darkhouse Books is located in Niles, California, an inadvertently
preserved, 120 year old, one-sided railtown, forty miles from
San Francisco. Further information may be obtained by visiting
our website at www.darkhousebooks.com.

Also Available from Darkhouse Books

Cozy Crimes
in
Libraries

Shhhh...

Murder!

Edited by
Andrew MacRae

Also Available from Darkhouse Books

Sanctuary

A Collection of Poetry and Prose
Edited by Susannah Carlson & Peter Bradbury

John Guzlowski

True
Confessions
1965 to Now

Also Available from Darkhouse Books

Duck Lessons

James M. LeCuyer